SLAMDOWN TOWN

★ ★ ★

AMULET BOOKS • NEW YORK

Library of Congress Cataloging-in-Publication Data:

Names: Nicoll, Maxwell, author. | Smith, Matthew, 1989- author.
Title: Slamdown Town / Maxwell Nicoll and Matthew Smith.
Description: New York: Amulet Books, 2020. | Summary: A birthday wish and
    vintage chewing gum transform eleven-year-old Ollie into wrestler Big
    Chew, which might win back his older brother's respect but destroy his
    friendship with best friend Tamiko.
Identifiers: LCCN 2019026723 (print) | LCCN 2019026724 (ebook) |
    ISBN 9781419738852 (hardcover) | ISBN 9781683356394 (ebook)
Subjects: CYAC: Wrestling—Fiction. | Brothers—Fiction. | Best
    friends—Fiction. | Friendship—Fiction. | Magic—Fiction.
Classification: LCC PZ7.1.N536 Sl 2020 (print) | LCC PZ7.1.N536 (ebook) |
    DDC [Fic]—dc23

Text and illustrations copyright © 2020 Abrams
Illustrations by Christian Garland
Book design by Hana Anouk Nakamura

Printed and bound in U.S.A.
10 9 8 7 6 5 4 3 2 1

Amulet Books® is a registered trademark of Harry N. Abrams, Inc.

ABRAMS The Art of Books
195 Broadway, New York, NY 10007
abramsbooks.com

To our mothers,
who shared their love of storytelling
and taught us to be good brothers

CHAPTER 1

"IF you want it so bad," mocked Hollis, "why don't you take it?"

Ollie Evander couldn't believe his rotten luck. For starters, Hollis had stolen *his* flyer. Ollie had jumped up and down trying to grab it back from him, but every time he got close, Hollis yanked it away. As if that weren't bad enough, Hollis had pinned him to the sticky, popcorn-covered floor of Slamdown Town Arena.

Ollie struggled to speak under his annoying—scratch that, *infuriating*—older brother's girth.

"Can't you just go get your own?" he groaned.

Ollie had first noticed the stack of neon-blue flyers on the side of the ticket counter.

SLAMDOWN TOWN ARENA

NEW WRESTLER TRYOUTS

THIS WEEK ONLY

TWO ENTER THE RING, ONLY ONE EXITS

He had pointed them out to his best friend, Tamiko Tanaka, who immediately dared him to try out. A dare was a dare. So he snagged one off the pile and pinky-promised that he'd be first in line *and* the first one signed to Slamdown Town. But then Tamiko had run off to grab snacks from the concession counter, and Ollie's jerkface brother had swooped in and started, well, being a jerkface brother.

"Go get my own? But I want *this* one. And you were so nice to hand-deliver it to me. Besides, they wouldn't let some ten-year-old kid wrestle anyway," said Hollis. "Especially not one as pea-size as you."

"First off, I'll be eleven in two days," grunted Ollie. "And secondly, at least I'm not pea-*brained*." Ollie's blond, shaggy hair fell over his eyes. He tried to push Hollis off him but failed. He didn't know how much more he could take.

"You know, I think I'll take this flyer for myself. Who knows. Maybe I'll try out."

"Sure. They won't hire an eleven-year-old, but a thirteen-year-old with a disgusting hair monster above his lip totally stands a chance," said Ollie, still straining to speak.

Hollis smiled and stroked his patchy lip hair. "I think it makes me look cultured."

"No. It makes you look like a . . ." But Ollie's mind blanked. He had never been great when it came to comebacks. Smack talk was more Tamiko's thing.

What's taking her so long? thought Ollie.

He mustered all his strength to push Hollis off him, again, but failed, again. Well, he guessed strength wasn't really his thing, either. Saturdays weren't supposed to be spent wrestling and smack-talking his brother. They were supposed to be spent *watching* wrestling. Real wrestling. Something he and his brother used to watch together all the time.

If he didn't find a way out of this grapple soon, he might miss the first match.

And he hadn't *ever* missed a match.

"Why don't you pick on someone your own size, Hollis," said a familiar voice.

Finally! Ollie turned an eighth of an inch—it was all he could muster under the circumstances—to find Tamiko standing over them. Her hair was a familiar, tangled mess. She wore her wrinkled Slamdown Town official tee. And she had only one sock on with a big hole that went from her ankle all the way up to her kneecap. He wondered if she always had only one sock on; Ollie hadn't seen his friend from this angle before.

"You know. Like a hippo," Tamiko went on, her voice casual. "Or a baby giraffe. Those things are bigger than you think."

In her right arm she held a stack of sour strips, a super slushie brimming with sugar, and nachos doused in cheese. In her other hand, as always, she held her phone.

Tamiko was always playing games on her phone. Last month it was *Ninja Kitten*, and before that, *Postcard Detective*. This month's mobile game was *Jewel Heist*, an addictive-but-simple game where you tap-tap-tapped away to uncover hidden treasure.

In every game she played Tamiko held the first, second, and third highest scores. She could play—and win—while carrying on a conversation, or taking a math exam, or, in this case, balancing a tower of snacks.

She was *that* good.

"By the way, Ollie, I think I got enough snacks to get us through the first match." She cradled her armful of food to her chest, a strand of cheese marring the white of her tee with a vivid orange stripe. "But we'll definitely need to make another run at intermission."

"Oh, joy," grunted Hollis, pulling his torso off Ollie at the sound of the word *snacks*. Ollie seized the opportunity to roll out from under him. "It's the second member of the baby brigade. What's on today's agenda? Let me guess. Naptime and sippy cups?"

Ollie stood carefully and checked his shins for bruising.

"I'm free!" he gasped.

"How long were you under?" asked Tamiko, ignoring Hollis entirely.

"Too long." Ollie took several deep breaths to regulate his breathing, as recommended by his favorite online video series on calming meditation.

"And too close to Hollis's butt, it looked like." Tamiko's upper lip quivered in distaste. "I'm shocked you held on to your sanity."

"Hey, Tamiko. Those nachos look heavy," said Hollis as he lumbered toward her and grabbed a chip right out of the tray. "Lemme help you make it a little easier to carry."

Hollis popped the best, saltiest, most cheese-drenched chip in his mouth.

"Hey! Get your sweaty paws off *my* snacks!" yelled Tamiko, pulling the chips away as fast as she could. Her sudden movement sent a blob of gooey cheese soaring into the air. It hovered above them for one deliciously cheesy moment before falling and landing directly on Hollis's oversize belly.

"My shirt!" yelled Hollis like a screeching monkey who just dropped his lunch. Hollis used the flyer to wipe the cheese from his shirt. Under other circumstances, Ollie might have tried to stop him. But the damage was done. Hollis wiped himself clean with the flyer—*Ollie's* flyer—then crumpled it up without a second thought.

He tossed it to the ground.

"Really? After all that?" Ollie cringed at the sound of his own squeak.

"You got cheese all over my most photogenic shirt," groaned Hollis. "Now I gotta teach you a lesson." He pointed and lunged toward Ollie, who squeaked again despite himself and leapt out of the way, causing Hollis to double over in laughter.

Ollie rolled his eyes at Hollis's use of the word *photogenic.* Using big words was clearly a part of his unending desire to prove he was more mature than he actually was.

Hollis was taking this whole newly *thirteen-year-old* thing very seriously. He was older than Ollie, yes—Hollis was in eighth grade (*barf*) and Ollie was in sixth—but he certainly wasn't more mature. If anything, Ollie thought that Hollis had become less so.

"Let's go, Ollie. You know your bro is way out of your weight class," Tamiko said, nudging Ollie in the rib cage with her elbow. Ollie would have squeaked again—Tamiko's elbows were sharp—but he had his pride to consider.

"But," pleaded Ollie, "I can't just let him get away with it."

"Oh, he won't. There's more than one way to beat a level

ninety-nine boss." She was referring to their favorite fantasy adventure co-op computer game, *Revenge of Kragthar*.

"Hey, Hollis!" called Tamiko over to Hollis. Tamiko pointed to his shirt. "Say cheese!" She snapped a photo with her phone.

Ollie almost fell over laughing.

"You just wish you were half as sophisticated as I am," said Hollis. With that, he lumbered off in the direction of the restrooms, exhibiting all the dignity he could muster with a blob of cheese on his shirt. Ollie knew that Hollis would find some way to spin this—he'd probably say that cheesy-blob shirts were "in" and that Ollie just didn't *understand*.

Ollie dove forward onto the sticky lobby floor and reached for the crumpled flyer just as a passerby—oblivious to Ollie's plight—ground into it with his heel, nearly smashing Ollie's fingers in the process. It was not Ollie's day.

"Dude. Not worth it," Tamiko told him. "We can just get you another one."

Ollie smoothed out the gooey, dirty, foot-printed flyer.

"No. I won't let Hollis win," he said, folding the paper gently into a square and pocketing it. "This one is fine. And besides, it's printed on Slamdown Town letterhead. Do you even know how much this thing will be worth someday?"

"Just as much as this one without any gross slime on it," said Tamiko, waving her own cheese-free flyer. But Tamiko didn't understand. Sure, they were identical flyers. But keeping the one he'd chosen meant Hollis's blundering attempt to steal it had failed. And that made this flyer a trophy of sorts, one worth holding on to.

Ollie's room contained many treasures from his wrestling adventures. The ticket stub from his first-ever match, where Mini Fridge defeated Rick Rodgers. A first-place ribbon that he and Hollis had won for best tag-team outfits at fan costume night, back when they still got along. The photo of him and Tamiko with huge smiles as they sat in the stands, cheeks stuffed with kettle corn.

But none held a candle to the signed poster of Professor Pain, Ollie's favorite wrestler, which his mom had gotten him for his birthday a few years back. He was certain no other, future gift would come within a mile of topping that one.

Even so, the cheese-stained flyer would fit nicely into the tableau.

"Ladies and gentlemen, boys and girls. Please take your seats," said a crazed voice over the Slamdown Town speakers. "The matches are about to begin!"

The hairs on Ollie's arms stood straight up. A surge of energy shot through his body.

"Come on." He tugged on Tamiko's wrist. "Let's get to our seats!" Hollis forgotten, the two dashed through the buzzing fluorescent archways and into the belly of the arena.

CHAPTER 2

WRESTLING was *exactly* what Ollie needed to get over Hollis. Their mom said Hollis's behavior of late was all part of getting older—but if that were the case, would his brother ever *not* be terrible? As much as Ollie wished he could take Hollis down a peg or two, he knew he was too small to kick his brother's butt, and that his brother's ego was too big to reason with. So instead, he'd watch *other* people kick each other's butts, which usually ended with a chair to the gut.

"Let's do this!" yelled Tamiko, freeing her hand from a bag of sour strips to give Ollie a high five. The friends marched across the sticky, unwashed lobby floors. Ollie had entered the arena more times than he could count. But he still felt goose bumps travel up his arms the moment he entered the belly of the arena and saw the wrestling ring in all its glory, far below in the center of the room. Above the ring, a flickering, worn marquee displayed the following message:

SLAMDOWN TOWN ARENA
TONIGHT'S MAIN EVENT
"WEREWRESTLER" VERSUS "THE BOLT"

"Today's gonna be the day Werewrestler loses," Ollie predicted as they headed toward their regular seats. He inhaled the familiar smell of body odor and vigor.

Mainly body odor.

"He better," said Tamiko, rolling her eyes. "This unbeaten streak is about as exciting to watch as my dad's talent-show auditions."

Having witnessed several excruciating audition tapes himself, Ollie couldn't help but agree that it was time for Werewrestler's streak to come to an end.

They passed a number of floor-to-ceiling hanging posters that depicted the current lineup of popular Slamdown Town wrestlers. Fan favorites like The Bolt, Werewrestler, Big Tuna, Gorgeous Gordon Gussett, Silvertongue, Lil' Old Granny, and Barbell Bill. And last but not least, a poster of Linton Krackle, the greasy, slimeball owner and CEO of Slamdown Town. The poster was adorned with green-and-yellow graffiti that read LINTON SOCKS, which Ollie had always assumed was supposed to say LINTON SUCKS.

But the typo had spawned an arena tradition.

He and Tamiko snapped their socks—or, in Tamiko's case, sock—as they passed.

"Linton socks!" they shouted.

It was true. Linton did sock—*er*, suck. He would make appearances—which were met by uproarious boos from the audience—every so often to set up big matches or make an important announcement. But usually he just sat in his back office counting money.

"Last one to our seats has to touch Hollis's dirty underwear!" shrieked Tamiko as she ambled up the steps toward their seats: center row, center column, with the best view in the house.

Ollie knew firsthand that Hollis had a whole hamper, bathroom, and bedroom floor full of dirty underwear. In fact, Ollie wasn't sure Hollis even *owned* clean underwear. But he chased after Tamiko anyway. They bolted up a flight of uneven stairs, took a hard left at the first broken window, leapt over the old pothole that was created when Lil' Old Granny pile-drove Barbell Bill in an out-of-the-ring brawl, and—finally—arrived at the set of rickety seats they claimed as their own.

"Too slow. I win!" yelled Tamiko. She hoisted her arms up in a victory celebration.

"Yeah, because you had a head start," he panted.

"See this?" Tamiko slowly ran in place. She exaggerated her movements, as if she were jogging on the moon. "This is you running."

Ollie laughed. She wasn't wrong. Plus, he could never be *mad* mad at Tamiko. She was his best friend, after all. The one who'd added her name—in permanent marker, no less—to the back of the seat she was currently sprawled across.

"It's tradition," an even tinier Ollie had squeaked all those years ago. "Look!"

He had pointed to his own name on his seat and to his brother's name in the seat adjacent. He and Hollis had gotten quite the talking-to from their mom at the time, back when they were still an inseparable tag team—but they didn't care. These seats were their thrones, the arena their palace, and they wanted everyone to know.

But now of course Hollis was too adolescent—in the literal sense rather than the insulting sense—to sit next to Ollie and Tamiko. He was seated several rows down, the lone kid with the huge water stain engulfing a slightly less huge, faded orange splotch on his shirt. But wishing things could go back to the way they used to be wouldn't make it happen. They had grown apart as Hollis started getting older, and he would just keep on getting older. Luckily, Ollie had met Tamiko in third-grade math class and found out that she liked wrestling just as much as he did. He had traded his brother for a best friend. Well, not traded.

Tamiko couldn't replace what he'd had with Hollis. Not entirely anyway.

Ollie buried the pang of their faded friendship, turning from the sight of his brother and refocusing on the scene unfolding below.

The arena was never very full. Even less so in recent years. Probably because it was run-down and lackluster and it hadn't been updated since Linton Krackle had taken over as owner and CEO. He prioritized ticket sales—and money—over improving the arena, and it had subsequently fallen into disarray. But to Ollie, that was all part of the charm.

Besides, fewer people meant that when they were there, the arena *belonged* to them. To Ollie, there was no better wrestling arena in the tristate area.

No. No better wrestling arena in the *world.*

They scarfed down most of the nachos, sizzled their taste buds on sour strips, and slurped the slushie dry before scraping the bottom of the cup for remnants.

The two friends bounced with cheese- and sugar-fueled excitement.

"So how long would it take you to pin The Bolt?" asked Tamiko.

Ollie smiled. It was their favorite pre-match discussion.

"Before she even had time to pull off a Static Shock," he said casually.

Tamiko grinned and tossed a gooey nacho into her mouth. With her other hand she continued to tap away furiously at the game on her phone.

Ollie, meanwhile, took out the flyer and began to doodle a drawing on the back. While Ollie may have been too small to actually wrestle, and too timid to smack-talk, he did possess a talent for drawing wrestlers.

He drew a sketch of himself, but beefed up to look the part of a huge wrestler, landing an epic takedown on Werewrestler, the reigning champion.

Tiny stars circled Werewrestler's head.

"No way," Tamiko said with her mouth full of cheese. "The Bolt would totally shock you at least, like, five times before you even had a chance for opening smack talk."

"What? You're joking. I'd have her pinned before she even entered the ring."

"Mm-hmm," said Tamiko. "And I'm gonna grow up to be as big and smelly as Big Tuna and win the championship belt with one hand tied behind my back."

They laughed. But Ollie knew something Tamiko didn't.

What she didn't know was that Ollie believed, deep down, that one day he'd be a wrestler. Then he'd show Hollis. And the competition. And anyone else who doubted that he didn't have what it takes. Because he totally did have *it*—what it took to be a wrestler. Just no one knew it yet.

The lights dimmed and the excited buzz gave way to hushed silence. A spotlight shone on the ring, highlighting a diminutive man in an outrageous, bright orange suit. His greased-back, electric-blue hair framed a large pair of neon green glasses.

Everything about the man was loud. But that was exactly why Screech Holler had been hired to be Slamdown Town's resident announcer.

Screech tapped his throat. Then slowly—*very* slowly—he raised his microphone to his lips. "Ladies and gentlemen, boys and girls." His high-pitched voice bounced off every surface in the arena and sent chills down Ollie's spine. "Welcome to Slamdown Town!"

CHAPTER 3

OLLIE watched the referee leap over the ropes and sail into the ring. She was big. No, huge. She never missed a date with the gym or a single one of her morning, afternoon, and evening protein shakes.

She intimidated everyone, in and out of the ring. Except Ollie.

She was his mom, after all.

His mom had the second-coolest job in the whole world. Because the *actual* coolest job in the world was—obviously—being a wrestler.

But his mom had been one once. This was in the pinnacle of her youth, before she sustained a career-ending injury to her funny bone, which, despite its name, was no laughing matter. Her wrestler name had been the Brash Banshee, and in her glory days, she was considered by all to be the fiercest, meanest, and toughest wrestler at Slamdown Town. She felled every opponent who faced her in the ring, and for two whole years was the undisputed champion of Slamdown Town.

Ollie had never known his mom as a wrestler, but he'd admired her old photos, videos, and posters from her time as the Banshee. The Brash Banshee was not only a terror in the ring but also a terror to behold. Her striking white eyes pierced through the long strands of hair that covered her face and through her opponent's heart. Pale, ghostlike strips of cloth wrapped up her torso and dangled lazily off her arms.

Scary wasn't a scary-enough word to describe the Brash Banshee.

She even had her own action figure, which he and Hollis used to play with, making their mom topple block towers with her bulging plastic biceps, or stomp on little green army men with her knee-high boots.

Ollie would stare longingly at the championship belt around her waist, both proud of his mom and sad that he never got to see her actually wearing it.

Her career had been cut short when she was challenged by an upstart new wrestler named Werewrestler. He was quickly making a strong reputation for himself, and he had his sights set on the championship belt. The Brash Banshee accepted—she never turned down a challenger—and many thought her victory a foregone conclusion.

After all, she'd defeated every other challenger.

But all good things must end, and her reign as champion, and as a professional wrestler, did exactly that when she stepped into the ring with Werewrestler.

Ollie had seen old, grainy footage of the match online and

was always struck by two things: one, how awesome and fierce his mom was, and two, how many people had been in attendance at Slamdown Town Arena that night. Each time he pressed Play on the video, he felt his heart race, as if he were watching it live for the first time. He'd gasp as his mom put Werewrestler into a choke hold, cheer when she pulled off a devastating backbreaker on him, and leap from his seat when she dove off the top rope and delivered her infamous Brash Bodyslam.

Victory was near. Instead of finishing the match, the Brash Banshee soaked up the crowd's admiration. Which explained why she didn't see that Werewrestler, having knocked out the referee, had grabbed an illegal chair. A well-aimed dirty strike sent the chair smack into her funny bone.

Ollie had whacked his funny bone before and knew how painful it could be, but his mom's injury looked ten times worse. After all, he had just hit his arm on his doorframe when he wasn't paying attention. Compared to a chair assault, that was nothing. Werewrestler had the momentum behind him and used that momentum to pin Ollie's mom. He had won by cheating, but in wrestling the rules were meant to be broken.

Or, if not broken, followed loosely.

Well, Brash Banshee wanted to put a stop to that. So she hung up her wrestling outfit and traded it for referee stripes. Her mission? To ensure that everyone involved in the matches would play by the rules. And not just the wrestlers.

"Our most esteemed referee," started Screech, "would like me to remind you that running in the arena is strictly forbidden. And also to stop wrestling your brother in the lobby, or you'll both lose video game privileges. That one seems oddly specific . . . !"

Ollie groaned.

"Called out by your mom in front of everyone! I love it!" said Tamiko, slapping her knee.

Ollie sank farther into his seat. A few rows down, he saw Hollis do the same.

"Bolt is going to take it," Tamiko reminded him, bringing the conversation—blessedly—back to wrestling.

"Please, please, please!" Ollie shook his clasped hands skyward, in the general direction of the wrestling gods. "If I have to see Werewrestler win again, I'm gonna barf."

"Me, too. It's like, give it up already, dude! But if we do barf, let's both aim at Hollis."

Werewrestler had been undefeated ever since that fateful day he claimed the championship belt from Brash Banshee. Since then, he'd toppled wrestler after wrestler. And after each victory, he'd raise the shimmering, diamond-encrusted belt above his head to remind everyone that *he* was the champion. Ollie hoped today would be different.

"Just wait," said Ollie. "Eventually somebody's gonna come along that can beat him."

"Whoever *someone* is, they better get here soon," moaned Tamiko. "Having the same champ was boring the first five hundred times it happened."

The lights went down. A chill ran through the arena. As if the stadium were a giant beast waking up from a deep slumber, blood-pumping music blared from the speakers lining the walls. The entire floor shook, sending reverberations rumbling through Ollie's chest. He got goose bumps.

It was time.

Screech Holler's voice cut through the air. "Folks, prepare for storm clouds, because the forecast calls for a *shocking* amount of lightning. Give it up for *The Bolt*!"

Ollie felt his eyes widen as The Bolt appeared at the top of the entrance ramp in a blinding surge of light. She held her hands high and soaked in the applause from the ten people sitting in the arena. Then she zipped headlong toward the ring, vaulted over the ropes, and landed smack in the center of the mat.

"Zap, zap! Zap attack!" Ollie yelled.

"We love you, Bolt!" shrieked Tamiko, her hands cupped around her mouth.

Just like always, Ollie and Tamiko screamed until their throats were sore.

The Bolt's character bio was one of Ollie's favorites. He knew it by heart. She'd been born during a freak thunderstorm and had grown up chasing storm clouds—that is, until the tragic day a million volts of electricity connected with the metal tip of her umbrella, sending her crashing into a wrestling arena. Her shoes sparked, her hair stood on end, and her leather jacket flashed lightning yellow every time she charged up an attack.

She was, in a word, *electric*.

Just then, a sudden, deafening roar echoed throughout the crowd.

"It must be a full moon," said Screech Holler as he struggled to hold the mic still. "Someone better call animal control, because there's a rabid dog on the loose. Your champion, the mighty *Werewrestler*, has entered the building!"

Smoke poured out of the entrance ramp. And out of the smoke walked the largest man legally allowed in the tristate area. He was half man, half wolf, and all wrestler.

He had blood-red eyes framed with dripping black face paint. His ripped shirt swayed eerily in the smoke. To cap it off, a silver chain with a large pendant that resembled a howling wolf dangled around his neck.

"Boo!" yelled Ollie at the top of his lungs. The rest of the crowd booed along with him. Many loved to hate Werewrestler, but Ollie and Tamiko just plain hated him.

"Get that cheating, walking muttonchop outta here," demanded Tamiko.

Both wrestlers stood in the ring. Ollie's mom checked The Bolt and Werewrestler for illegal items. She removed a hammer, a spiked glove, and a long-overdue library book. All from Werewrestler. Then she checked Werewrestler again. After removing a hidden container of thumbtacks, she cleared both wrestlers to start.

But of course, before any actual wrestling came the smack talk.

"Do you smell that?" asked Werewrestler. He sniffed the air. "That, loser, is the sweet smell of *pain*." He sniffed again. "And maybe burnt nacho cheese. But *mostly* pain!"

"I smell it! It's gonna hurt so bad!" squealed Tamiko. "For Werewrestler, I hope!"

"The only thing I smell is your foul chance of winning this match," countered The Bolt. "Just like your smack-talk game, you're lacking the energy-efficient, long-lasting voltage necessary for victory!"

Werewrestler snarled.

"Prepare to be chomped, stomped, and whomped."

"Dream on. Nobody steals The Bolt's thunder!"

"She said it!" shrieked Ollie with glee. "She said the catchphrase!"

Ding, ding, ding!

The Bolt sprinted toward Werewrestler. Now it was time to let her fists do the talking. More specifically, her stunning(ly electric) hammer fists of fury. They rained down from above in a blistering, unrelenting combo that rocked Werewrestler. The Bolt landed a flying leg kick. A surprised Werewrestler reeled against the ropes.

"The Bolt is wasting no time," said Screech Holler.

Werewrestler retreated into the corner. It was a bad move—Ollie knew wrestling strategy by now and he knew each wrestler's weak spot. Sure enough, The Bolt charged shoulder-down into Werewrestler, slamming him into the corner of the ring. The Bolt grabbed Werewrestler by the scruff and went for an anaconda vise hold.

Ollie glanced at Tamiko—she was watching, rapt. Hopeful even.

But this time, Werewrestler was ready.

"He countered the grapple. Werewrestler's got her now," predicted Screech.

"No!" screamed Ollie. Tamiko clasped his arm with one sweaty palm.

Werewrestler yanked The Bolt straight into a headbutt. Stunned, The Bolt lurched backward. Werewrestler was on her in a flash. A knee to the gut doubled The Bolt over. A chop to the larynx threatened to end the match right there. But The Bolt saw it coming. She dodged and pivoted, spinning back around to face Werewrestler.

"These two are giving it all they got, folks!" yelled Screech. Ollie couldn't say for sure from that distance, but Screech looked like he might be foaming at the mouth.

The Bolt caught Werewrestler with her shoe, setting off a flurry of sparks. One stray spark landed directly in Werewrestler's left eye, sending him to the mat.

"That's gotta be an illegal move there," said Screech. Ollie watched as his mom approached The Bolt with a stern look and a wag of her finger. Ollie had seen that look and finger wag before, usually when he and Hollis stayed up too late on a school night.

"Yep, there's the ref giving her a talking-to," said Screech.

"Ah, come on, Mom. He barely got burned!" Ollie shouted down to the ring.

Ollie's mom pointed her formerly wagging finger straight at The Bolt's shoe.

"Improper use of foot apparel," warned Ollie's mom into her mic.

"What?!" shouted The Bolt, outraged. "Come on, ref. I barely touched him."

"I'm giving you a warning. One more and—"

"Look out!" yelled Tamiko.

The Bolt realized too late that she had made a mistake. She left herself exposed as she argued with Ollie's mom. Werewrestler had always been one to flout authority, and now was no exception. He positioned himself directly behind The Bolt. Before Ollie's mom could say or do anything at all, Werewrestler grabbed The Bolt, raised her into the air, and used all his body weight to slam her onto the mat.

"Hot dog, that woman has a family!" screeched Screech Holler.

The Bolt lay on the mat wriggling like a worm, unable to stand.

Ollie watched as his mom gave Werewrestler a fierce reprimand. Werewrestler clearly paid her no mind. The blow, while dirty, wasn't technically illegal, but it was close.

Werewrestler turned away from Ollie's mom and waved his arms for the crowd.

"Boo!" roared the crowd.

"Aroooo!" he roared in response.

Werewrestler circled The Bolt like a ravenous shark as she slowly got to her feet. He snapped his yellow teeth, mimed taking a big bite of an imaginary turkey leg, and dramatically wiped his mouth clean.

"Oh, no! He's preparing the jaws!" said Ollie, turning to Tamiko. He felt his faith in The Bolt faltering, then crumbling into a million pieces. Werewrestler didn't always pull out this maneuver, but when he did, it was all over.

This signaled that Werewrestler's finishing move, Full Moon, was impending.

"Full Moon! Full Moon!" chanted Werewrestler, trying to get the crowd on his side. Ollie and Tamiko didn't participate. Even Hollis refused to do the chant. At least their mutual dislike of Werewrestler still united the brothers. It wasn't much. But it was something.

Maybe the only thing these days?

The Full Moon involved Werewrestler locking his opponent in a devastating sleeper hold, much like the jaws of a wolf trapping its prey and leaving them for dead.

Or, in the case of wrestling, pinning them.

Werewrestler wrapped his giant arms around The Bolt and squeezed. And squirm as she might, there was no breaking loose. The last thing poor Bolt saw was the sweat stains of Werewrestler's torn shirt as she was squished deeper into his armpits.

Caught between a muscly arm and a sweaty pit, The Bolt couldn't break free. The noxious fumes must have gotten to her, because she slid down on the mat and remained passed out. The Bolt had officially suffered a power outage.

Ollie and Tamiko groaned in unison.

Werewrestler flopped down on top of The Bolt and pinned her. Ollie's mom dove beside them. For one brief moment, her eyes locked with Werewrestler's. Ollie held his breath. What he wouldn't give to see his mom get her revenge and take down Werewrestler right there, right now. But she had a job to do, a job she took *very* seriously, and so she began the count. She slapped the mat with her palm as she shouted, "Eight! Nine! Ten!"

Ding, ding, ding!

The bell sliced through the roar of the arena, signaling the end of the match. Werewrestler climbed onto the top rope and soaked in the crowd's disappointment.

"Already?!" shouted Ollie. "But she didn't even get to use any of her special moves!"

"Man. I thought for sure The Bolt would take it," said Tamiko, sounding distressed.

"Boo!" yelled the crowd again.

Ollie could feel the audience's displeasure. Who wants to see the same wrestler win every weekend, especially one as unlikable as Werewrestler? Though he didn't know this for certain, Ollie guessed that Slamdown Town's steep decline in attendance had less to do with the run-down, broken arena and more to do with a champion that no one could root for.

One day, Ollie hoped, Werewrestler would get what he deserved. Which was to get his butt kicked and have his belt taken away.

And the sooner that happened, the better.

CHAPTER 4

THE following evening, Ollie tiptoed into his brother's room. Right past the sign on the door that read NO BABIES ALLOWED along with a crude drawing of Ollie in a diaper.

The only reason he was even in Hollis's lame room was because Hollis had refused to let him borrow *their* laptop to play his favorite computer game: *Revenge of Kragthar.*

"Dream on. It's *my* laptop. And you're not using it," Hollis had told him when he'd asked to borrow it. So Ollie was taking matters into his own hands.

Hollis's room was decorated with unwashed, dreary black clothes, bottles of acne cream, and unopened packs of deodorant. A minefield of squished hair-gel tubes and crushed soda cans littered the floor. Strange, unidentifiable smells oozed out of the drawers, closet, and trash bin. His room seemed to be in a perpetual state of messy. Even when their mom ordered him to clean it up, the room somehow, like magic, immediately reverted back to a teenage garbage dump.

Man, eighth graders are the worst, thought Ollie.

He finally located the laptop under Hollis's pillow.

The second Hollis knew the laptop was missing he'd come looking for it, because he spent most of his free time using it to "build" his website: the Officially Unofficial Slamdown Town Fan Club. The site itself was a jumbled mess, kinda like Hollis's bedroom: littered with photos of wrestlers, banners, pop-ups, and—for some reason—a poorly photoshopped image of Hollis's head on Big Tuna's body. Each weekend he'd blog about the matches and, using the site's built-in forum, chat with other members of the Slamdown Town wrestling community.

"You have no idea the struggles of being a web developer," said Hollis dramatically one afternoon when they ran into each other in the hallway on their way to the bathroom.

"You aren't a web developer, Hollis. You're a thirteen-year-old with a fan site that has, like, five people on it, including me, you, Mom, and Tamiko."

"I'll have you know I am up to seven users," said Hollis as he slammed the bathroom door in his brother's face. Ollie was certain that the other three were just alternate accounts Hollis had made himself. But still, Ollie would take any opportunity to discuss wrestling with anyone.

Even Hollis.

✳✳✳

Ollie tucked the laptop under his arm and, making sure to be as sneaky as possible, tiptoed quietly back into the hallway.

Ollie and Hollis had shared a bedroom until Hollis turned thirteen and decided that he needed "his own space." Ollie didn't understand why they couldn't continue to share a room. He didn't take up much space, and he really liked falling asleep knowing his brother was right there with him. Having someone in the room during thunderstorms to talk about how *definitely not scared* they both were had always been a relief. And though he never openly admitted it, he even found Hollis's snoring kinda comforting.

But Hollis insisted, and so their mom cleared her stuff out of her office and let him move into that room. When Hollis moved out, he took all his stuff *plus* the stuff they shared, like the laptop. Sharing, to Hollis, meant keeping their stuff in his room all the time.

So Ollie tried to beat Hollis at his own game. He would hide the laptop in his room whenever it was his turn to use it, which usually ended with him in a headlock and revealing the hidden location to his brother. After a few weeks of this, Ollie begged and begged his mom to buy him his own. She refused.

"You don't need two laptops," she said as she shook her head. "You need to respect each other and share. And if you can't do that, then I'll have to lay down the law."

Ollie knew she wasn't kidding around. She never joked when it came to the rules . . . and in this case, *laying down the law* meant they'd *both* lose out on the laptop.

Which meant that he wouldn't be able to play *Revenge of Kragthar*.

Back in his own room, Ollie dove onto his beanbag chair and opened the computer. His room was *way* cooler than Hollis's.

There were action figures and comic books lining the shelves. Clothes, some of them clean, were strewn everywhere other than in his dresser drawers and laundry basket. And of course, his pride and joy: Years of accumulated wrestling treasures, including the signed poster of Professor Pain—his most prized possession— hung on the wall by the window. Just the way it had been before Hollis left.

With significantly less-smelly clothes.

The *Revenge of Kragthar* menu-screen music drew his attention back to the game. He threw on his headset and saw that Tamiko was already waiting for him online.

"There you are. Thought I'd have to clear out this dungeon myself," said Tamiko, her voice blaring through his headset. "Hold on a second while I get the stream started."

As a streamer, Tamiko, under the handle T@M1k0, would broadcast her games so that other gamers could watch her play. Ollie tended to feel a bit odd knowing that someone he didn't know was watching him fight waves of pixies and giant toads. But Tamiko insisted that her magnificent gaming prowess be witnessed by the masses.

Or at least the dozen or so followers who tuned in to watch.

"We are live! Let's do this!" shouted Tamiko.

Ollie winced and lowered the volume. "Think we can defeat Kragthar this time?"

"We better," said Tamiko. "I just got all my potions restocked from the last time we failed. Not to mention my acid gauntlets for maximum face melting."

Kragthar. A level ninety-nine endgame boss. A half goblin,

half troll bent on stopping would-be plunderers from leaving his dungeon with his loot. For months, Ollie and Tamiko had grinded and leveled up in order to be strong enough to defeat him. For months, they entered his dungeon cave only to be defeated and sent back to the entrance to try again.

Today would be Kragthar's downfall.

Probably.

Tamiko, who Ollie had to admit was the more skilled gamer of the two, played a wizard class. Lightning bolts. Fireballs. Blizzards. The elements were under her control. She played support to Ollie and shielded him from any and all harm. Managing the forces of evil while keeping Ollie's character safe proved no challenge at all for her.

But Ollie preferred a more direct, fight-everything-in-front-of-him approach. A knight, decked out in armor, with a sword and shield that were twice his character's size.

And of course, all his skill points were placed into strength.

"We're gonna hit Kragthar so hard, he's going to feel it in all five games in the series," said Tamiko. Ollie laughed. Tamiko really had a way of inspiring confidence in him.

He was ready.

"Wait," said Tamiko. "Before we go in, we gotta equip the right outfit."

She was right. You couldn't go into battle wearing rags and soiled underwear. For months, they had worked together to unlock the best gear: a helmet that emitted blue flames; diamond-encrusted gloves of dexterity; plate armor that resisted poison *and* stun damage; shoulder pads that, when fully charged with gemstones, allowed the wearer to teleport short distances; and a little friendly hedgehog that followed their characters.

The upgraded gear provided additional health and other class-specific benefits, and, most important, it looked really cool. And the hedgehog was just cute.

Now fully equipped, Ollie's knight charged forward into the dungeon and Tamiko's wizard followed. Ollie could hear Tamiko's fingers mashing buttons over the headset. They cleared the first area—a room full of poison-spitting bats—without breaking a sweat.

As always, the calming nature of gaming mayhem allowed Ollie's thoughts to drift back to wrestling. Discussing the action of Slamdown Town wrestling matches paired surprisingly well over the epic battles against the pixelated forces of evil.

"I still can't believe that Tommy TV Remote defeated Iron Duckie with two dead batteries last night," said Ollie as they arrived at the first gate. Ollie's knight produced a key, inserted it into the lock, and pushed the gate open. They ran forward.

"Really?" asked Tamiko. "I thought that was pretty obvious. Now, Emerald Emma offering Barb Haywire an alliance? That was shocking. Speaking of shocking . . ."

Tamiko's wizard zapped a horde of undead spiders.

". . . who woulda thought Captain Cashew would defeat Immunity?" she continued.

"Because of a peanut allergy? I know. You couldn't write that!"

They turned the corner and encountered a giant silver snake with three heads. Ollie and Tamiko tried to hack away at her, but nothing they did caused any damage.

The snake raised her three heads and began to speak.

"Brave wizard and noble knight, for you both, the end's in sight. But to pass, you must first state why you seek such a terrible fate."

"Oh, wait," said Ollie. "This snake lady is trying to say something to us."

"I know what to pick." Tamiko scrolled through the available lines and selected. "We are here, oh slithering snake, to free the realm and our vengeance take."

Having chosen the right dialogue option, Ollie's knight and Tamiko's wizard ran past the snake and into the next and final area.

"Sucks about Werewrestler," he said, bringing the conversation back to wrestling.

"Yep," said Tamiko. "Now we gotta watch *another* championship match with Weredoofus in it. Seriously, no one can beat his stupid face? I'm starting to think that the whole thing may be rigged."

For years, Ollie had waited for justice to catch up to Werewrestler. Someday, someone would avenge his mother's loss. He didn't care who it was. He'd be satisfied as long as Werewrestler didn't wear the championship belt around his waist.

"Bolt should've opened with Zap Attack. Something quick and nimble to set the pace of the match. That's what Professor Pain would have done."

"Not this again," whined Tamiko. "I know Professor Pain's your favorite wrestler of all time, but come on, dude."

"I'm just saying. I love The Bolt. I really do. But if Professor Pain were around today, he'd totally be the one to beat Werewrestler," he argued.

Their knight and wizard avatars cleared the final room and

made their way to the boss gate. Her wizard produced the boss key, placed it into the lock, and turned it.

This was it. It didn't matter what armor you wore or what dialogue options you chose. Kragthar was a test of half-goblin, half-troll, all-gross strength. If you were strong enough, and fast enough, you could win. But if you weren't, it was GAME OVER.

Ollie leaned in toward the screen. "Okay," he whispered. He didn't know why he was whispering, but he was. He wiped his sweaty hands on the back of his pants.

"Let's think about this before rushing in. It's—"

At that very moment, Hollis barged into his bedroom.

"Hollis?!" Ollie shouted.

"Hollis?!" screamed Tamiko. "What are you talking about? It's not Hollis; that's Kragthar! Okay, so set your power attack to—"

But Ollie wasn't listening. For one brief moment, Ollie was convinced, or perhaps hoped, that Hollis had actually come to play the game with them. But the fiery look in his eyes when he spotted the laptop quickly put an end to that thought.

"Give it back," said Hollis, grabbing at the controller.

Tamiko was still giving directions into the headset. "Ollie, are you listening?"

He wasn't. He yanked the controller away before Hollis could snatch it.

"Get out of my room!" Ollie yelled.

"You snuck into my room and stole my computer. Now give it back!"

Ollie could hear Tamiko screaming into the headset. "Ollie! I need backup!" On the screen, Tamiko's wizard blasted spells while Ollie's knight swung his sword. Then Ollie's knight stood still. Until he didn't.

Ollie saw Hollis's meaty hands grab the laptop. He froze and stared into his older brother's eyes. He felt his heart speed to the pace of one of Professor Pain's patented powerhouse pile drivers. And those were deadly fast. "What are you doing?! We're in the middle of fighting Kragthar!"

"I'm taking *my* computer to *my* room," said Hollis. He yanked the laptop forward, but Ollie held on for dear life and was pulled directly into Hollis's chest. The momentum made them both tumble to the floor.

On the screen, Ollie's knight ran around erratically, pulled and pushed in all directions as the two boys wrestled on the ground over the computer.

Before he and Hollis had been enemies, they had shared things. Even in recent months, as Hollis decided he didn't need Ollie anymore, they had played by their mom's rules. But the rules had just changed without Ollie even realizing it.

"Give it back," groaned Hollis.

"It's both of ours," replied Ollie with a strain.

Ollie dug his heels into the carpet and pulled the laptop toward him. Hollis gritted his unbrushed teeth and pulled the laptop back in his direction with all his adolescent might. The computer, caught in the middle, remained suspended between the two.

That is, until Ollie felt it slip from his hands.

"Kragthar, I'm sorry!" shouted Ollie.

"No!" yelled Hollis, to Ollie's great surprise.

Ollie watched, horrified, as he realized why Hollis had also yelled. He saw the laptop not just get pulled from his own grip but also slip from his brother's sweaty hold. Ollie knew all too well how sweaty Hollis got now that he was a teenager.

For a brief moment, the laptop almost seemed to hang in the air. Then, with a sickening crash, it fell to the ground.

The two boys leaned down and saw a large crack across the center of the screen. Ollie hardly dared to breathe. This was not a problem some tape could help fix.

Now the screen was frozen. For the briefest of moments, Ollie's knight and Tamiko's wizard were stuck in stiff parodies of attack . . . And Kragthar, only a few hits from *finally* being defeated, was, well, frozen. Then the screen faded to black.

"Great job, dweeb," said Hollis, his scruffy upper lip contorted in disgust. "Look what you did. Now how am I supposed to run the Officially Unofficial Slamdown Town Fan Club?"

Ollie didn't have long to consider the consequences. Their mom strode into the room—through the din of utter chaos, he hadn't even heard her come up the stairs. No longer in her referee uniform, she sported a tank top and a sweatband to hold her hair back. Her sweat-covered face let Ollie know she'd just come from their makeshift basement gym. She did *not* appreciate being interrupted during a workout.

"What in the blazes is going on up here?" she demanded.

The look on her face made Ollie realize how much trouble they were potentially in. He caught Hollis's eyes and saw that he realized the danger, too. The stern gaze of their mom united the brothers, who had fallen under that look too many times to count.

"Boys. We've talked about this. Destruction of household property *and* unsanctioned roughhousing?" She arched a brow. "Two major infractions in one romp. Not okay."

Ollie couldn't believe that just moments ago he was sad that his brother had moved out. Hollis had shifted from ultimate brother to ultimate villain.

Puberty. Just a phase. A teenager thing. Blah, blah, blah. Ollie had heard many excuses. None seemed right or reasonable. Hollis was just a jerkface. Why couldn't Hollis go back to the way he used to be when they were younger?

Good thing Ollie had met Tamiko.

"Now, apologize. And then no more video games for either of you for the rest of the night. No—the rest of the week. And I mean none of them. Not on your computers or phones or anything," said Ollie's mom.

"But—" started Ollie.

"Trust me. I'll know. And do you have any idea how expensive it will be to repair that laptop? So no buts, mister."

Ollie giggled. *Butts.* There was a time when Hollis would have laughed, too. But he didn't even crack a grin. Ollie guessed Hollis thought *butts* were for babies or something.

Under their mom's watchful eyes, the two boys muttered their apologies.

"Sorry I got mad after you snuck into my room without permission," mumbled Hollis. It looked almost painful for him to say.

"That's okay. And sorry I got mad after you caused me to lose when we totally would've beaten Kragthar," offered Ollie.

He waited for Hollis to accept his apology. It never came.

He couldn't help but feel a pang of disappointment.

"Shake hands and go to your corners. I mean, rooms," corrected their mom.

The two boys shook hands, Ollie straining under Hollis's grip.

With that, Hollis stormed out of the room, cradling the broken laptop.

"You know better than to fight your brother," said his mom when they were alone.

"I know. If I were stronger, I could've taken him," said Ollie.

His mom opened her mouth and then closed it. She hesitated, as if choosing her words carefully. "You *are* strong Ollie," she said, planting a kiss on his forehead.

"No, I'm not. Look." Ollie flexed his arm with all his might. No muscle appeared. In fact, his arm somehow looked even more noodley. "Not like you, Mom."

His mom shook her head, her neck muscles bulging as she did so. "You don't need to be big and strong in order to be big and strong. Someday you'll understand."

As Ollie lay in bed that night, he replayed their conversation in his mind. He wondered what strength his mom saw in him. He lay wondering about it until his brain hurt and he finally drifted to sleep.

After all, tomorrow was a big day.

CHAPTER 5

MONDAY mornings meant two things: Ollie would have to wait five more days for wrestling. Also, school. But this Monday was different, because today was Ollie's birthday.

And not just any birthday. It was his *eleventh* birthday!

That meant he was no longer some little ten-year-old baby, as Hollis would occasionally refer to him. After all, he'd been in double digits for a whole year now. And eleven felt just so much *older* than ten. Something about two ones, side by side, inspired confidence.

He leapt out of bed and rushed to the mirror. He pulled at his cheeks, looked behind his ears, and spun around to try and examine himself from all angles.

Well, he certainly felt older, but he couldn't be sure if he looked older. There was only one way to find out. He rushed out of his bedroom and sprinted downstairs.

Ollie's mom was always going on and on about how much Hollis was changing now that he was a teenager. Every day it would be a comment about how he was a "young man" or that he "grew overnight." Well, Ollie could see that Hollis was changing, all right. Strange and random body hair, sudden and swift mood changes, voice cracking and deepening, and a life-consuming and complete desire to "fit in" and "be cool."

Thankfully, Ollie seemed to have avoided all of that. There was, however, one part of growing up he was looking forward to: the growing part!

Over the years, his mom had tracked their heights near the doorframe of the kitchen. Each birthday, they would stand tall (well, as tall as they could) and use a pencil to mark the tops of their heads. While he doubted he would ever reach the high bar set by his mom, Ollie held out hope that today of all days he'd see a marked improvement.

He leaned back against the frame and stood tall. Holding his breath, Ollie marked his height with the nearby pencil attached to a piece of string. He checked his progress.

Nothing.

Ollie ran his finger over the birthday marks and noted that he hadn't grown at all since he was nine. Well, maybe *at all* was an exaggeration, but it was such a small amount that he didn't even know what to call it. What's less than a millimeter? Maybe an olliemeter? He made sure to keep that to himself. He didn't want to give Hollis any big ideas.

Speaking of Hollis, he had grown steadily taller each year and, according to the mark for his last birthday, had grown at least a head taller when he turned thirteen. But if the price of getting taller was turning into the teenage monster his brother had mutated into, maybe Ollie would pass.

With a sigh, Ollie headed into the kitchen. Hollis, barely awake, spooned soggy cereal into his mouth but kept missing and spilling on his shirt.

"Morning," said Ollie. Despite not growing, he was determined to have a great birthday, and not even his brother could get him down. He took his seat at the table. "Got anything to say to me?"

"Yeah," grumbled Hollis. "Keep it down."

"Happy birthday!" bellowed their mom from behind. She leapt into the kitchen. In one arm she had a handful of wrapped presents and in the other a huge stack of buttery pancakes with eleven lit candles jabbed into them.

Ollie nearly jumped out of his seat.

"Now, it appears to me as if we have a pretty major violation at this breakfast gathering," said his mom as she placed the presents and pancakes in the center of the table.

"I didn't do it," said Hollis as he furiously wiped his shirt clean.

"You can't start your birthday without a happy birthday song!"

Ollie's mom walked over, belting out the song heartily. Hollis, embarrassed, sank into his chair in an attempt to hide as their mom sang each note.

"There ya are. Make a wish!"

Ollie thought about it.

"I wish that wrestling was every day of the—"

"No!" said his mom, cutting him off. "Don't waste your wish! If you say it out loud, it won't come true."

Hollis rolled his eyes. "Oh, please! Wishes aren't real," he insisted. "And why would saying them out loud make them not come true?"

"Hey, I don't make the rules. I just enforce them."

Ollie was hungry, so instead of finishing his wish, he blew out the candles.

His mom scooped up the candles from the table and started running them under cold water. Ollie knew she'd make sure the full recommended rinsing would be done before the candles were rolled up in a health-and-safety-approved, fire-resistant wrapper.

"Come on, birthday boy. Dig in! Now that you're an eleven-year-old, you need to make sure you eat like one!" She served them both a wobbling stack of pancakes and poured a waterfall of syrup on top of the fluffy, golden pile.

Ollie dug in, shoving pancakes into the corners of his mouth and slurping up every drop of syrup. He peered at Hollis over the pancake tower and watched as his brother inspected each present. Ollie could tell he was trying to guess the contents and already formulating plans to somehow say that it was "theirs" and therefore they should share.

What was Hollis's was Hollis's and what was Ollie's was also Hollis's.

Ollie tore open the packages: Some new clothes that would quickly find their ways into various piles on his bedroom floor. An extensive homework organizer he planned to use to prop up his desk, which had started leaning a bit. And a whole new set of drawing notebooks and pencils!

"Thanks, Mom," he said, giving her a kiss.

"You're very welcome, young man." His mom's face broke into a smile. "We should do this again sometime. What do you say? Same day next year?"

Through the window, Ollie saw the school bus turn onto their street. He hurriedly tossed the gifts into his room, grabbed his bag, and ran toward the door.

"Hold up," said his mom, blocking Ollie's path. "Good luck at school. Pay attention. Don't run in the halls. Listen to your teachers. I want a good, clean fight—*erm*—school day, understood?" she asked.

"I'll try!"

The driver, idling in front of their house, honked the bus's horn angrily.

"Oh, and one more thing," said his mother sternly. "And this is extra, super, duper important . . ." She wrapped her arms around him and squeezed him tight. "I hope you have the best birthday ever! I love you!"

"Thanks, Mom. Love you, too," he gasped, struggling to breathe through her loving iron grip.

CHAPTER 6

OLLIE'S teacher sighed. Mr. Fitzgerald always looked tired. But today he looked downright exhausted. He ran his hands through his thin gray hair, fluffing a few stray strands to cover his bald spot.

Ollie had messed up. Again. When he had been called on to comment on the short story they'd just read in class, he had (of course) been busy thinking about wrestling. So, instead of giving the correct answer, he dreamily blurted out what was on his mind. "Daring Donna's Dive of Doom?"

The response had sent Tamiko tumbling out of her desk with laughter. It took some time for Mr. Fitzgerald to settle the class and get everyone back to work. Now Ollie sat at his desk after the class had been dismissed. Mr. Fitzgerald gazed down at him.

"Sorry, Mr. Fitzgerald," he said.

"I know what's going on here, Ollie," said Mr. Fitzgerald.

"You do?"

Mr. Fitzgerald produced Ollie's most recent quiz. Across the top, a drawing showed The Bolt about to drop a shock elbow on the elderly—but ripped—Lil' Old Granny.

"This is pretty good," said Mr. Fitzgerald, pointing to the drawing. Ollie had been doodling wrestlers on his quizzes and homework for years. At first they had started out as stick figures, but recently he'd really started to advance his skill. "But this? This isn't so good." He pointed to a series of wrong answers and the quiz grade: 60 percent.

"Ouch," whispered Ollie.

"You need to focus." Mr. Fitzgerald held up his hand. "And to be super clear, you need to focus on something other than wrestling."

"Okay," Ollie mumbled.

Mr. Fitzgerald sighed. "There's a time for everything. When you're at Slamdown Town, you can think about wrestling all you want. But when you're here, in school, you should leave wrestling in the ring. You can really go places, if you apply yourself."

Mr. Fitzgerald wanted Ollie to apply himself. His mom wanted him to follow "the rules." And Hollis wanted him to take the first available flight to Antarctica.

"Only you can get yourself there. And hey," said Mr. Fitzgerald as he handed the quiz back to Ollie. "Maybe consider signing up for an art class after school or this summer. I think you have some real talent."

As long as *there* was where wrestling was, that would be fine with him.

Ollie spent math class studying how often The Bolt performed specific moves. During history, he doodled muscular bodies and wrestler outfits on top of the portraits of presidents. At lunchtime, he imagined his fries were wrestlers and made them pile-drive and perform a suplex into ketchup.

"Incoming!" yelled Tamiko as she dodged ketchup splotches from the collision.

But not everyone was so lucky. The impact had sent ketchup flying into the air, across the lunchroom, and smack into the back of the head of the biggest kid in school.

Hollis.

Hollis was sitting, as usual, at the eighth-grade table with his eighth-grade friends. They were all big—to Ollie, they practically looked like adults—and they were always making fun of everyone else who wasn't them, because everyone else wasn't cool.

Why?

Well, because everyone else wasn't *them*.

Ollie never really liked any of Hollis's friends, because, well, none of them liked wrestling. And Ollie couldn't trust anyone who didn't like wrestling.

Ollie noticed that Hollis didn't really talk to his eighth-grade friends about his love of wrestling. Probably because they didn't think it was cool. And because it wasn't cool, it wasn't discussed. When it did come up, he'd say he went to the matches just because his mom was a referee. He didn't like it, but his younger brother did, and hey, isn't he dumb?

The eighth graders were insufferable, annoying, and just plain jerks.

Especially to the sixth graders.

Hollis turned red, and not only because he had ketchup all over his head. His friends howled with laughter as he wiped it off and turned around to see who he had to beat up.

He saw Ollie and the pile of ketchup in front of him, and he squinted his eyes.

Ollie felt his throat fall into his stomach.

Hollis and his group of eighth graders got up from their seats, walked over to Ollie and Tamiko's table, and sat down around them like a pack of hungry hyenas.

"Well, well, well. If it isn't the birthday butthead," said Hollis.

Hollis's friends giggled.

"Sorry, Hollis," said Ollie. "It was an accident."

"Yeah! Get lost, you zit-faced teen loser," said Tamiko.

"Not helping, Tamiko," whispered Ollie.

Hollis grabbed a fry, dunked it into the pile of ketchup, and ate it.

"Get lost? But I haven't even given Ollie his birthday present yet."

Ollie didn't like the sound of that.

Hollis pulled out a small gift from his pocket. At least, Ollie assumed it was a gift. When he looked closer, it appeared to be a slightly dented gift box wrapped in a wad of dirty newspaper.

"What is it?" he asked.

Hollis wagged a finger. "You gotta open it to find out."

The eyes of the eighth graders fixed on Ollie. Opening the gift felt like walking into a trap, but curiosity got the better of him. Ollie lifted the lid. He squinted as he peered closely at the object within, then pulled it out of the box and held it up to his eyes. It was a piece of already-been-chewed gum. The color had been chewed out of it. It looked hard and crusty, and it was covered in bits of food and hair and dust and who knows what else, like it had spent way too long on the ground and been stepped on too many times.

"Gum?" he asked, holding it up for Tamiko to see.

The eighth graders snickered.

Good joke, Hollis, thought Ollie. *You found a piece of gum under a desk or something and wrapped it up to give to me for my birthday. You're sooo clever . . .*

"Not just any gum," Hollis declared proudly. "That gum belonged to—drumroll please—Professor Pain himself."

"No way. You're lying," said Tamiko.

"Me? Lie? Here." Hollis shoved a certificate of authentication into Ollie's hand.

Ollie skimmed the paper. *Blah blah . . .* "official" *. . . blah blah blah . . .*

It was uncanny. An official Slamdown Town letter proved that Hollis was, remarkably, telling the truth. The gum he was holding had belonged to the legend himself, Professor Pain. The self-proclaimed instructor of the ring dealt homework in the form of head kicks and extra credit as body slams. Hollis knew that Professor Pain was Ollie's favorite wrestler of all time. He wouldn't mess around with this. Would he?

Ollie stopped himself. Of course he would.

"How—" he started.

"Bought it on eBay," interrupted Hollis. "Cost me a whole dollar, plus three dollars shipping and handling. You like it?"

The eighth graders snickered even harder.

Ollie did. He *really* liked it. A piece of wrestling history sat in his hands.

"Yeah. Thanks," he said.

"And you know what gum is meant for, right?"

"Um, duh. Wait. Do *you* not know what gum is for, Hollis?" said Tamiko with mock concern.

"Gum is for chewing," Hollis continued, ignoring Tamiko. "Don't you wanna chew it?"

The eighth graders crowded closer, straining to get a good look at Ollie. They raised their phones up to film him. He wanted to climb under the table and hide. But that might attract even *more* attention than he already had.

"It's a wrestling collector's item, not a—"

"Chew the gum! Chew the gum!" Hollis chanted, turning to his friends.

They joined in.

"Chew the gum! Chew the gum!"

Ollie looked more closely at the wad of gum. He groaned. A strand of hair, a piece of corn, and something green that caused him to turn his head away were only a few of the items stuck to the gum that he was able to identify. His stomach clenched.

Ollie raised the gum to his lips. He felt the eighth graders lean in.

He took a deep breath. Then lowered the gum. "No . . . I'm not doing it."

The eighth graders shook their heads. Some tsked; others laughed. Everyone watched him, leaving him feeling as though he'd forgotten to put pants on.

He wished he could turn invisible.

"Happy birthday, butthead," said Hollis, looking gleeful. "Enjoy your crusty, old gum."

Hollis walked away, and everyone else dispersed, leaving Ollie and Tamiko alone.

Ollie may have grown an olliemeter this morning, but now he felt smaller than ever.

CHAPTER 7

THE rest of the day plodded on. No matter where Ollie went, the eighth graders whispered and giggled and pointed. And since the eighth graders did it, that meant that the seventh and other sixth graders did it, too. They didn't even know why they were whispering and giggling and pointing at Ollie. If the eighth graders were doing it, then it was cool.

"Ignore them. They'll find something else to talk about soon," Tamiko said.

As Ollie lay in bed later that night, he couldn't escape the embarrassment. He'd tossed the gum on his bed stand as soon as he'd set foot into his room.

The incident played out like a bad movie over and over in his head.

So instead of replaying the bad memory for the thousandth time, Ollie whipped out his phone and pulled up one of his favorite videos of Professor Pain. The person who uploaded it seemed to have originally recorded it themselves using old tapes. The footage was choppy and slightly out of focus. But Ollie loved it. The bad quality made it feel more authentic.

Professor Pain was an old-school wrestler from years ago, even before Ollie's mom's time as the Brash Banshee. Other than videos he'd watched online, Ollie had never seen him wrestle. But Professor Pain was a Slamdown Town legend. He'd enjoyed a long and accomplished wrestling career before retiring to spend more time sleeping on tropical beaches and being paid to make terrible local business commercials.

"Hey, you," barked Professor Pain in his signature, raspy tone. "Yeah you, the one sitting right there watching this video at this very moment. You seem kinda small and afraid. Tell me. Do you wanna be big enough to stand up to your bullies?"

Ollie nodded. "Sure do."

"Do you find that growing up changes people and wish you could just get into some sort of ring and wrestle all your problems away?" asked Professor Pain.

"Yeah," squeaked Ollie. It felt like Professor Pain was talking *to him*.

"Well, I ain't talking to you," snarled Professor Pain. "I'm talkin' to the future you. The one that's destined to become a 'rassler. Welcome, friend, to my *Anyone Can Be a Wrestler* series," barked Professor Pain.

In addition to his deep voice, the speaker managed to emit Professor Pain's smacking noises; he was always chewing a piece of gum.

"Just do everything Professor Pain does, friend," said

Professor Pain as he worked the gum, "and you'll be a gen-u-ine 'rassler in no time. Because remember—"

"—anyone can be a wrestler if you believe in yourself," said Ollie in time with the video. He had seen this enough times to recite nearly every line, memorize every loud smack of the gum.

The very same gum that Ollie now owned. The gum that Professor Pain chewed during his championship match against Mega Maniac. The gum he'd chomped on when he'd fought both Lieutenant Freedom and Captain Dependence. The gum he'd munched on when Rick Colossal had shockingly offered his hand in a tag-team alliance before they both defeated the Dreadful Five.

And all of a sudden, the overwhelming urge to chew the gum came over Ollie. The gum may have been disgusting. Yet *something* was pulling him to the gum. Maybe it was the connection to his idol. Maybe it was the desire to one-up his brother; to prove to Hollis that he was tough enough to try it. Or maybe it was the gum itself, seemingly calling to him . . .

"Like I was saying before," continued Professor Pain, "there's a 'rassler waiting inside each and every one of us."

Wrestling was everything to Ollie. Maybe even *beyond* everything. And with one cruel gift, Hollis had turned wrestling into humiliation. When Hollis had asked to move into his own room, Ollie had been hurt. But now Hollis had crossed a line. Using wrestling against him was just flat-out wrong. It was a betrayal Ollie hadn't anticipated.

The sound of Professor Pain chomping away on the gum echoed out of his phone.

"And if you're willing to follow my five-part *Anyone Can Be a Wrestler* series and do everything—and I mean everything—I say, then I promise you, your wish of being a 'rassler will come true. Chew on that, and you'll be as big and strong as ol' Professor Pain himself."

Ollie shot out of bed and scooped up the box that contained the gum. He was surprised thirty-year-old gum could still be *that* sticky. He was *not* surprised thirty-year-old gum could be that gross.

Sticky or not—disgusting or not—he had made up his mind. Today was his eleventh birthday, after all. He wouldn't let Hollis push him around anymore. It was time to grow up.

After all, Professor Pain had said to chew on that. Maybe "that" was a piece of knowledge gained from a self-help series. Or maybe "that" was an already-been-chewed piece of bubble gum.

"I wish I was as big and strong as Professor Pain," said Ollie to the gum.

And with that, he popped the gum into his mouth and chewed.

CHAPTER 8

OLLIE had prepared his mind and mouth to taste the most horrible thing ever.

Instead, it was kind of flavorless. Like that time his mom had let Hollis cook spaghetti and he forgot to turn off the stove and they had watery, limp noodles for dinner.

He wasn't sure what he'd expected. After all, this was thirty-year-old, already-been-chewed gum. Of course it was going to be flavorless.

That is, until it wasn't.

Suddenly, the gum turned icy hot. Like cinnamon, but cinnamon coated in lava. Then, just as quickly, it turned super sour. Way, *way* sourer than the sourest sour strip he'd ever tasted. And then he was blasted by an overwhelming fruity flavor.

Strawberry? Or maybe cherry?

Or maybe—

Ollie didn't finish that thought. Rather, he *couldn't* finish that thought, because right then the gum did a bunch of really, really weird stuff.

He could feel the bubble gum in his mouth shooting and expanding in all directions, as large and destructive as an atomic bomb, but worse. Ollie felt a rush of power flood through every muscle in his body. The sensation of careening down a steep roller-coaster drop started from his stomach, spread through his torso, crept up his arms, caused his hair to stand up straight, and shot out of his toes.

He was spinning. Or maybe the room was spinning. Or maybe the world was spinning so fast that merely standing demanded all his focus.

He felt his body expanding. Upward, outward, in all directions. It was too much to feel at once, but the one thing he was still aware of was the sticky gum in his mouth.

And in an instant, the sensation stopped. His stomach rolled, threatening to bring his birthday pancakes back for round two. When his eyes stopped bouncing around in his head, Ollie noticed that he was *much* closer to the ceiling than he had ever been before. He lurched forward and fell toward the ground. It took a lot longer for his face to hit the carpet than it usually did.

He found his footing again and spotted himself in the mirror. But his reflection wasn't . . . *him*.

The giant that stared back at him was six and a half feet tall and had arms the size of dump trucks. He was covered in muscles, and his muscles were covered in muscles. His neck and jaw were as wide as a beach ball; his hair was long and flowing, and looked perfectly conditioned; and his skin was spattered with a golden, muddy spray tan.

"Whoa," said Ollie. In a really deep voice that wasn't his own. The gravelly, spine-chilling voice definitely matched the gargantuan creature that stared back at him.

Ollie had never felt anything quite as exhilarating, or as terrifying.

Or maybe both?

This is nuts, thought Ollie. It didn't feel like a dream. Or a nightmare. And yet, how was any of this happening? People didn't transform into muscly giants by chewing bubble gum. Or did they?

Ollie wasn't a regular gum chewer, so maybe he'd missed out on some gum secret that others already knew? Were gym memberships a cover by the bubble gum–making companies?

That's crazy, thought Ollie. But then again, turning into a giant was crazy, too.

"Exhilarating. Terrifying. That's how you'll feel after you've completed my five-part series and found the 'rassler inside yourself!" shouted Professor Pain from his phone.

Ollie, surprised, leapt into the air and smacked his head on the ceiling. He had completely forgotten he was watching the Professor Pain video. It continued to play uninterrupted.

"Stick around for part one of my five-part series," declared Professor Pain. "Coming to you right after these messages from our sponsors!"

Ollie leaned over to pause the video. His meaty finger tapped—well, slammed—into his now-tiny phone, creating a large crack that snaked across the screen.

"Oh, no," moaned Ollie.

He didn't know his own strength. Before this, he had no strength. And now he (apparently) wielded a lot of it. He needed to be careful. If he broke anything else, his mom might put a stranglehold on his allowance. He turned and bumped into the lamp, which knocked over onto the ground. He dove to grab it, but he missed and ended up sliding headfirst into his desk. His momentum sent his head straight through the cheap wood.

He tried to pull it out and, in his panic, ended up lifting the entire desk off the ground. He spun around, wearing the desk on his head like a helmet, and threw it off.

The desk crashed on the bedroom floor with a loud thud.

He flinched and waited for his mom or his brother to call for him.

Luckily, they were asleep and, both being heavy sleepers, didn't seem to hear.

He looked around and collided face-first into a model of a spaceship that hung down from the ceiling. The spaceship took flight. It was aimed directly at a bookshelf, which, after being hit with a high-flying spaceship model, tilted suddenly to one side.

Ollie sprang forward to catch the falling bookshelf but succeeded only in ripping the entire shelf right off the wall.

He put the shelf, and the large stack of books it supported, on top of his overturned desk.

He had made a mess of his room. Well, *more* of a mess. He crawled back over to the mirror and looked at the person staring back at him.

The person that was apparently him.

What is happening to me? thought Ollie. *I'm . . . big . . . I'm strong . . . I'm . . .*

Ollie started to panic. This kinda stuff only happened in

books or movies, and he was pretty sure that he wasn't in one of those. But with the way things were going, nothing would surprise him at this point. Was he going to be stuck this way forever?

He opened his mouth to scream, but before any sound came out, the gum fell from his mouth and onto the floor. And when he stopped chewing the gum, the hulking dude in the mirror deflated, as if the air had been let out of a balloon or a bubble-gum bubble had been popped.

He looked down at Professor Pain's wad of gum. He crawled over, picked it up, and held it close to his face. He was almost a little afraid of it. Well, not *it*, but what it did.

He didn't know how, he didn't know why, but somehow, someway, chewing Professor Pain's thirty-year-old gum turned Ollie into a huge, lumbering hulk.

Hollis had said birthday wishes weren't real, but his wish had come true.

Ollie was—*finally*—big and strong.

CHAPTER 9

OLLIE'S mom's voice drifted up the stairs from the kitchen.

"Ollie! Come on now. You're going to be late for the bus. Again."

Ollie wiped his eyes. His head pounded, and he felt nauseous, like the time he and Hollis rode the spinning ride at the carnival over and over again until they puked.

Only, this was much worse. When his vision finally steadied, he realized that he was sprawled on his back on the floor of his bedroom.

The sun sliced through the curtains. It must be morning.

Ollie sat up slowly and rubbed the back of his head. He felt like he might have a bruise.

And it felt . . . *sticky?*

And then he touched *it*. The wad of gum.

It was stuck to the back of his head and clinging to his long, unkempt hair. He yanked it out, pulling some strands of hair with it, and winced. That had really hurt. His eyes watered as he looked down at the gum he now clasped in his palm.

Ollie had spent all night inspecting the gum and searching the internet for answers. There were many articles that popped up, with titles like "Chewing Gum Makes You More Productive!" and "Seven Surprising Benefits of Chewing Gum," but none of them mentioned anything about magically transforming into a brawny giant. He must've passed out mid-search and landed in the gum.

"Ollie!" his mom shouted again from downstairs. "Hurry up!"

Last night, he had chewed the gum and had become *big*. But that had to have been a dream, *right*? Gum didn't make people transform. At least not any gum he knew of. He'd been having vivid dreams lately, but that one was the most realistic he'd ever experienced . . .

There was only one way to find out. He slowly placed the gum onto his tongue, closed his mouth, and chewed. A dash of icy-hot flavor. An explosion of power. An eruption of adrenaline. And just as he had done the night before, Ollie shot upward. He shot outward.

And just like last night, he transformed into a giant, hulking version of himself.

He couldn't believe it. "Not a dream!" yelled Ollie, and he let out a cheer.

There was a knock at the door.

Ollie's heart nearly burst out of his bulging pectoral muscles. As quickly as he could, he spat out the gum. And just like a balloon being popped, the hulking figure deflated back into Ollie again. And not a moment too soon.

"You aren't even dressed," exclaimed his mom as she opened

the door. "I've been calling up to you all morning. Buses wait for no one! Just because you're eleven now doesn't mean you can be lazy."

She shut the door and headed back downstairs.

Ollie's phone chimed. It was a text from Tamiko.

Dude. Check out this video for beating Kragthar.

Kragthar? How could he think of video games at a time like this? Somehow, Professor Pain's already-been-chewed gum was . . .

Magic?!

He knew that sounded ridiculous, but how else could he explain what was happening? He remembered that he had wished he were big enough to take on Hollis.

Had this disgusting piece of gum granted his wish?

Or had the wish made this disgusting piece of gum magic?

He had heard of people wishing on stars or birthday pancakes, but wishing on a disgusting wad of gum? It was ridiculous! It was insane! It was impossible!

It had happened.

His mind raced. He had to tell someone.

He typed a response.

Tamiko!

Tamiko replied:

what

SOMETHING HAPPENED

He could see that Tamiko was typing. He had considered telling Hollis last night, but knew that was a bad idea. Sure, anyone, even Hollis, would think this was amazing. But considering his brother was being a puberty jerkface lately, Hollis might take the gum away from him and keep it for himself, just like the laptop; or worse, he'd tell their mom and then she'd take it away from both of them. Ollie was pretty certain that transforming into a mammoth beast violated some unspoken rule he didn't know of. He wasn't willing to chance losing the gum. His phone chimed again.

YOU BEAT KRAGTHAR WITHOUT ME?! :'(HOW COULD YOU?? Lol jk you'd be lost without me. You doing okay after yesterday? Don't worry. We'll show Hollis who's boss

I made a WISH. I chewed the gum! and

???? . . . and????? Also gross

Ollie tried to type an explanation but kept deleting whatever he typed.

I GREW HUGEEEEE

. . . whut

Ollie had a brilliant idea. He knew how to convince Tamiko. He tossed the gum back into his mouth, chewed, and transformed. He lifted the phone to his face and took a photo.

He messaged it to Tamiko. She responded a second later.

. . . who is that?

it's me!

lol . . . ok . . . so anyway . . . back to the real reason i texted you. my parents are doing that *wellness* thing again. UGH i need you to sneak me some junk food THIS IS NOT A DRILL

"Ollie. I'm not playing around!" yelled his mom from downstairs.

Right. He still had to go to school.

He still had to be Ollie.

He spat the wad of gum into his hand and returned to his puny, normal self. He threw on his clothes, heart pounding. He looked like he had gotten caught in a windstorm. But there was no time. He needed a wrapper or something to store the gum in—there was no way he was letting it out of his sight after what had just transpired. He spotted a piece of neon-blue paper on his desk, snatched it up, and rolled the gum inside.

He ran out to the bus . . . just as it pulled away from the curb.

"Wait! Come back!" he yelled. But his mom was right. Buses didn't wait for anyone. Hollis pressed his lips against the back window and blew a giant raspberry as the bus left without Ollie.

So Ollie's mom drove him to school on her way to her other job as a personal fitness trainer. Her hair was wrangled into a bun, and her sleeveless T-shirt flapped in the breeze from the open window. He didn't mind driving with his mom, but it definitely came with a price. She regaled him the entire ride with a lecture about the importance of being on time. She also yelled at random pedestrians for violating basic traffic rules.

"The crosswalk is *clearly* painted for the safety of both me, the driver, and you, the pedestrians," she explained to a confused-looking elderly couple who had veered slightly outside the lines. "The rules are rules for a reason, people!"

He heard only bits and pieces. He had to talk to Tamiko. She was smart and watched a ton of movies. She would know what to do. His mind spun round and round.

All his life, Ollie wanted to be big and strong. And now, with a simple chew, he could be. For years he had waited for someone to come along and defeat Werewrestler. That someone would finally avenge his mom and give the Slamdown Town fans someone worthy to root for. Maybe, with a new champion, more people would come back to watch and the stands would be full again like they used to be. But with the gum, he wouldn't need to wait for *someone*. He could take matters into his own hands.

He thought this sort of awesome event happened only to mysterious orphans or aliens in disguise. Or wannabe superheroes. Yet here he was, a regular kid who could not be bothered to tie his shoes correctly or pass a math test, with the power to turn into someone huge. And muscly. And surprisingly hairy. He was more than okay with all of it.

CHAPTER 10

OLLIE sprinted from the car the moment his mom pulled up to school, clutching the wrapped gum firmly in his hand. Taking the steps two at a time, he vaulted up the stairs, flew down the hallway, and skidded into Ms. Middleton's class.

"Tamiko! I have something to tell you," he shouted.

The whole class snapped their heads toward Ollie. And then they all turned to Tamiko. Tamiko's face scrunched up as she felt all eyes on her.

He ripped the gum out of its neon-blue wrapper and waved it in her face.

"You're not going to believe it. It's—"

"Whatever it is, it *can* wait till after class, Ollie," said Ms. Middleton. She motioned to his seat. The class giggled. In all his excitement, Ollie had forgotten one important fact:

School was still happening.

"And you know the rules. No gum in class," she said. Before

he could stop her, Ms. Middleton swiped the gum out of his hand and casually dropped it in the trash bin.

Ollie could have screamed. He didn't, but he could have. He felt all the blood drain from his face. He must have looked as pale as a ghost.

Tamiko shot him a weird look and took her seat.

"Okay," began Ms. Middleton, "everyone take out your textbooks."

He took his seat and pulled out his science book, never once taking his eyes off the trash can. He couldn't believe his rotten luck. He'd just found out he had magic gum, and then of course it'd been confiscated.

Don't panic, he told himself.

Once class ended, he would casually stroll past the bin and retrieve the gum. He started to feel better. After all, it wasn't like the gum could get up and walk away.

Just then, the school custodian entered the room.

Ollie watched in horror as the custodian grabbed the trash can, walked back into the hallway, and dumped it into his own, much larger bin. Then the custodian returned the now-empty trash can back to the classroom.

This time Ollie actually *did* scream, cutting Ms. Middleton off mid-lecture.

"Ollie?! What now?"

The custodian closed the door and wheeled his bin out of sight.

Ollie had to move. And fast! Before he lost the gum forever.

"I have to use the bathroom. And so does Tamiko," he announced.

"I do?" she asked, confused.

He turned to Tamiko and fixed her with a pleading stare. "You do. Right now."

Tamiko raised her hand. "Ms. Middleton, I really need to use the bathroom."

"Inside voices please," groaned Ms. Middleton. She looked at Ollie, then at Tamiko. She sighed. "Since you clearly will not stop disrupting my class until you've settled . . . whatever it is you're doing . . . Fine. Make it fast."

Ollie took off down the hall. Tamiko appeared seconds later right behind him.

"For the record, I do not have to go to the bathroom," said Tamiko.

"We need to get my gum back."

Tamiko stuck her tongue out, disgusted. "No. It's in the trash, Ollie. Where it belongs. Honestly, what is going on with you? You've been acting weird all morning."

Ollie was only half listening. He scanned the hallway for the custodian. He spotted the trash bin outside the science lab. The custodian was inside, grabbing another trash can.

"There!" he said. He turned to Tamiko. "Just trust me."

He and Tamiko ran over to the trash bin and peered in. It was filled with, well, trash: a banana peel, a soda bottle, several used tissues, a wrapper, a half-eaten tuna fish sandwich. And, buried somewhere beneath all that and more, Professor Pain's magic gum.

"Oh, barf," said Tamiko. She shielded her nose. "Seriously, Ollie? What's going on?"

"No time to explain." He rifled through the trash bin.

"Have you lost your mind?" asked Tamiko.

"Where is it?" He tossed trash over his shoulder and just barely missed hitting Tamiko with a browned apple core.

"Hey!" she yelled.

"Sorry."

It had to be close. It had to be! Wait . . . There! At the bottom, wedged between a broken stapler and a half-finished yogurt container, was the neon-blue paper wrapper and, inside it, the gum. He thanked himself for wrapping it. Hopefully very tightly.

He grabbed the gum as quickly as he could.

Ollie pulled Tamiko away into the gym. After checking that no one else was around, he shook the wad of gum in front of her face.

"I have something incredible to show you," he said.

"Wow. Gum. I don't know if I'll ever be the same again," said Tamiko sarcastically. She turned her attention to her phone and started playing *Jewel Heist*. She glanced up in between lightning-fast finger-tapping. "Well, c'mon, let's see this *life-changing event* before everyone thinks I've been in the bathroom this entire time."

Ollie unwrapped the gum. He threw it into his mouth and chewed. He transformed. The now-big and -muscled Ollie waved down at Tamiko. Tamiko's jaw dropped. So did her phone.

"Tamiko? You okay?" he asked.

She slowly pointed a shaky finger straight at him.

"Giant hairy monster demon!" screamed Tamiko at the top of her lungs. Which, for Tamiko, was loud *to the extreme*. Ollie wouldn't be surprised if the whole world had heard that. She bolted away, clearly wanting nothing to do with whatever was going on.

"Tamiko, wait!"

Ollie lurched forward and used his massive hand to scoop

her up by the back of her shirt. He lifted her up to his face. Tamiko spun in the air as she swung wildly at him.

"Hey, put me down," she demanded. "I'm ranked first, second, and third in the *Ninja Kitten* online leaderboards, and I am not afraid to kick your butt!"

She squirmed and threw a lame swing at Ollie's chest.

"Ow!" she yelled, nursing her arm. "Jeez, what are you made of? Bricks?!"

Despite all her struggles, she could not wriggle free of Ollie's bubblegum iron grip.

"Would you cool it, Tamiko? You're gonna get us caught."

"It knows my name! What did you do with my friend? Is he inside you? Did you eat him? Don't eat me okay?! I swear I don't taste good," pleaded Tamiko. "But I can get you other kids to eat. Plump, juicy ones that are way better tasting than I am!"

Ollie sighed. "Tamiko! It's me! When I chew this gum, I grow big! And when I spit it out, I shrink back to me. See?!" He spat the gum back into his hand and he shrunk.

Tamiko slipped from his deflating grip and fell to the ground. She breathed heavily, her eyes thick with disbelief. Then, acceptance. Then, wonder.

"That guy in the photo you sent. That was you?" she asked.

"I wasn't making it up," he answered.

"This is Professor Pain's already-been-chewed gum?" Tamiko's eyes shimmered with excitement, as if truly seeing the gum for the first time.

"Yes."

"The same Professor Pain's gum that Hollis gifted you yesterday?"

"Yes."

She paused. She seemed to be struggling with what she had seen. She kept shaking her head and blinking rapidly, as if trying to see if she'd wake up. He couldn't blame her.

"Whoa." Her face lit up, full of wonder. "That *is* the coolest thing I've ever seen."

"You wanna try it?" he asked.

Several seconds passed. Her still-open jaw slowly closed.

"Umm. I'm going to pass. You know I'm weird about eating food that has fallen on the floor, and that thing looks like it's spent thirty years on the floor."

He tossed the gum back into his mouth and transformed again.

"I gotta see something."

He ran over to the pull-up bar. Earlier that year, during the school fitness exam, Ollie had been able to do only one and a half pull-ups. Okay, one and a quarter.

The worst in his class.

He leapt into the air, wrapped his palms around the bar, and pulled himself up.

One. Two. Three.

And then he proceeded to do forty-seven more.

"Fifty!" shouted Tamiko. "I think that's a new school record!"

As he heaved himself up for the final pull-up, the bar sagged and snapped under his weight. He fell to the floor and landed on his feet. The bar might have been done, but he wasn't yet. He ran over to the rock-climbing wall.

He'd never been able to reach the bell at the top of the wall.

In fact, he'd never been able to reach the second foothold. He'd never been strong enough.

He grabbed on to one rock.

Then another and another.

He climbed and climbed until he reached the bell at the top of the wall. He punched it with his fist. It rang, broke free of the wall, and fell to the ground.

"That was the fastest I've ever seen anyone climb the rock wall!" said Tamiko. "Also, I'm not paying to fix that bar or that bell. That was all you, big guy."

He climbed down and did a victory lap around the gym.

Even with Tamiko's epic shout, they had managed not to get caught by any students or teachers yet. But he was not interested in finding out what would happen if someone noticed a big hairy dude wrecking the gym equipment. He spat out the gum. A few moments later, eleven-year-old Ollie pulled out the wrapper. He placed the gum inside.

And that's when he noticed *what* piece of paper he'd grabbed to wrap the gum in. He had tossed the neon-blue flyer on his nightstand after the match on Saturday.

He had forgotten all about it. Until now.

There it was, next to the doodle he had drawn of himself as a wrestler.

NEW WRESTLER TRYOUTS

THIS WEEK ONLY

"Hey, Tamiko," he said. "I have an idea."

CHAPTER 11

WHEN the school bell rang at the end of the day, Tamiko and Ollie sprinted out the door and down the steps. As usual, they did not immediately head home.

They marched straight to Mrs. Ramirez's tiny house.

Mrs. Ramirez was a little old lady who lived down the block from them and had ten standard poodles. She was too old to walk them herself, so she had enlisted Ollie and Tamiko's help.

Each afternoon, the two friends groomed, brushed, and walked the enormous dogs. They'd hit the pavement with five dogs each and hang on for dear life as the poodles dragged them up and down the block. It was hard work, but it was better than going home and doing homework; plus, it meant Ollie got to hang out with Tamiko for a little longer each day.

Wrestling tickets were not cheap. In fact, Linton Krackle had recently raised the entrance fee another whole dollar. Ollie didn't know why he thought making the tickets *more* expensive would help sell *more* tickets And while his mom was the sole referee at Slamdown Town, *employee discount* was a phrase that Linton wasn't familiar with.

"Employee discount?" Linton had said with confusion when Ollie's mom had asked. He looked up the definition on his phone and spat out his cup of watered-down bargain-brand coffee. "I pay *you*, don't I? So you and your family can afford to enjoy full-price wrestling entertainment."

So instead, Mrs. Ramirez paid Ollie and Tamiko ten dollars each—two dollars per dog. That covered the tickets and—just barely—the snacks.

Ollie called his mom after they'd safely returned the poodles and had their ten dollars in hand. He read over the tryouts flyer again as he waited for her to answer.

His mom worked as a personal trainer during the day, so she didn't always pick up. She was most likely breaking down some workout rule or another with her latest overwhelmed client who was beginning to have second thoughts about their beach-body dreams. He didn't like lying to his mom, but he thought this was a special situation.

She picked up.

"Can I go to Tamiko's for a bit and work on, uh, homework?" he asked.

"Sounds good. Be home by supper. And no more than fifteen minutes of wrestling videos tonight, and then it's straight to bed. Promise? No, not you," he heard his mom tell her client. "You need to give me seventy more squats on the double!"

He promised. He hoped he wouldn't need wrestling videos anymore.

He'd have the real thing now.

Later that afternoon, Ollie stood in the back parking lot of Slamdown Town Arena. He popped the gum into his mouth, transformed, took a step forward, and tripped over his own feet. They were far bigger, and they took much larger steps, than he was used to.

"Look out below!" yelled Ollie as he crashed into some nearby bushes. Leaves and berries went flying all over the sidewalk, and a bird who was nesting peacefully in one of the bushes buzzed angrily around his head. He ran around the parking lot awkwardly, his massive legs pounding the pavement and his mighty arms swatting at the bird. Changing back and forth from an eleven-year-old kid to a giant wrestler would take some getting used to.

Once he steadied himself, he approached the door—not his usual door, the one all the arena patrons used, but the side entrance.

He had discovered the side entrance with Hollis years ago. They'd tried to sneak in a couple times when they were short on the admissions fee, but arena staff always chased them away and informed their mom. Those dudes were tattletales.

He and Hollis weren't trying to do anything bad. They'd just wanted to see what happened behind the scenes. They'd always joked that backstage was an ancient colosseum where the wrestlers would practice wrestling rock columns like in those old stop-motion movies, or maybe a futuristic training facility with robotic wrestlers who said things such as "Destroy all humans!"

It had been a few months since they'd joked about that.

Ollie ran his hand along the sign that was painted on the door.

"Nah, I can't make it," replied Tamiko when he had asked her earlier to tag along. "I got dinner with my grandma, and I never miss meat loaf night. If I did, my grandma would serve *me* for next week's dinner. Besides, the arena won't just let some kid run around backstage. Remember?"

True. The farthest either of them had ever gotten was when Tamiko made it a full four steps in before arena security escorted them out. Even Hollis was impressed.

"But what if I mess it up?" He bit his lip. Tamiko was the one who laughed in the face of danger. Without her there, what would he do if he got into trouble?

Tamiko placed her hands on Ollie's shoulders and gave them a reassuring squeeze.

"Listen, Ollie. You know I'd wanna be there, but this is a solo mission. Wrestlers only. I'm not a wrestler. But you are."

"You're right," sighed Ollie.

Now that he was here at Slamdown Town and looked the part of a wrestler, there was no one to stop him. Nothing standing in his way. It was all on Ollie now.

All he had to do was walk through the door labeled WRESTLERS ONLY.

He took a deep breath and stepped inside.

Ollie entered a dimly lit hallway. The overhead lights flickered on and off. A water pipe spat and leaked muddy water. The ground was carpeted in scuff marks and bronzer.

Not quite the grand entrance he had imagined.

He turned the corner and collided with a wall of muscle and anger.

"Watch where you're going, punk!" yelled the burly wrestler he had just walked into. He noticed an unmistakable lightning bolt tattoo across her face.

His heart leapt up into his throat.

"Um, holy cow. Wow. You're . . ." Ollie struggled to talk. "You're The Bolt!"

"Yeah, I am. And *you're* in my way," she snapped.

Ollie was at a loss for words. Here he was, standing in the wrestlers-only section of Slamdown Town, having an actual conversation with one of his favorite wrestlers.

"You hear me?" she grunted. "I said beat it, or else!"

Or else what?! Ollie couldn't believe his luck. *The Bolt? Threatening me?*

His mind raced with the possibilities.

"What are you gonna do? Tesla Coil? Zap Attack? Thunder Knee?!" he asked.

"No. Worse," she muttered, taking a step forward.

"Worse?!" For a moment, Ollie thought he might faint from excitement.

The only move worse than any of those was . . . *Oh, no.*

"Lightning Strike," said The Bolt as she leapt into the air, spun around, and used the momentum to roundhouse kick Ollie in the chest. He was sent flying back toward the door he'd just walked in. The Bolt screamed and sprinted toward him with both fists raised.

Ollie, having seen this move a thousand times before, knew that lightning *did* strike twice. In fact, it struck dozens of times—in the form of rapid-fire fists to the face.

"I'm gonna punch that gum right outta your mouth!"

Ollie focused on keeping his mouth shut tight as her fists connected again and again with his cheeks, until the storm finally passed. He lay on the floor, looking up at The Bolt as she stood over him, fists still clenched.

Ollie saw stars. This was the greatest day of his life. He wouldn't wash his face ever again, no matter how many times his mom told him to do it before bed.

He chomped down on the gum, which he'd stored in his left cheek for safekeeping.

"Good luck today, you big chew," she said. "You're gonna need it."

The Bolt pushed past Ollie and stormed out to the parking lot.

"This is the best day ever!" he declared to no one. He wished Tamiko could have seen this. He'd be sure to commit every incident to memory to share with her later.

He continued down the hallway until he reached the locker room.

"Best day ever" was about to get better. Because as he entered the Slamdown Town locker room, Ollie found himself surrounded by a treasure trove of the most amazing, spectacular, and jaw-dropping wrestling artifacts. He felt a dizzying sensation, as if his brain were melting. Then the adrenaline took over. And he shot forward for a better look.

You gotta be kidding me, he thought as he approached.

There, sitting in a locker directly in front of him, was the *actual* stinger Queen Bee had used to take down Rey Rocket after Queen Bee discovered Rey was allergic to bees. Then he spotted what lay next to it. He froze.

"No way!" he whispered. "Is that—"

"Oy, mate!" croaked a voice behind him.

Ollie froze. He knew that voice. He spun on his heel, lockers temporarily forgotten. There, before his very eyes, was Reggie Highwayman.

"Biscuits and gravy! You're the British Terror. No way," exclaimed Ollie.

"Excitable bloke, this one," Reggie commented, wincing. "Inside voices, mate."

"You're even flying the colors," Ollie said, awed, as he reached out to touch the patriotic scarf around Reggie's neck. Then he proceeded to rub it against his face. "So cool. And it smells just like my mom's tea."

"Keep yer mitts off the ol' Union Jack," grunted Reggie.

Reggie freed his scarf from Ollie's grip and walked away, muttering.

I got to touch Reggie Highwayman's scarf. Ollie knew he must have been a strange sight to behold: a towering wrestler practically drooling over everything and everyone. Sure, Ollie was a huge, overly muscled wrestler now. But he was also still an eleven-year-old kid standing backstage alongside his lifelong legends. Ollie could hardly believe what he was experiencing. It felt like a surreal dream. A smelly, surreal dream.

Because Ollie smelled something fishy.

Fishy like when Hollis would jam seaweed down his swim trunks at the beach, or when his mom made him a tuna fish sandwich for lunch.

"Big Tuna!" he exclaimed.

Big Tuna, staying true to his name, was both large and

smelly. Ollie squealed, as much as a huge wrestler with a voice as gravelly as a mountain can squeal, and stared. He knew he shouldn't—and his nose begged him to walk away—but he couldn't stop. Big Tuna, the terror of the sea, stared right back. And if those eyes could talk, they would have said to get lost, quit staring, and that it was time to get out of the water, because swimming hours had officially ended.

But Ollie just kept right on gawking. Big Tuna snorted, pushed past him, and knocked his shoulder into Ollie on the way out. Ollie, still getting used to his massive size and weight, stumbled to maintain his balance. But he didn't care.

He'd officially taken a blow, sorta, from Big Tuna! He had to physically think about not smiling so hard. He closed his lips, furrowed his brow, and tried to look tough.

Just keep chewing. Just keep chewing.

Ollie spotted a long line of wrestlers who he didn't recognize. He guessed that had to be the line for the tryouts. So he took one final look around the locker room.

He hoped it wasn't the first and only time he'd get to see it.

CHAPTER 12

OLLIE moved to take his place in the tryout line. He realized this was the first time in his life he could actually see over the head of someone standing in front of him.

He looked around the room at his competition. Well, what passed for his competition. The hopefuls gathered were wrestler wannabes. And judging by their strange wrestler gimmicks (a woman in an anteater outfit named, yep, The Anteater, was chatting excitedly with a set of twins who were wrapped head-to-toe in tinfoil and who called themselves The Leftovers) and the general lack of any athletic build (a guy with a toilet seat around his neck and a plunger in hand who proclaimed himself The Flusher was having a stare-down with a fellow in snazzy shorts named Toot Toot McSnazzy Shorts), these "wrestlers" were far from top-tier talent. In fact, they might not even be bottom-tier talent.

This should be easy, thought Ollie. *Right . . . ?*

A wave of uncertainty washed over him. What if he didn't

make it? Or worse, what if someone found out that he wasn't actually a wrestler?

He chewed the gum so hard that he thought he might break a tooth.

After a few minutes, an attendant arrived and ushered them into the arena. Ollie noticed a few important people wearing suits sitting in the stands. At least, he assumed they were important, because only important people would bother to wear suits in the arena. In the center of the suits was the biggest (metaphorically anyway) suit of all: Linton Krackle, the greasy, stocky CEO and owner of Slamdown Town.

The flickering lights from the arena bounced off Linton's polished, balding head. His bushy mustache rested on his upper lip and danced when he spoke, and his custom-made suit wrapped around him like a boa constrictor.

Ollie signed important-looking papers that the attendant blabbed on and on about—something about waiving his rights in case he got injured and that Slamdown Town was in no way responsible for anything, ever.

"Yeah, whatever. Is it time to wrestle yet?" he asked.

"Okay, listen up," interrupted Linton Krackle to the group of hopeful wrestlers. "We're looking for the best of the best. The type of wrestler who will instill fear into the hearts of their opponents. The type of wrestler who will instill so much excitement in fans that they'll wet themselves and need to buy an official Slamdown Town diaper at the souvenir shop. Most importantly, though, we need the type of wrestler who will instill money into the pocket of their CEO."

The wrestlers mumbled in agreement.

"Okay," said Linton. "Time is money and I ain't paying the bill. Let's kick this off. You in the lobster suit. And, uh, big guy chomping on the gum. Get in the ring."

Ollie looked at the guy in the lobster suit.

"Name's Larry Lobster," the guy said. He extended a friendly claw. Ollie shook it.

"Name's Ollie . . . uhh . . ."

"Pleased to meet you, Ollie Uhh!"

Ollie and Larry Lobster made their way toward the ring. Above them, the very important business people watched closely while taking notes on their laptops.

The other wannabe wrestlers took seats in the front row.

Ollie climbed over the ropes and walked around the ring. He had imagined this moment his entire life. Now, with the mat beneath his feet, it felt like a dream.

But it wasn't. It was real.

"Somebody pinch me," said Ollie out loud to himself.

"Okay!" said Larry Lobster.

Ding, ding, ding!

The bell sounded.

Larry Lobster whacked Ollie on the back of the head with his lobster claw. Luckily, since Larry was in a giant lobster suit, the claw had a lot of padding. The blow didn't do much of anything.

Ollie spun around and grappled with Larry. The big, padded suit made it hard to grab on to anything. So every time Ollie thought he had him, Larry wriggled away.

But Ollie didn't give up.

He ran straight toward the ropes, bounced off them, and used the momentum to fling himself back toward Larry Lobster.

This time, he connected.

He secured a front facelock on poor Larry Lobster, hooked a meaty arm under his left leg, hoisted him up and over his head, and sent him straight back down in a blistering fisherman's driver.

Larry Lobster was right on time for a face-to-face meeting with the mat.

He hit it and flopped around like a fish out of water.

Ollie saw his chance to pin his opponent, and he didn't hesitate.

He threw his body into the air and slammed directly on top of Larry.

Ding, ding, ding!

The ringside bell sounded out his first victory in the ring. Wrestling staff rushed up to remind Larry Lobster that Slam-down Town was not responsible for his injuries. And that his car had been double-parked and towed.

The matches that followed were some of the least entertaining matches Ollie had ever seen. The ragtag pairs barely managed to pull off the simplest of moves. One wrestler, Snackie Jackie, managed to knock herself out with her own haymaker. The Human Paper Clip stopped mid-match to take an "important call" from his mom about what to order for dinner. The Flusher didn't even make it into the ring before tripping and rolling his ankle.

I got this, thought Ollie.

After all the tryouts were finished, Linton had a discussion with the people next to him. Ollie did not understand what they could be talking about. He *had* won, after all. Did this mean he was now officially a wrestler? No one else had won as quickly as he had.

"All right, listen up!" yelled Linton from the stands after a few moments. "Bubble gum, you've got size, you've got guts, and you've got strength. Which is more than I can say for these other basement dwellers. The rest of you, get outta here."

"Thanks." The word emerged as a squeak even with Ollie's new, deep "adult" voice. The crowd of hopeful wrestlers, dreams dashed, mumbled and grumbled as they shuffled out.

"But you've also got a long way to go if you wanna be a professional wrestler. You don't have a costume. You don't have smack talk. And you don't have any signature moves," said Linton, raising a finger with each infraction. "Sure, you made dinner out of Larry Lobster, but who is Larry Lobster? A real wrestler doesn't just win; they win with style! And style wins the crowd," he added, gesturing to the empty arena. "So you tell me: Why should I reach into my pocket and pay *you* to wrestle for Slamdown Town?"

Ollie hadn't thought of that. He had figured that winning the tryout was most important. He hadn't considered that *how* he won would matter more.

"I'll, uh, wrestle for free," he offered. Besides, he already had an after-school job.

"You're hired," said Linton. Behind him, the suits nodded their agreement. "What do we call you?"

"What do you call me?"

"Yeah. What's your name?"

"My name?" Ollie thought for a moment. *What was it that The Bolt had called me?*

"Call me Big Chew."

"Welcome to Slamdown Town, Big Chew."

CHAPTER 13

AS soon as the tryouts were over, Ollie sprinted over to Tamiko's house. When he told her he had been hired, she screamed and did victory laps around her basement.

"Quiet down there!" yelled Tamiko's mom from the top of the stairs.

Her mom, a professor, was grading papers upstairs while her dad, a professional napper, slept on the couch. Tamiko's parents didn't like when she and Ollie yelled or played too loudly. Tamiko found it annoying, but Ollie didn't mind. Hanging out at her house meant he didn't need to keep his eyes out for random older-brother attacks.

He told her everything, from encountering The Bolt in the hallway all the way to when he dramatically announced his wrestler name as Big Chew.

"Do you like it?" he asked.

"Like it? I love it!"

Ollie was relieved. Tamiko always came up with the best video game character names. She even went so far as to give them their own fictional backstories. There was Diamondz McThievey, the jewel thief with a (stolen) heart of gold; Oakenbear Manypants, the shape-shifting wizard with a keen eye for adventure and fashion; and Sensei Kitty Litter, the feline martial arts master who flexed her claws of vengeance following a betrayal by her apprentice. He knew Tamiko could be particular, and he was happy to have passed her test.

"So, who would you want to wrestle first?" asked a breathless Tamiko. "Brad Baby Stephens? Lil' Old Granny?"

Ollie paused for dramatic effect. "Werewrestler."

"Ollie . . . ," she said. "I get it, but . . ."

"Don't you want to see me avenge Brash Banshee?"

"Come on. Of course I want to see you avenge your mom, Ollie. But it's *Werewrestler*."

"Someone has to teach that bully a lesson. Why not me?" he demanded to know.

"That's crazy talk, Ollie. He'd destroy you. You may be able to turn into someone who *looks* like a wrestler, but that doesn't mean you *are* one, or that you can take on the reigning champ. Think of all those wrestlers who've trained for years to defeat Werewrestler—and all with a zero percent success rate, I might add."

Tamiko's phone buzzed. She scooped it up.

"Um, why is Slamdown Town calling me?" she asked.

"Oh." He knew he had forgotten to mention something important. "They said I needed a manager, and I panicked, so I gave them your number."

"You did *what*?!" yelled Tamiko.

"Volume. Lower it," called Tamiko's mom from upstairs.

Ollie lowered his voice. "Yeah. They said I needed a manager to arrange the fights and stuff. It all happened so fast and was kind of a blur. But—the phone! Hurry, pick it up."

"Okay. First: You should have asked," answered Tamiko, blowing a loose strand of hair out of her face. "And second: I'm eleven years old. I can't be a manager."

"Please, Tamiko," he begged. "My wrestling career depends on it!"

She considered this. "All right. Quit your crying. I'll do it. On one condition."

The phone in her hand continued to buzz.

"Anything. Whatever it is, I'll do it." He really needed her to pick up that call.

Tamiko turned her full attention to Ollie. There was no joking around in the look she gave him. "Promise me that we're still a team on this."

"What do you mean?" asked Ollie, confused.

"Sure, you can change into some crazy magical wrestler now. Which, yeah, that's so awesome. But, like, we're best buds. We gotta do this together. Just like always!"

Ollie was shocked. Was Tamiko jealous that he had found the gum and not her? Or upset that she couldn't go to the try-outs? He hadn't noticed her acting any differently, but then again, he had been kind of distracted. "Of course. You're my best friend."

She looked relieved. "And also your manager!"

Tamiko grinned, picked up the phone, and put it on speaker.

"This is Ms. Manager," said Tamiko in a super-serious, super-deep voice.

"Ms. Manager?!" mouthed Ollie. "That's the best you could think of?!"

Tamiko waved him off and continued. "Yes, Ms. Manager, and I'm an extremely important businesswoman with lots of famous wrestlers to manage. Who is this?"

"Well, uh, Ms. Manager. Linton Krackle here. I'm sure I need no introduction," began Linton on the other end of the line, who then went on to introduce himself in great detail anyway.

"You know, the rich, extremely talented, and also handsome owner of Slamdown Town," said Linton in a tone dripping with self-admiration. "Mom always said my older brother was the one destined for greatness. Well, does he own a semi-successful wrestling arena with a less-than-semi-talented lineup of stars?"

"No?" guessed Tamiko.

"No, he doesn't," confirmed Linton. "All he's got is his stupid *medical degree* and his *long list of celebrity patients*. I sure showed him. And he thinks I forgot about that five bucks I lent him in middle school. Well, let me tell you something about compound interest—"

His voice sounded even slimier over the phone. Linton's tone reminded Ollie of the time he had gone with his mom to the used-car dealership. The car dealer had tried to make Ollie feel like he was his friend, but Ollie could tell that it was all an act to get his mom to buy a more expensive car. That's kind of how Ollie felt every time he saw Linton Krackle.

Like it was all an act.

"Listen, Linton," said Tamiko, cutting him off. "About Big Chew's first match ..."

"Straight to business. I like that." Linton smacked his lips. "Newbies don't necessarily bring in the crowds. Which means I don't make bank. And I love making bank. So we're gonna *ease* the big guy into it. Make him all warm and fuzzy for the fans. And *then* they'll pay top dollar to see him dance. That's why he's gonna face Bertha Blunder on Saturday."

Ollie looked at Tamiko. Bertha Blunder, whose claim to fame was failing her way to victory, was a decent opponent, but she was no champion. Bertha wasn't the goal. Ollie realized that Tamiko could actually stop him from facing Werewrestler if she wanted. If she folded now, Big Chew would be taking on Bertha Blunder. He held his breath.

"We want Werewrestler," announced Tamiko.

Tamiko had to cover the speaker on her phone to stifle the laughter coming from Linton. "Oh, man. You are something else, Ms. Manager. Very funny."

It took Tamiko some time to convince Linton that she was, in fact, *very* serious. And then he was even more confused.

"Listen," started Linton. "I get that Big Chew wants to wrestle the best of the best. But even if I wanted to pair him with Werewrestler—and believe me, I don't—I can't."

"But you're Linton Krackle. The CEO and owner of Slamdown Town. Aren't you, like, the most powerful man alive?" asked Tamiko.

"Flattery will get you everywhere," replied an amused Linton.

"Except in the ring with Werewrestler. Guy's a freak. You don't challenge him. *He* challenges you."

"Easy peasy. So how do we get Werewrestler to challenge us?"

"You drive a hard bargain," said Linton after a long pause. "I can see why Big Chew picked you to be his manager. You want the best? Then your guy's got to prove himself and start winning some matches. If he proves himself, I'm sure Werewrestler will come howling. What do you say we start with the crown prince of fashion himself? Gorgeous Gordon Gussett."

Tamiko put her hand over the speaker. "What do you think?" she asked.

"Whatever it takes to get to Werewrestler," Ollie answered.

She uncovered the phone. "Yep. Bring him on!"

"Your funeral. Or rather, Big Chew's. He's got Gorgeous this Saturday."

And with that, Linton ended the call.

Ollie and Tamiko erupted into relieved laughter.

"Keep it down, down there!" yelled Tamiko's mom from upstairs.

"Sorry, Mom!"

"You're the most amazing best friend ever," said Ollie.

"Tell me something I don't already know."

"I just have to kick Gorgeous's gorgeous butt, and then I'm one step closer to facing Werewrestler."

"Hold on there," said Tamiko in her Ms. Manager voice. "Sure, you got the fight. But now you gotta start training."

"You don't think I can beat Gorgeous?"

"I'm saying a level one warrior can't take on Kragthar the

Destructor and live. And you're at, like, level zero right now. Barely even pushed Start to begin the game."

She had a good point. He would need to work on his wrestler. Even Linton had barely let him join. He had strength, sure, but no costume, no smack talk, and no finisher.

"Well, you know . . ." Ollie flashed his friend a smile. "It takes both of us to bring down Kragthar. I know we can do this, too, if we work together."

"You're right! Let's level up, Big Chew!" shouted Tamiko.

CHAPTER 14

THE next morning, Ollie got dressed in record time. He paid no attention to how he looked. Then he stretched out on the couch. He had a little time to chill before the school bus arrived, so he pulled up part one of Professor Pain's *Anyone Can Be a Wrestler* video series on the family tablet.

"Hey there, 'rasslers," said Professor Pain, his long, oiled hair blowing in the wind. He was standing outside the entrance to Slamdown Town, back when it had been new and shiny. The arena from the glory days was hardly recognizable compared to what it had become now.

"Pull up a beanbag chair, friends, because today's topic is all about the first important part of being a 'rassler: your outfit. Let's start off by taking a look at a true masterpiece. Mine."

Professor Pain's outfit was both professional and painful. A tie dangled between an open suit jacket with the sleeves ripped off. Choosing not to even bother with a shirt, he wore an XXXXL pair of school-uniform pants that were held up by a leather belt with a skull buckle. And he kept a ruler in his back pocket for sizing up his opponents.

"A wrestling outfit should be the embodiment of your 'rassler. A great costume will work with you, not against ya. Want to stand out amongst the crowd? Your outfit will help you do that. Want to be an icon? Make a fashion statement for the ages."

Ollie watched as Professor Pain walked into a large closet full of glittering robes and wrestler singlets. "Some people say a picture is worth a thousand words. Well, friend, let me tell you something. That's a lot of words, and we don't have that kind of time. Crowds want to see style. So instead of talking, I'm gonna show you some stylish costumes."

A slideshow with floating pictures set to club music showed Professor Pain modeling various costumes, including a chicken suit, a barbarian, and a can of refried beans.

"Now, each one of these says something different," announced Professor Pain over the video. "One says that I'm super tough and intimidating, one says that I'm a little puny wimp, and one says that beans are the true musical fruit. I found that one out the hard way."

Ollie laughed. He and Professor Pain shared the same brand of humor—humor that Hollis now thought was immature.

"Point is, the outfit is the first part of your 'rassler that people are gonna notice. You can use your outfit to say whatever you want about the kind of 'rassler you want to be. Before you say a word of smack talk or raise your fist, your outfit says, *Hey. This is me.*"

"Give me that," interrupted Hollis.

Hollis grabbed the tablet right out of Ollie's hands.

"Hey, not cool. I was watching something," he said.

"It's an emergency, Ollie. I need to catch up on *Sasquatch Mysteries*. I missed last night's episode, and if I don't watch it, I won't be able to talk with my friends about it. And if I can't talk to my friends about it, then what will I talk about?!"

Hollis headed toward the kitchen. Ollie leapt off the couch in pursuit. Only, his foot caught his shoelace. Ollie thought people tripping over their untied shoelaces was an urban legend. A myth his mom spread to get him to tie his shoes every morning. But the mouthful of carpet he ate after falling to the floor proved him wrong.

"You are the worst." Hollis laughed, doubling over. "And I didn't even have to do anything this time. You make it too easy."

Hollis left and took the tablet with him.

Later, Ollie brought his bad mood with him all the way to the bus. He plopped down in the seat next to Tamiko and let out a long, exasperated groan.

He sounded kinda like a sasquatch from *Sasquatch Mysteries*.

"Well, hello to you, too, Mr. Sunshine," joked Tamiko.

"One day I'm gonna beat him."

Tamiko glanced up from her phone. "Who, Hollis? Forget your brother. We got bigger problems," said Tamiko. With her free hand, she pointed her finger right in Ollie's face. "And by we, I mean you. And by big problems, I mean Gorgeous problems."

He already knew he was in trouble. He had no costume for Big Chew. And he had challenged the one wrestler who had been recognized by no less than five fashion designers for his ravishing outfits. Gorgeous Gordon Gussett did not simply walk a runway. He commanded it. And Ollie knew that Gorgeous's runway of choice was the wrestling ring.

"I know," he moaned. "I didn't really think this one through."

"Well, you'd better start thinking, because the match is this Saturday," said Tamiko. "We gotta get you high-tier loot! I'm talking a flaming-blue helmet, diamond-encrusted gloves, ultra-resistant plate armor, teleporting shoulder pads, and why not a little hedgehog companion for fun. Or, you know, something cool like that."

"But where am I going to be able to get an outfit like that?"

Tamiko rolled her eyes. "Duh. You just need to come up with a kick-butt costume for Big Chew. We can make it ourselves."

"But I can't design an outfit," he protested.

"You can't design an outfit?" Tamiko sighed and closed her game. She reached over, unzipped his backpack, and pulled out one of his many notebooks.

"Look," she said, pointing to a random page. Ollie had drawn a picture of Slammin' Sammy delivering his patented Sam Slam finishing move. Then she turned to another random page. She pointed out a picture of The Bolt uttering her catchphrase.

"Nobody steals The Bolt's thunder!" yelled the illustrated Bolt into a speech bubble.

"You do this stuff. All. The. Time." She tossed him the note-book. "You're an amazing artist. So, what's the big deal? Make a new design for Big Chew."

She was right. His drawings of wrestlers filled the corners of nearly everything he owned. They were pretty good, too. And he often embellished them, adding extra stuff from his imagination. Plus, he wasn't the only one who thought he was creative. Mr. Fitzgerald had said so. So had his mom. Even Hollis was reluctant to say that his drawings were "bad," which, coming from Hollis, basically meant they were great. Maybe getting an awesome costume for Big Chew would not be so impossible after all.

"Yeah, I can totally do it," he said. "I'll draw up the best costume ever."

"So there ya go," she said, returning to her game. "Just do what you already do best!"

Ollie made drawing the outfit his number one priority that day. His teachers were accustomed to him doodling all over his tests and homework and textbooks and any spare scrap of paper that floated his way. So he drew up his costume design largely uninterrupted during classes. It took him all morning to finish. He added the final touches the moment the bell rang for lunchtime.

When he revealed his completed drawing to Tamiko at the lunch table, she gasped.

"Is that a good gasp or a bad gasp?" he asked.

"You can call it an amazed gasp," said Tamiko. She held up the drawing. "That is the single coolest, most awesomest wrestling outfit of all time."

Ollie had left nothing out. He had started with a basic wrestler singlet. From there, he added a ton of cool accessories, including two large gold gloves, a jeweled crown, a pair of shoulder pads, a huge sparkling belt, golden knee-high boots, leather elbow braces, a red cape draped around the shoulders, and, to top it all off, the words *Big Chew* emblazoned across the chest.

"I couldn't decide on one idea," he admitted. "So instead, I put them all in there."

"Genius," said Tamiko. "Maxing out your stats. I love it. Why didn't I think of that?"

Ollie smirked. He felt proud that his sketch impressed Tamiko. If she liked it, he knew everyone at Slamdown Town would, too.

Tamiko arched her brow. "There is one problem, though . . ."

"What? Is it the boots? I thought about drawing wings on them, too."

"So first off, do that. Right now," demanded Tamiko. "But second, you agreed to wrestle for free."

"Yeah . . ."

"Well, you kinda went all out on this create-a-character thing. Which, again, I love. Don't change a thing. But I was kinda expecting the outfit to be a lot less . . ."

Flashy? Bold? Ridiculously epic? What problem could Tamiko possibly have with—

"Expensive," she finally managed.

"Oh."

"Yeah, dude. How are you gonna pay for this stuff?" she asked.

He doubted Mrs. Ramirez had enough dog-walking needs to pay for even half of what he'd drawn. And he wouldn't be able to ask his mom for any money. Even if he and Hollis hadn't just busted the laptop, it wasn't like they were made of money. Between both her jobs, his mom still made the same diagonally cut tuna fish sandwiches for his and Hollis's lunch every day. So what was he going to do?

CHAPTER 15

"THIS day is taking forever!" moaned Ollie to Tamiko.

Tamiko looked up from her textbook. "The first bell hasn't even rung yet, Ollie." She was studying for a rumored pop quiz they had later that day in math class while simultaneously tap-tap-tapping away for gold and jewels on her phone.

"Don't remind me," said Ollie, raising his fist at the school bell. "Ring, already! Ring!"

His mind had always been on wrestling. But since he was now a real-life wrestler, his attention span at school was nonexistent. The gum had changed him into a wrestler. But it didn't change the fact that he still needed to go to school.

"We should be out trying to find a costume for Big Chew." Ollie doodled a mini Big Chew on his homework. "Not doing fractions."

"Dude. You're not even doing them, though," pointed out Tamiko. A sound from her phone signifying success indicated that she had unearthed another treasure chest. She pointed to the shining treasure. "And remember, this isn't real gold. You still don't have any money."

Sure, he had drawn an amazing costume. But a drawing wasn't going to beat Gorgeous Gordon Gussett in the ring. A full day of classes stood in his way of assembling his costume.

When the first bell finally rang, Ollie was reminded of the ringside bell in the arena that sounded the end of a match.

Later that day, when Ms. Glenbottom raised her hand to silence the class and announce the not-so-surprising surprise pop quiz, her jangling arm bracelets reminded him of The Bolt's electric arm gauntlets.

And when Mr. Pinkley, his history teacher, asked Ollie who wrote the Declaration of Independence and he instinctively replied "Gorgeous Gordon Gussett," he was reminded of, well, Gorgeous Gordon Gussett and how he still didn't have an outfit for Big Chew.

"The Declaration of Independence," replied Mr. Pinkley, "was most certainly not written by someone named Gorgeous Gordon Gussett."

Tamiko raised her hand. "Thomas Jefferson did it."

"Correct. Very good," said Mr. Pinkley with a smile.

"That one I actually know because of *Warriors in Time,*" whispered Tamiko to Ollie. "Who says you don't learn anything from gaming?"

When the end-of-day bell finally rang, Ollie cheered.

"Awesome costume, here I come!"

Later at home, Ollie rummaged through the attic. He looked for any oversize pieces of clothing that he might be able to use for Big Chew's outfit.

Back when they *actually* used to hang out together, he and Hollis would sneak into the attic while playing treasure hunt. So he remembered where to find some old clothes that belonged to his mom, his uncle, and his grandparents.

At the time, the clothes had seemed enormous, and to Ollie they still were. But his mom *was* pretty big. Not Big Chew big, but close. They might actually fit.

There was only one way to find out.

Here goes nothing, he thought as he tossed the gum into his mouth and transformed.

He tried on every piece of clothing in the attic, and by the end of the night had gathered a purple wet suit from his mom's surfer days, a pair of dusty old snow boots, Hollis's old football shoulder pads, a pair of mismatched gloves, an unused red shower curtain, a pair of old knee- and elbow pads that his grandma used to wear roller-skating, and a prop crown that his uncle had worn performing in the local theater.

Separately, they were just a bunch of random items that he found in the attic. But together, they could become a costume.

Hopefully.

The following day in study hall, Ollie showed Tamiko the clothes he had gathered.

"This is great," she said. She placed the crown on her head and admired herself in her phone. "I always knew I was royalty. We can totally work with this. My dad has a bunch of art supplies that we can use to cut some of this stuff up and make it even more awesome."

"Shh!" shushed Mrs. Martino. "Study hall is for studying."

They apologized and pretended to go back to studying.

Tamiko's dad was an Elvis impersonator. He went to contests and everything, and he had even made his own custom Elvis costume. It looked like the real thing! And he was a pretty good Elvis, too. More important, that meant he had a whole bunch of materials lying around Tamiko's basement in case he ever needed to repair his outfit.

"I can't believe you're actually going to be wrestling Gorgeous Gordon Gussett," whispered Tamiko. "I think I'd even consider washing Hollis's dirty tighty-whities for a chance to touch the *actual fabric* of the prince of fashion's costume."

"Yeah. About that . . . ," he whispered back.

"Please tell me you don't actually have a pair of Hollis's soiled underwear on you."

"No."

Tamiko looked relieved. "Don't scare me like that, Ollie."

"They're not Hollis's."

Ollie pulled a giant pair of his grandpa's underwear from his backpack.

"My eyes!" shrieked Tamiko. "They burn!" She dove out of her seat, as if Ollie had pulled out a giant bug from his backpack. "It's like they follow you from everywhere in the room. Put them away! That underwear is staring into my soul and judging me!"

"Ms. Tanaka!" yelled Mrs. Martino. "This is study hall. *Not* talking hall. Study now!"

"Sorry, Mrs. Martino."

Tamiko took her seat only after Ollie put the underwear away.

Almost all wrestlers wore underwear as part of their costume. Ollie had suspected that his grandpa's might just do the trick but then realized he'd have to wear his grandpa's old underwear to find out. So he figured he'd wait till he was *completely* out of options before trying. After finding nothing else in the attic that would work, he finally mustered the courage to try them on and, of course, they were a perfect fit.

They were actually pretty comfortable.

Wrestling history ran in Ollie's family. His grandpa had been one of the people who helped build Slamdown Town Arena. He was renowned for two feats: his ability to lift gargantuan cement blocks and his extreme distaste of buying new clothes. For all Ollie knew, his grandpa had worn this very pair of underwear while laying the foundation of the arena. In a way, wearing them would kind of be like bringing them home.

"Don't worry," he reassured her in a whisper. "I washed them on extra hot. And then again on extra, extra hot."

"No amount of washing will get me to touch those things," she hissed back.

CHAPTER 16

THAT evening, Ollie and Tamiko raided Mr. Tanaka's arts and crafts drawer. It was time for him and Tamiko to make Big Chew's costume a reality.

First, they used the purple wet suit as the base of the entire outfit. Next, they turned the red shower curtain into a cape. They splashed the snow boots and gloves with gold paint and dunked the shoulder, elbow, and kneepads in a pile of glitter. Tamiko added jewels onto the already-overjeweled crown. And to top it all off, they cut letters out of white construction paper to spell out BIG CHEW and slathered them in glue to make sure they stuck to the chest.

They left the underwear as is. Neither of them, especially Tamiko, wanted to handle Ollie's grandfather's ancient underwear any more than they needed to.

They waited until everything was dry and not a moment later.

"Let's see how it looks!" squealed Tamiko.

Ollie went into the bathroom. First, he transformed into Big Chew. Then he changed into his new outfit. He admired himself in the mirror. Everything looked perfect! He spun around and inspected the cape, the crown, the boots, the underwear . . .

And that's when it hit him.

Oh, no, he thought. *Everyone's gonna see me in my underwear.* He gulped and tried to push the thought out of his mind.

He stepped out of the bathroom and crept down the hallway. He found it a little difficult to move under the weight of all the clothing, but he thought that maybe it was because the stuff hadn't dried yet. Once it dried, he'd be able to get around without a problem.

"Well? How do I look?" he asked.

"It's a lot," offered Tamiko. "Like, a lot, a lot."

Ollie spat the gum out into his hand and returned to being Ollie. All the oversize clothing fell off him into a heap. "You're right. It's missing *something*."

"Do you not know what 'a lot' means?"

"Professor Pain says that your outfit helps define who you are. Which means that my outfit needs to be big, it needs to be bold, it needs to be exciting! I know that's not who I am, but it's who I need Big Chew to be. But more importantly, it needs to be bigger, bolder, and more exciting than Gorgeous Gordon Gussett's."

He marched straight over to her dad's Elvis costume.

"These pants," he said. He ran his fingers through the pants' white, glittery tassels.

Tamiko shook her head. "No way, Ollie. Absolutely not."

"C'mon, Tamiko! These pants are so cool."

Tamiko crossed her arms. Ollie could tell from the way she

was biting her lip that she wasn't convinced. He knew he was asking a lot from her.

"Look, I get it. They're your dad's and everything, but . . ." He looked down, embarrassed. "You know, if I had them, then you and everyone else won't have to see me in my underwear," he offered.

"Wrestlers wear underwear, Ollie! It's kinda their thing."

"There's a reason people have nightmares about being out in public in their underwear, Tamiko! I'm not being crazy!"

"Although . . ." She considered this. "You make a solid argument. Those tighty-whities give me the heebie-jeebies." She eyed Ollie's grandfather's underwear and took a dramatic step backward.

"Can I at least just try them on?" asked Ollie.

She sighed. "Fine, but hurry up."

He transformed back into Big Chew. Then he grabbed the pants and pulled them on. Just as he'd hoped, they fit Big Chew perfectly.

"Ta-da!" he yelled as he struck a dramatic pose.

"They really bring the whole costume together," admitted Tamiko. "But . . ."

His face dropped. "But what?"

"If anything happens to those pants, I'm dead. Like, seriously dead, Ollie. My dad spent months making that costume. He may love it more than he loves me."

"I won't let anything happen to them," he promised.

She chewed her lip. For what seemed like forever, she said nothing.

"Okay," she relented at last. "But only as long as *nothing* happens. And we get them back here right after the match."

He jumped up and down.

"You got it. There's no way I'll lose now," said Ollie.

"Agreed," said Tamiko. She stood back to admire the costume. "Gorgeous Gordon Gussett better look out, because there's a new fashion icon in Slamdown Town."

Very soon, Ollie would take his first step toward challenging Werewrestler. And once he had the belt, he'd reclaim the Evander family wrestling legacy back from that no-good cheater and give the fans of Slamdown Town someone worth cheering for.

And he'd look good doing it.

CHAPTER 17

THE day of the first match finally arrived. When the coast was clear, Ollie shoved the Big Chew outfit into his backpack. Then he quietly snuck down to the garage and stuffed his backpack as far back as he could reach into the trunk of his mom's minivan.

He hid the backpack without much difficulty. The trunk was crammed full of protein powder kegs, dumbbells, and more sweatpants than he could count. So he tossed it underneath a pile of junk.

They would be leaving for the arena in just a few minutes. Ollie had barely slept the night before. On the one hand, he was ecstatic that he was actually able to wrestle today. On the other hand, he was terrified that he was actually able to wrestle today. Both feelings threatened to make him lose his lunch.

Ollie was just about to hop in the car when Hollis appeared

out of nowhere. His brother had apparently attempted to style his hair. Probably to look more *mature*; to Ollie, Hollis looked like he'd dunked his head in jelly and let it freeze. And the look on Hollis's face told Ollie he was not going to like what his brother had to say.

"I smell something . . . suspicious," said Hollis. "What are you doing?"

"Nothing," lied Ollie in a panic.

"Now, now. No lying." Hollis patted his nose. "I've trained my nose to detect when someone lies. I read about how to do it online. So why don't you tell me what's going on?"

Ollie's mind raced for an answer. "I was, uh, cleaning out the car?"

Hollis sniffed. "The nose says two things. One"—Hollis held up a finger—"this car hasn't been cleaned in a *long* time. And two"—he held up another finger—"that was a big lie. You're acting *odder* than usual this morning. In fact, you've been acting odder than usual this whole week. And I wanna know why."

Hollis pushed Ollie out of the way and dove into the trunk of the car.

"Aha! What's this?!"

Big Chew's costume was bold. It was sparkly. It was *supposed* to catch the audience's attention. And Ollie was sure it caught Hollis's attention now. His backpack remained unzipped. He noticed the golden boots poking out.

The outfit had done its job—just at the absolute wrong time.

My wrestling career is over before it started!

"Contraband!" shouted Hollis from inside the trunk.

Ollie was already formulating an excuse for why he had stuffed a fabulous wrestling outfit into the back of the trunk. But Hollis didn't emerge from the trunk holding the outfit.

Instead, he emerged brandishing a lime-green water gun.

"I was wondering where this had gone. You said you didn't know," accused Hollis.

"I didn't!" He and Hollis hadn't played water tag in forever.

Hollis sniffed again. "The nose says that's another lie. Is there anything left in this thing?" he asked as he inspected the water gauge. "Only one way to find out!"

He pulled the trigger. A sad trickle of water hit Ollie in the face.

"Guess so!" Hollis laughed as he ran back into the house.

Ollie caught his breath.

That was a close one. He'd have to be more careful moving forward.

"You all right, Ollie?" asked his mom after she got in the car and they left for Slamdown Town. "You look a little pale."

The drive over to the arena didn't have any crazy incidents. What the drive did have was a spirited discussion about the "mysterious" new wrestler, Big Chew.

"Whoever he is, he doesn't stand a chance," predicted Hollis. "Gorgeous Gordon Gussett is gonna toss him out of the ring like last year's leopard-skin outfit. Which, for the record, I still hold is top five for him."

Ollie fought the urge to pop the gum into his mouth and show Hollis *exactly* what he could do. "Yeah, well, I think he'll be great and should totally be given a chance."

"As long as he follows the rules and abides by all instructions,

I'm sure he'll be fine," assured their mom, decked out in her referee outfit. "But Gorgeous Gordon Gussett for his first match? Seems like Linton wanted to offer Gorgeous some fresh meat."

Hollis and their mom laughed. Ollie didn't.

When they all got inside the arena, he met Tamiko, who was buried in her phone at their usual seats. He didn't want to do anything differently for fear Hollis—or worse, his mom—would suspect something was up. He'd already had a hard time not speaking up in the car ride over.

Ollie looked down at the ring. He couldn't believe that within an hour he'd be inside it wrestling while Tamiko sat right here watching him. He had been coming to the arena with her for years. But this was the first time she'd be watching without him by her side.

Ollie felt a pang of sadness.

"Yeah, I'm gonna miss you, too," she said, as if reading his mind.

Tamiko seemed to be compensating by ordering double the amount of snacks. She opened her mouth, closed it, and chewed her lip. "Listen," she finally mumbled. "As your friend and manager, I just want to say one thing."

She smiled.

"Go kick Gorgeous Gordon Gussett's butt!"

"But what if he kicks my butt?" he asked.

"Don't worry," assured Tamiko. "Your mom is the best ref there is. She'll make sure you don't get *too* messed up. And if you do, well, that's wrestling! You'll be fine. And I'll be cheering for you!"

He could stand there all day, or he could get ready. So he slung his backpack over his shoulder and said goodbye to

Tamiko. Then, in the safety of a bathroom stall, he popped the gum into his mouth. Ollie had entered the stall, but Big Chew left. He was ready.

Or as ready as he was going to be.

He made his way back into the locker room. All around him, the other wrestlers put on their outfits and prepared for their matches. So he began to do the same.

Ollie bounced up and down with nervous energy. Or he would have bounced, had his new awesome outfit not weighed him down. A small price to pay for fashion excellence.

He examined his costume in the mirror.

I look really good!

He noticed a few of the wrestlers glancing at him. Everyone was probably thinking he had one really impressive costume. For the first time all morning, he started to feel confident about the upcoming match.

They were talking about him, too. He couldn't hear exactly what they were saying, so he moved closer and strained to listen to their conversations.

"I don't give him five minutes," said The Rhino.

"Five minutes?" The Bolt laughed. "He won't last thirty seconds!"

"I got two minutes!" said Mack Truck.

The only wrestler who believed in him was Lil' Old Granny, the shockingly well-built senior citizen who doled out suplexes and home-baked goods in the ring. She pulled out her purse and bet the other wrestlers a whole five dollars, in nickels and pennies.

"Not only will he last longer than two minutes, but he'll win," predicted Granny. "I should know! I've seen a thing or two."

"Please! With those eyes, you haven't seen anything in years," said The Bolt.

So, they all took the bet.

Ollie slumped down. His confidence faded. But he didn't have long to think about it.

"You're needed in the ring, Mr. Big Chew," barked a lanky Slamdown Town attendant.

It was time to wrestle.

CHAPTER 18

OLLIE chomped on his gum as he made his way to the top of the ramp. He needed to wait for Screech Holler to introduce Big Chew before heading out to the ring.

"Ladies and gentlemen, boys and girls!" screamed Screech. "Take your seats, because it's time for some wrestling."

As he peeked out of the curtain, Ollie could see his mom in the ring, stretching and reviewing the rule book. In the stands, Tamiko gorged on her pile of snacks. A few rows below her, Hollis leaned back to take a selfie of his hair. But he leaned back too far and fell over. Ollie hoped to get his hands on *that* photo later.

But his attention was drawn to the ring. The lights had gone dim. Screech Holler stood and raised the microphone to his mouth.

"Now give a big Slamdown Town welcome to the newest member of our wrestling family. He's big! And he chews gum! He's *Big Chew*!"

Ollie took a deep breath. Then he took his first step and

walked down the ramp toward the ring. As he walked, his senses were assaulted with familiar wrestling entrance traditions. Crackling music blared over the blown-out speaker system. Lights flashed and spun from the aging electrical grid overhead. Fire and smoke fizzled and plopped out of pyrotechnic tubes that lined the runway and hadn't passed a safety inspection in years.

He had seen wrestler entrances hundreds, if not thousands, of times. But to be here in his own entrance felt like a weird, awesome, out-of-body experience.

"My goodness, folks!" Screech's voice was thick with admiration. "Would you get a look at Big Chew? Now, that is one impressive-looking outfit!"

The handful of people in the arena buzzed with excitement. Especially Tamiko, who yelled louder than he had ever heard her yell.

Ollie winced. But it felt good to know that he had at least one fan.

He picked up a nearby microphone.

A wave of nerves crashed over him. Ollie hated public speaking. But then again, it wasn't really *him* speaking. Ollie was a small, timid kid. But Big Chew? Big Chew was a big, awesome wrestler. *He* could talk to crowds, no problem.

With renewed confidence, he addressed the crowd as he walked toward the ring. "That's right, Slamdown Town!"

He found that walking and talking proved a slight challenge, as the outfit's weight became more and more apparent with each step.

"Note the epic new shoulder pads designed for maximum intimidation."

He huffed and puffed. "Stand in awe of my gauntlets of extreme heaviness which—*phew*—are sure to—*man, these weigh a ton*—crush my opponent."

He barely managed to swing one leg over the ropes and into the ring.

"Be amazed by my impressive, awe-inspiring *whoaaaaa*—"

Ollie tripped over the ropes and tumbled face-first into the ring.

"A whoaaaaa? What's a whoaaaaa?" asked Screech. "Is that some new wrestling accessory I don't know about? Somebody get me a fashion guide."

Ollie tried to stand up as quickly as he could. He didn't have to worry. He just had to get used to the costume. This was his first time wearing it for a match, after all.

His mom walked up to check Big Chew into the match.

He gulped.

"Are you here to wrestle, or are you going to a costume party?" she asked.

"Sorry, Mom. I mean ma'am."

He wondered if his mom had been this nervous when the Brash Banshee made her wrestling debut. He had heard the stories: how she had put her pants on backward, how she had forgotten her smack talk, and how she had messed up her finishing move. But he had also heard how she pinned her opponent, Lizzie Leprechaun, in record time, a record she still held to this day. His mom had said that she was nervous, but Ollie seriously doubted his mom had ever been nervous in her life. At least not when it came to wrestling.

She reviewed Big Chew's outfit with a critical eye. She chewed intensely on her referee whistle, which Ollie knew meant that she was deep in thought. A moment later she spat it out. "Well, it's not conventional, but technically this is all legal. You're clear for the match. Good luck." Then she added in a whisper, "You're gonna need it."

Suddenly the lights went down again. Ollie turned and looked up the ramp.

"Folks," began Screech Holler, "our next wrestler needs no introduction, but that's what they pay me to do so I'm gonna do it. He's the ten-time winner of Slamdown Town's Most Dashing Head, Brow, and Nose Hair Award. Give it up for the crown prince of fashion himself, Gorgeous Gordon Gussett!"

Gorgeous Gordon Gussett appeared at the top of the ramp. And then immediately locked eyes with Ollie. Watching him from the stands for years had not prepared Ollie for the intense level of gorgeousness that radiated from him. As Gorgeous stepped into the flashing lights, Ollie was immediately blinded by his head-to-toe, diamond-encrusted white suit.

Gorgeous made his way down the ramp. His golden cane *tap-tap-tapp*ed as he walked.

"Hello, Slamdown Town," said Gorgeous Gordon Gussett in a silky smooth tone. Even Gorgeous's voice oozed perfection. "It is I, Gorgeous Gordon Gussett. Feast upon my beauty, for it is bountiful."

He whipped out a mirror and gazed longingly at his own reflection. "I know I've already helped myself to multiple servings."

"Someone call the paramedics," said Screech. "I see multiple fans have already passed out due to gorgeous overload. Never look directly into Gorgeous's smile, folks. The sun has nothing on that shine!"

Ollie felt a pit in his stomach as Gorgeous slid through the ropes and into the ring. He was briefly checked in by Ollie's mom who, smartly, had donned a pair of extra-strength sunglasses to make the inspection.

Then Gorgeous turned to face him.

"Talk about a fashion disaster," said Gorgeous as he looked over Big Chew's costume. "Did you roll around in the clearance section of a chain department store and call it a day?"

Gorgeous shuddered. "Throw in the diamond-encrusted towel. It's obvious you cannot compete with my level of extreme gorgeousness. No one can share the stage with me."

"Well, get ready for me to wipe that extremely handsome smile off your face," Ollie said as he pointed his finger at Gorgeous's face in what he hoped was an intimidating fashion. "Because Big Chew is here, and he . . . I mean, I . . . am going to kick your butt."

Gorgeous was right. Ollie didn't know what he was thinking. There was no way he could out-fashion Gorgeous Gordon Gussett. He felt hopeless.

Ollie's mom stepped in. "Listen up, wrestlers. I want a clean match. Ready?"

Then he remembered why he was doing this in the first place. He needed to win preliminary matches to get Werewrestler to notice him. Then he'd beat Werewrestler, win the championship belt, and give Slamdown Town someone worth cheering for.

Ollie clenched his teeth, flexed his muscles, and took a deep breath. He nodded.

Gorgeous stole one last look in his hand mirror. Then he nodded, too.

Ding, ding, ding!

Ollie was immediately speared by Gorgeous, who had launched himself through the air without wasting a second. Ollie fell backward and hit the mat.

Gorgeous grabbed Ollie by the shoulder pads. Which Gorgeous then used to catapult his opponent straight off the mat.

Ollie flipped forward, hit the ropes, and rolled into the corner.

"That was your Full Morning Beauty Routine move," he said with wide eyes. "That was awesome!"

"Please. *Awesome* isn't awesome enough to describe my style," scoffed Gorgeous.

Gorgeous had gotten in a few quick moves. But there was no need to panic.

So Ollie stood up and readied himself.

"How's this for awesome?!" he shouted.

Arms outstretched, Ollie dashed toward the ropes in an attempt to build up momentum. He was going to knock Gorgeous straight on his perfectly chiseled butt.

But the costume was weighing him down, and Mr. Tanaka's Elvis pants were *super* restricting. He never got enough speed. Gorgeous bounced himself off the ropes, charged toward Ollie, and raised his arm. Ollie ate a faceful of Gorgeous elbow.

"Wow," he said, his nostrils buried in Gorgeous's gorgeous

tricep. "Your skin is so smooth. And smells like that flower spray we keep in the bathroom."

When he opened his eyes, he couldn't see anything.

"Help! I've gone blind!" he shouted.

But then he realized that his crown had fallen over his eyes. He couldn't see Gorgeous, but he could feel his opponent walking toward him.

"My skin-care products are all imported. And exclusive," clarified Gorgeous.

Ollie felt Gorgeous wrap his arms around his torso. Then he was yanked into the air. He crashed somewhere in the ring. Exactly where he didn't know, because the crown blocked his sight. Ollie couldn't wrestle if he couldn't see. So he pulled off the crown.

"Ah, much better," he said.

He found himself in the middle of the ring with Gorgeous Gordon Gussett looking at him in disgust. So he stood up and tossed the crown straight at him.

"Ew! Crowns are *not* in style. Keep it away from me!" shrieked Gorgeous.

"Watch it," barked Ollie's mom. "Wearing fashion accessories is one thing. Using them as weapons is another."

Gorgeous ripped the crown into two pieces. Then promptly tossed them out of the ring.

Ollie had bought himself a few seconds to catch his breath. He found his footing, raised his arms toward the ropes, and attempted to set up an aerial body slam right off the ropes. But his shoulder pads were too restricting. Try as he might, he couldn't raise his arms all the way up to the top rope.

On top of that, his kneepads weren't allowing him to fully

bend his knees, so he couldn't get any leverage. Gorgeous saw Ollie struggling with the ropes. He lunged forward and grappled him from behind.

"Gotcha!" said Gorgeous. "Let's see you deal with this!"

He flung Ollie forward toward the opposite ropes. After Ollie bounced off and shot back, he was immediately clotheslined by Gorgeous. The move slammed him onto the mat.

"The Dashing Dash," he groaned. "Much more intense than I thought it would be."

Ollie lay there, stunned, on the mat. This first match was not going according to plan.

In fact, his mom ran over and began to count him out. So humiliating.

"One! Two! Three!" she yelled.

Ollie knew that he had to the count of ten to get up off the mat. He realized now that he had been too ambitious in designing his costume. Maybe putting every cool item together wasn't a good idea after all. But he didn't have long to think about it.

So he got to his feet and began to shed as much of the clothing as he could. He kicked off his kneepads. Then he removed his shoulder and elbow pads. And his coat.

He tossed everything out of the ring.

His mom eyed him closely. "You best keep this within acceptable, family-friendly standards of clothing coverage."

"What do we have here?" asked Screech. "A mid-match costume change?"

Gorgeous laughed. "That's right. There can be only one prince of fashion. And you're looking at him. Thought you could face me in those rags? Well, you won't fare any better without them!"

Ollie was in the process of removing his gloves and tossing them out of the ring, too, when Gorgeous wedged a fist straight into his stomach. Then Gorgeous chucked him forward. He toppled to the floor.

But the worst was yet to come. Because then Gorgeous lumbered over. He put two manicured hands on Big Chew's cape.

"It's time to hang up that silly cape of yours," declared Gorgeous.

With that, Gorgeous grabbed the cape, swung Ollie around a few times, and sent him flying toward his mom.

Riiiiiip! He collided straight into her. Ollie was seeing stars.

Gorgeous Gordon Gussett wiped the sweat off his brow with Big Chew's cape.

Screech hollered into his microphone. "My goodness, folks! Linton Krackle certainly likes throwing his low-risk investment—that's fancy talk for 'cheap,' by the way—rookies into the deep end. Is Big Chew's wrestling career over before it started?!"

CHAPTER 19

ALL that remained of Ollie's costume was Mr. Tanaka's sparkling Elvis pants, his golden boots and gloves, and the purple wet suit. The rest of his outfit lay in tatters around the ring or had been flung out into the stands. His mom berated Gorgeous Gordon Gussett.

"Attacks on the referee are strictly forbidden!" she yelled. "And they will be met with a personalized and completely by-the-book smackdown from yours truly." She flexed her muscles and gritted her teeth.

She wasn't messing around.

"I can't help it if the rascal can't keep his footing," argued Gorgeous.

They bickered back and forth before she let him off with a warning.

A *stern* warning.

But the fight was back on. And Gorgeous wasted no time.

He caught Ollie with a Runway Walk spear move. Gorgeous looked like a diver plunging into a pool as he smashed straight into him. Ollie was knocked to the ground.

"Whoa, you're good," said Ollie.

Gorgeous waltzed around him, soaking up the admiration from the crowd.

"That's right, everyone!" exclaimed Gorgeous Gordon Gussett. "Pay attention to me! Slamdown Town fans have the best taste! Speaking of taste . . ."

Gorgeous lifted his leg and dropped a kick straight to Ollie's jaw.

"There's your complimentary sample."

Gorgeous grabbed Ollie by his pants' ankles and dragged him around the ring.

"Wait. Hold up. Not the pants!" yelled Ollie. If anything happened to those pants, Tamiko would kill him before her dad killed her. He tried to break free, but couldn't get a strong-enough grip while Gorgeous dragged him.

"You know," started Gorgeous, "I think these pants have committed enough fashion crimes for today. Don't you think so, Slamdown Town?"

The crowd roared their approval. But even over the crowd, he could still hear Tamiko.

"No! You promised!" she shouted.

But, try as he might, there was no stopping Gorgeous. So in one mighty pull, Gorgeous Gordon Gussett split the pants in two.

"Noooo!" he heard Tamiko scream from the stands. Ollie watched as Gorgeous held the torn pants in each hand and let both pieces drop to the mat.

Ollie had promised Tamiko that no harm would come to her dad's pants. Now they were destroyed. And, even worse, Ollie was probably going to lose his first match.

"You've got nothing to hide behind now, Big Chew!" said Gorgeous as he grabbed Ollie by the torso, swung him into the air, and held him up for the crowd to see.

If Gorgeous had just pinned Ollie instead of trying to humiliate him, perhaps the match would have gone differently. But he *had* tried to embarrass Big Chew. And when he did, Gorgeous found himself face-to-face with the single most terrifying article of clothing his fashionable eyes had ever witnessed.

Ollie's grandpa's underwear.

"I think I'm going to be sick," moaned Gorgeous.

Ollie fell to the mat as Gorgeous Gordon Gussett released him. He spun around to find Gorgeous stumbling around blindly.

"What happened?" he asked.

"Those happened!" screamed Gorgeous as he pointed at the underwear. "Those are positively criminal. Surely they must be illegal!"

His mom chimed in. "As it turns out, those briefs fall *well* within ringside undergarment regulations. They appear breathable, supportive, and possibly vintage? I don't know much about fashion, but I do know that vintage is in these days. Carry on."

He couldn't believe it. Out of every awesome article of clothing, it seemed that his grandpa's underwear was the piece that might win him the match.

He wasted no time. Ollie walked over to the ropes and climbed to where Gorgeous had left his cane. He grabbed it, reentered the ring, and approached Gorgeous, who was getting back on his feet after being knocked over by the mere sight of the underwear.

Ollie held the cane like a baseball bat. He thought of all the times in gym class that he had been picked last for softball and all the times that he had caused his team to lose.

Well, he wasn't going to lose now.

He leapt into the air and landed smack on top of Gorgeous Gordon Gussett.

"Ah! The underwear! It's touching me! It's touching me!" Gorgeous started to sob hysterically as Ollie's mom flopped beside them and began to count out the pin. "Good thing *Wrestler's Fashion Weekly* says manly tears are in."

"Um, that's last week's issue. Tears are out."

"Noooo!" screamed Gorgeous through a river of beautiful tears.

Ollie's mom slapped the mat and rounded out the count. "Eight! Nine! Ten!"

Ding, ding, ding!

She grabbed Ollie's meaty arm and raised it into the air.

"Big Chew is the winner!" screamed Screech Holler.

Ollie couldn't believe it. He had just won his first wrestling match.

And it felt better than he ever dreamed it would.

CHAPTER 20

OLLIE strutted from one corner of the ring to the other, soaking up the applause.

"That was easily the most impressive debut I have witnessed in years, folks," declared Screech, his voice brimming with excitement. "This Big Chew is one to watch!"

Although he knew deep down that there were even fewer people in attendance today than usual, despite the hope that new blood would draw a bigger crowd, it felt to Ollie like the roar of the crowd had never been louder. The last thing he wanted to do right now was leave the ring. But that's exactly what his mom was telling him to do as she marched toward him.

"Hey! Big Chew!" she yelled. "Congratulations on your first win, but you're holding up the rest of the matches. Slamdown Town rules clearly state that each victor is allowed no more than—"

Ollie had heard this rule a thousand times and instinctively cut her off.

"Thirty seconds of celebration post-match," he said in his deep, gravelly voice.

She looked surprised. Maybe even proud. "You know the rule." Then she frowned. "So why am I here telling it to you? Get your butt outta the ring before I kick it out!"

Even though he towered over his mother, Ollie still felt like he was four feet tall and being yelled at for not picking up his dirty clothes and getting his homework done.

"Sorry!" he bellowed.

Her face scrunched up. He was afraid that she had recognized him. Or maybe she was just getting angrier and angrier that he was still standing there and not exiting the ring as instructed.

Either way, he didn't want to hang around to find out.

"I'm going! I'm going!"

He scooped up the tattered remains of Mr. Tanaka's pants. Then he practically dove over the ropes and out of the ring. He knew not to mess with his mom, especially when she *didn't* know he was Big Chew. She would never hurt Ollie, but she might do serious damage to a wrestler not following proper protocol.

He ran up the ramp toward the wrestlers' entrance. Above him, the cracked jumbotron replayed highlights from the match. He made his way through the curtains just as the lights fell and the entrance music for Immunity began to blast from the speakers.

Ollie turned to make his way toward the locker room when he was stopped.

"Big Chew! Wait! Big Chew!"

Ollie couldn't believe his luck. He had won his very first match, and now he had his very first fan.

Could this day get any better? He turned around to greet the adoring fan.

"Big Chew," said a breathless Hollis. "Will you sign my elbow pad?"

Ollie's jaw dropped.

Hollis, leaning over the barricade, waved an elbow pad in Ollie's face. But not just any elbow pad. It was Ollie's right elbow pad that he had lost during the match. Hollis waved the pad even harder.

"Hello! Did you hear me? Sign my elbow pad, big guy!"

Ollie realized that his jaw was still open.

"Don't you mean *my* elbow pad?" asked Ollie. He reached to grab it.

Hollis pulled it away. "Finders keepers! Now c'mon. Just sign it!" He shoved a permanent marker into Ollie's hand. "Might be worth a few bucks someday!"

Ollie groaned. Of all the eight people in the arena who could've become a fan, why did it have to be his annoying older brother? But then Ollie was struck by a thought. Sure, he wasn't able to use Big Chew to get back at Hollis at *home*.

But at the *arena* was a different story.

The wrestlers were always doing things to their fans, good and bad. Depending on which wrestler he talked to, he'd either get a signature or a knuckle sandwich. And it was just totally accepted, because that's what people loved about wrestling.

"Yeah," said Ollie with a wicked grin. "I'll give you my signature, all right."

He reached out, grabbed Hollis by the shirt collar, and lifted him into the air.

"Hey!" said an annoyed Hollis. "What are you doing?!"

Ollie had thought that his day couldn't get any better after winning his first match. But hearing the panic in his older brother's voice took the cake. Finally, after years of being picked on and pushed around, Ollie was bigger, stronger, and scarier now. He wished he had a water gun so he could squirt Hollis in the face and get him back for earlier today. And now he wouldn't have to worry about his brother retaliating.

Then he was struck with a brilliant idea.

"You wanted my signature, didn't you?"

Ollie pulled the cap off the marker and pressed it down on Hollis's forehead. The black ink squeaked and squished as Ollie signed the words *Big Chew*. It looked good, but Ollie thought that it was missing a little something extra. So he drew a mustache on Hollis's lip and a monocle around Hollis's eye before dropping him to the floor.

"There you go," said Ollie.

His brother looked ridiculous. He was sure this was going to infuriate Hollis. He'd be so embarrassed, and it would take at least a week for the ink to be washed off his face. Maybe Ollie would even hide all the bars of soap in the bathroom.

Hollis pulled out his phone so that he could see his reflection. His face turned red.

Yes, thought Ollie. *He's so mad. Look at him!*

It turned even redder. Then purple. And then Hollis started to laugh.

"What are you laughing at?" Ollie demanded to know.

Hollis just laughed harder and harder until he was crying with amusement. Ollie didn't understand. Hollis was supposed to be angry, not happy. His plan hadn't worked at all. In fact, bullying Hollis had yielded the exact opposite of what he had wanted.

"Oh, man," said Hollis through fits of laughter. "That is amazing! This is way better than a stupid elbow pad! I like your style, Big Chew!"

"You do?"

"Plus, you have excellent taste in underwear." Hollis shook the permanent marker. "I can't wait to tell my little brother that you signed my forehead. He'll be so jealous!"

"No, don't do that—"

"Consider me a fan! You know, I'm the web developer and moderator of the Officially Unofficial Slamdown Town Fan Club. Have you heard about it?"

"Yeah," started Ollie, before catching himself. "Uh, I mean, not rea—"

"You have?! Oh, man! Wait till I tell my brother that a wrestler has heard about my website. I knew the site was gaining traffic, despite what the numbers say. Put it there!"

Hollis held out his hand for a high five. Ollie, annoyed, slapped it away, but Hollis thought he was just giving him a high five.

Getting revenge on his brother had totally backfired.

"In fact," said Hollis, "I'm gonna go find the pip-squeak now."

Hollis turned and ran back through the curtains and out into the arena.

Ollie's number one enemy was now Big Chew's number one fan.

CHAPTER 21

OLLIE returned to the locker room and saw The Bolt, The Rhino, and Mack Truck pulling out their wallets and begrudgingly handing over the money they owed Granny.

"Five minutes, my butt!" said a cackling Granny, the only wrestler who'd believed Big Chew would win his first match. "Pay up! All of ya!"

The Rhino paid Granny, lowered his head, and walked toward the locker-room doorway. He bumped shoulders with Ollie as he passed, let out a snort, and stormed away.

Ollie sat down by his locker and began to unlace his boots. He was afraid to make eye contact with any of the other wrestlers. Especially those who hadn't believed in him and had lost the bet. He knew all too well that wrestlers constantly had beef with one another. And he didn't want to be on the receiving end of any of it. After all, these people were his heroes. And potentially his future opponents, too.

"You proved us wrong, Big Chew," said The Bolt.

Ollie looked up to see The Bolt standing over him. She held out her hand. He instinctively flinched. But then he realized that she didn't want to wrestle him. It wasn't some high-voltage smackdown move.

She wanted to shake his hand.

"Oh, yeah" was all he managed to say.

Hoping he wouldn't faint, he reached out his hand and shook hers. His fingertips brushed her famous electric gauntlets, which, to his great shock, gave him the faintest of zaps. The sensation reminded him of when Hollis dragged his feet across the carpet in the living room and then chased him around the house, threatening to poke Ollie with his finger.

Mack Truck proudly slapped Ollie on the back, leaving a greasy handprint.

"Impressive costume," said Mack Truck. "Well, what's left of it anyway. I doubted it at first, but I think your look really came together out there. Between you and me, those pants were in desperate need of a tune-up. The briefs, though? They're firing on all cylinders!"

Ollie had to remind himself to speak. "Wow! Thanks! That means a lot."

He groaned. He was a six-and-a-half-foot-tall tough-as-nails wrestler, not an eleven-year-old kid.

"I mean, uh, yeah. Of course it came together out there. That was my plan all along."

"Well, could've fooled me!" said The Bolt.

Granny slotted her dentures into her gummy mouth with her muscled arms and smiled wide at Ollie. Despite her age and slouching posture, she was tall enough to look Big Chew straight in the eye. She'd been wrestling since before most of the Slamdown Town wrestlers had even been born, and old age hadn't slowed her down. Though her smack talk in recent years *had* become less about insulting her opponents and more about lamenting her hip pain, her grandkids' shenanigans, and the "good old days."

"You've got moxie, son. I never doubted you for a second. Now," she said as she pulled a number of plastic bags out of her locker, "help me bring these groceries to my car!"

He felt like he was already a part of the Slamdown Town family. Ollie had idolized these wrestlers for years. And now some of them seemed to think of him as a friend, or at least a coworker—a thought he could barely wrap his head around.

Granny shoved the groceries into his chest and slowly walked toward the doorway. Sure, she *could* have carried them to her car on her own. But why should she when there were plenty of helping hands around who could listen to her talk about that one "crazy" family vacation she took overseas all those decades ago?

"Hurry up, Big Chew. Can't wait around for the bananas to ripen! Not at my age! But you may want to throw on a pair of pants first," advised Granny.

Ollie looked down at his grandpa's underwear and remembered he'd had to sacrifice Mr. Tanaka's costume in order to defeat Gorgeous Gordon Gussett.

I really hope Tamiko isn't too upset with me . . .

"And word of fashion advice, deary? Maybe consider dyeing the underwear gold. It will tie the whole costume together. Besides, they look older than I am!"

After delivering the groceries to Granny's car in the parking lot, Ollie spat out the gum, folded it into the flyer, put it in his pocket, and met up with Tamiko in the lobby.

"Dude! You were amazing!" she said, playfully punching him in the arm.

He rubbed where she'd hit him. "I know! I'm still shaking!"

They practically bounced up and down with excitement.

"But as your manager," she began, bouncing less, "we gotta get down to business. You said *nothing* was going to happen to my dad's pants. If I wasn't so pumped about you winning and everything, I'd totally kick your butt. I'm so busted."

"I know." He reached into his backpack and pulled out Mr. Tanaka's destroyed Elvis pants. "I'm really sorry, Tamiko. It just sort of happened. Maybe we can fix them?"

Tamiko cradled the destroyed pants in her arms.

"I'm no doctor, but I think if those pants had a pulse, it would have flatlined," said Tamiko. "They deserved better than to be torn to shreds by Gorgeous Gordon Gussett. May they rest in peace."

Ollie struggled with that to say. "It was my fault. I'm sorry."

"Yeah, but I knew this wasn't going to end well. I shouldn't have let you borrow them in the first place. I guess I can kiss video game privileges goodbye."

She raised her phone to her lips and kissed it.

"Goodbye."

"How can I make it up to you? I can talk to your dad."

Tamiko waved her hand dismissively. "If I get grounded for a few days, then no big deal. If you get grounded for a few days, you won't be able to wrestle, and then you won't be able to get that championship belt. Keep your eyes on the prize."

She looked over the destroyed pants and sighed.

"As your manager, I'll take the fall for this one. But you're buying me nachos. Mega-size. Consider it my fee."

"It's a deal," assured Ollie.

"Hey, Ollie!" shouted Hollis as he lumbered over toward them. He was pointing gleefully to the signature on his forehead. "I got something to show ya!"

"Dude. What happened to his face?" whispered Tamiko.

"Long story."

"Ollie," said Hollis as he arrived, out of breath, in front of them. "Check it out! That new wrestler, Big Chew, signed my face and gave me a monocle! Aren't you jealous?"

"Umm . . ." Ollie didn't know exactly how to respond.

"I'm gonna frame this and hang it on my wall," said Hollis as he snapped a selfie.

Tamiko crossed her arms. "Any wall with a picture of your face on it deserves to be quarantined and demolished."

"Plus, I got this awesome elbow pad, too," continued Hollis. He chose to ignore that Tamiko was even there. "It kinda looks like those old ones that Grandma used to wear roller-skating, but like *way* cooler 'cause it's Big Chew's."

Tamiko snorted with laughter.

Ollie gulped. "Grandma roller-skated? I didn't even know."

"Um, duh. She only talks about being high school grand champ every time we visit." Hollis rubbed his face against the elbow pad. "I can feel the awesomeness." Ollie knew that what

Hollis was really feeling was the sweat of both Big Chew and their grandma. But he kept that information to himself.

"I'm totally Team Big Chew now. So back off." Hollis snapped another pic for good measure. "Anyway, I'm off for a soda refill. Chip chip, cheerio!" he said in a mock accent and pretended to lower his monocle.

"Dude," said Tamiko. "Hollis is a Big Chew fan? Guess I'm going to have to say he's the worst wrestler ever now. It was fun while it lasted."

CHAPTER 22

OLLIE sat in the back of English class. Mr. Fitzgerald droned on and on about their upcoming group presentations. Or something like that. Ollie wasn't paying attention.

He was huddled behind his backpack with his nose pressed against the screen of his phone, watching part two of *Anyone Can Be a Wrestler*. Professor Pain's voice shouted through his headphones.

"So now that you have your costume, next we're going over the power of smack talk," yelled Professor Pain over the music. "Smack talk allows you to get into the *mind* of your opponent."

Professor Pain was considered a connoisseur of fine insults. His words bit, stung, jabbed, and berated his opponents. Wrestlers had feared what he might say as much as they feared his raw strength.

"But what *is* smack talk? It's carefully analyzing your opponent and using that knowledge to insult not just them but the very essence of their being. We aren't talking simple name-calling. Anyone can call you a doodoo head or a slackjawed jibberjabber or a fool for choosing a wrestling career over a lucrative partnership at your dad's pathetic firm."

To be fair, Ollie doubted anyone would ever call anyone else any of those things (as far as that last one, at least not in the ring). But the Professor knew more than he did, so he listened on.

"Truly astounding smack talk will pick apart the invisible armor wrestlers put around themselves to hide their very real and very vulnerable insecurities. It's a chance to verbally tear them apart limb by limb without raising a finger. If your smack-talk game is on point, then you'll almost certainly—"

"Ollie!" said Mr. Fitzgerald. "Phone. Away. Now."

He'd been caught. He closed the video and tossed the phone into his backpack.

"As I was saying," Mr. Fitzgerald continued, "you and your partner will be expected to read a short story from the assigned list, write a report on the short story, and then present your report to the class. This is a group project, but you should divide the work equally between each other. Is that clear to everyone?"

The class murmured in agreement. Of course he and Tamiko would be partners.

They always had been since they became friends. They huddled together and thumbed through the list of stories. It wasn't that Ollie didn't like reading. He would go home and read about wrestling, followed by more wrestling, every single night. He just didn't like reading the stuff assigned at school.

"Well, we gotta pick one," insisted Tamiko. "How about 'The Deadliest Pigeon'?"

They ended up selecting it because Tamiko's grandma owned a sassy parrot who could sing television-show theme songs on command. That, and a short story about a murderous pigeon on a revenge quest actually sounded pretty cool. But there was still the problem of having to get up in front of the class and speak.

Even the thought of it made him nervous.

"Your class presentation will be worth a quarter of your grade, so make sure you work with your partner for the rest of the week. And take it seriously. This is a chance for you to work on your reading, writing, and public-speaking skills."

Later that day, he and Tamiko grabbed stuff from their lockers for math class.

"Let's get together after school tomorrow to work on the presentation," said Tamiko.

"Sounds good," said Ollie. It didn't but, again, he had no other choice.

Suddenly, Tamiko's phone buzzed. It was Slamdown Town Arena.

Ollie looked at her. She looked at him. She picked up the phone.

"Hello?" she answered.

"Ms. Manager? It's Linton Krackle. Fabulously wealthy and successful CEO of Slamdown Town." Linton sounded as if he were ready to make a deal. But then again, Linton was *always* ready to make a deal. Provided he came out on top.

Tamiko cleared her throat and lowered her voice. "Yep. It's me. Ms. Manager. Now, spill it, Krackle! I'm a really important manager with a lot of important people to manage!"

The bell rang. So they walked toward math class while Tamiko continued the call.

"Congratulations on Big Chew's first win. But one win won't get the attention of Werewrestler. And things are only going to get more profitable—*er*, harder—from here. I've got another match for your guy this weekend. That is, if he's still up for it."

"Who's the unlucky opponent?" asked Tamiko.

"He'll be wrestling the viper herself, *Silvertongue*."

Tamiko gulped. Ollie felt his palms get sweaty.

"Hello?" asked Linton. "I have other money—*er*, calls—to make, ya know."

She covered the phone and turned to Ollie. "Silvertongue. Are we in or out?"

Ollie knew that Silvertongue was going to be twice as difficult as Gorgeous Gordon Gussett, and he'd barely beaten him. Her fists were dangerous, but her words were deadlier. She possessed divine-level smack-talking skills. Time and time again, Silvertongue would disarm her opponent without even lifting a single finger.

Ollie nodded. "I'm in."

Tamiko screamed into the phone. "He accepts, obviously! And he'll win! Obviously!"

"Win or lose, I still make money, and that's what's most important of all," said Linton. "Speaking of which, I've got a stack of hundred-dollar bills that are just begging to be counted. Wait. These are singles?"

Tamiko hung up the phone just as they arrived in Ms. Glenbottom's classroom.

"Stop the math presses!" yelled Tamiko as she stood up on her desk. "Big Chew is facing Silvertongue on Saturday!"

The class reacted the same way they always did when

Tamiko shouted breaking wrestling news. They winced, massaged their ears, and then went right back to whatever they were doing before. Everyone's obvious lack of interest never stopped Tamiko, who felt an almost moral obligation to share any tidbit to as many people as possible.

"Shh," said Ms. Glenbottom. "This is math class. Not wrestling class. And no standing on desks for grand announcements, Tamiko. We've talked about this."

Ollie spent all of math class writing potential smack talk in between pre-algebra problems. He'd never really considered himself that great of a talker. That was kind of Tamiko's thing. But he'd watched a lot of wrestling and heard a lot of smack talk.

How hard could it be?

✳✳✳

That afternoon, he and Tamiko discussed the upcoming match against Silvertongue while they walked Mrs. Ramirez's dogs around the neighborhood.

"She mentioned that Thespian should consider mime work instead, and *bam!*" Ollie smacked his fist into his open palm. "He ran sobbing from the ring."

Tamiko's eyes shimmered with admiration. "I want to be her when I grow up."

"There's no way Big Chew can compete with smack talk of that level!" Ollie knew his strengths, and being mean, intimidating, and insulting were not any of them.

"Glad you said it and not me," said Tamiko. "Smack talk is one of the most important parts of wrestling. Big Chew needs to ramp up his smack-talk game to the next level. And honestly, a few levels beyond *that*. Manager's orders."

"Well, I have been working on some stuff. Insults and all that."

He and Tamiko struggled to keep the poodles on the sidewalk as the pack spotted a nearby squirrel—an apparent thrill seeker—that sat chewing on an acorn instead of scampering away in fear.

"You've been holding out on me?" asked Tamiko. "Bring on the smack talk."

He pointed at Tamiko, imagining her as Silvertongue. "You must be hungry. Here's some food." He pretended to pull it away. "Psych!"

Tamiko blinked. He waited but received no response.

"Okay. I admit. I was just really hungry for lunch when I wrote that. Let's see." Ollie sifted through his notes. "Here's a different one." He straightened up. "Do you know why they call me Big Chew? Because I'm big!"

Fake snores and impatient dog whining were the only responses he received this time.

"Huh? What?" Tamiko dramatically looked around, pretending that she had only just woken up. "Oh, hey, Ollie. Silly me. I thought we were here to practice smack talk. Not tell each other bedtime stories, because you literally put me to sleep! Sorry, Ollie. But that smack talk is, well, bad. Like, five-alarm-fire bad. Like, dead-last-in-the-*Ninja-Kitty*-online-leaderboard bad. What do you think, poodles?"

The poodles all looked up and barked.

"Okay, let's workshop this," said Tamiko. She scrunched up her face in thought. "So if I was dishing out smack talk to my opponents—*er*, victims—I might say something like 'You must be hungry. Because I've got a plate of insults for ya!'"

"Oh! That's good!" said Ollie, writing down *plate insults* in his phone while being dragged down the street by his five poodles. "See? That's the kind of smack talk I need."

"And maybe something like 'Do you know why they call me Big Chew? Because I chew up big opponents. Like you!' And then I'd leap off the top ropes and body-slam them."

"This is great! Man, if only I was as good as you at smack talk."

"Well, it's not *that* good. It's just not terrible." She unraveled one of the doggie doodie bags and leaned over to pick up a fresh, smelly specimen. "As long as your smack talk no longer ends up smelling as bad as this," said Tamiko as she pinched her nose, "you'll be good."

✳✳✳

Over the next couple days, Ollie spent every lunch, bus ride, and class coming up with potential smack talk with Tamiko. After school each day, he went to Tamiko's to work on their presentation and practice smack talk.

They had read the short story together several times and reviewed the question prompts that they had to answer in their report. Well, Tamiko had read the short story several times.

Ollie, on the other hand, had been too focused on coming up with smack talk.

"Ollie, you gotta focus," implored Tamiko. "This presentation is a huge part of our grade."

"I know, I know. Sorry. It's just—"

"—the smack talk. I know. I'm helping ya with that, too, remember?"

She was right. Ollie put the smack talk down for the moment and reviewed the questions with her. They were deep, confusing questions. Questions like:

1. What are the main themes of "The Deadliest Pigeon"?
2. What is the pigeon's motivation?
3. How do you think the pigeon was feeling when he finally confronted his brother and said, "Coo! Coo!"?
4. What would you have done if you were the pigeon? And why?

Ollie's eyes glazed over. Why was he reading about stupid pigeons when he should be practicing his smack talk? There were only a few days before his match.

✿✿✿

The next day, the smack talk wasn't going as well as either of them had hoped.

Tamiko demanded he chew the gum and turn into Big Chew every time they practiced. "It's not remotely scary when *you* say it. When Big Chew says it, I can feel my heart stop!"

So he'd pop the gum into his mouth, transform into Big Chew, and pretend that Tamiko's basement was Slamdown Town Arena and that Tamiko was Silvertongue.

"Why aren't you talking? Cat got your tongue?" Ollie tried. "You know, 'cause her name is Silvertongue." The realization that they could play on her name was a big breakthrough for him yesterday. But he could tell that it fell flat for Tamiko.

She held her hand up to her heart. "It's still beating, which means you aren't insulting me nearly enough! C'mon, dude! Hurt my feelings! Make me cry!"

After their sessions, Ollie tried to get his homework done. But try as he might, every time he sat down to do his pre-algebra practice exam or answer the questions for "The Deadliest Pigeon," he ended up thinking about smack talk instead.

Part of what made Silvertongue so strong were her words. She used them as a shield, a way to put an unseen wall between herself and her opponents. But what she was able to dish out, she was not so willing to receive. Ollie picked up her weakness after reviewing all her old matches online. Wrestlers who were able to dig into Silvertongue with their own smack talk knocked her off her game. Which was exactly what he would have to do.

If he didn't come up with better insults, he would never be able to go the distance against Silvertongue.

CHAPTER 23

THAT night, Ollie stared at himself in his bedroom mirror and glanced down at the note cards in his hand. He looked up into the mirror and said, in his deepest voice:

"What's on the tip of your tongue? Oh, yeah. My fist."

He laughed. He and Tamiko had come up with that one earlier today. He shuffled the note cards and found another line that he was particularly proud of.

"You look hungry. Well, here's my elbow on a silver platter ..." Then, like Tamiko said he should, he elbowed the air. In the ring, he would elbow Silvertongue's face.

He took a deep breath and flopped onto the floor. He had been practicing his smack talk—like Tamiko had told him to—all night after dinner. It was getting late and, in addition to practicing his smack talk, he still needed to finish his note cards for their presentation tomorrow. But try as he might, he couldn't get himself to focus on the boring "The Deadliest

Pigeon." Especially not with his match against Silvertongue only two days away. Sure, smack talk was only *one* part of his match against Silvertongue. He would still need to actually wrestle her to win. But considering she was the queen of mean, Ollie knew he'd be at a serious disadvantage if he couldn't fight insults with insults.

He pulled out his phone. Maybe a little break would help.

Wrestling was on his mind, so his fingers naturally brought him to the Officially Unofficial Slamdown Town Fan Club site. Ollie found himself looking at Big Chew's smiling face as it filled the landing page. The headline "Big Chew: Awesome or Extremely Awesome???" leapt off the screen.

Ollie read Hollis's most recent blog post:

S'up internet. It's your favorite mod and number one wrestling FANatic, me, here with some super important news. And that news is Big News. Cuz it's about Big Chew. AKA the best new wrestler at Slamdown Town. He's new, and cool, so we're going to dedicate today's WRESTLER SPOTLITE to him. Why? Cuz he's new and cool and

Hollis never proofread his articles, which meant spelling errors and unfinished thoughts were constant. That may have had something to do with why no one new ever visited the site.

Why? Cuz I said so. And also because he's awesome!!! Did you see him put on that cool display with Good-for-nothing Gorgeous?! He was like OH NO MY COSTUME IS FAILING and then was all like PSYCHE I GOT THIS and then WHAM!! He kicked that crybaby's butt. He started out with a really cool costume, and then sort of like lost it, which I think was like intentional. Like he was trying to show that COSTUMES WEREN'T IMPORTANT. Deep stuff, folks. Either way, I got an awesome elbow pad out of it, and (DRUMROLLLLLLLLLLLLL) he signed my forehead. aLTHOUGH, total bummer permanent marker isn't permanent permanent.

In conclusion, extremely awesome. That's what he is. Because he's totally not afraid to take on the "supposed" big wrestlers. Silvertongue, you're gonna be a nother crybaby just like GGG when Big Chew chews you up on Saturday.

Everybody leave your likes and comments below.

Their mom was, as always, the first to comment below:

This is my son who wrote this. I'm so proud of you! Don't forget to take out the trash like I asked. Love you. —Mom

Tamiko added her own reply below:

You heard your mom, Hollis. Take yourself outside AT ONCE.

Ollie laughed. If only he could talk smack as easily as Tamiko could. Ollie began to type his own reply, but stopped himself. He was supposed to be working on the presentation, not wasting time online.

Focus, Ollie, focus, he thought.

He tried to work on his presentation, but after a couple failed attempts, he figured he'd grab a snack from downstairs. He couldn't write note cards for his presentation on an empty stomach! Once he had his snack in hand, he'd totally get to work and finish them.

He exited his room and made his way down the hallway.

As he passed Hollis's bedroom he stopped and examined the sign on the door.

NO BABIES ALLOWED

Ollie pulled a pen out of his pocket and rewrote the sign to say:

~~NO BABIES~~ NO OLLIES ALLOWED!!!

He also made sure to turn the drawing of Ollie as a baby into Ollie as a wrestler. It pretty much ended up looking a lot like Big Chew in a diaper.

Then he pressed his ear against the door and listened. It sounded like Hollis was watching a wrestling match on his phone. Suddenly, Ollie heard Screech Holler's voice:

"That was easily the most impressive debut I have witnessed in years, folks," declared Screech, his voice brimming with excitement. "This Big Chew is one to watch!"

Hmm . . . , thought Ollie.

Hollis wasn't watching just any match. He was watching Big Chew's debut.

Ollie turned the handle, opened the door, and let himself in. After all, the sign on the door said he was allowed.

The overwhelming smell of body odor that greeted Ollie upon entering reminded him of walking into Slamdown Town. At the arena, it was the sweat of hard-fought victory. Here, it was the sweat of an adolescent teen who refused to shower. The stench threatened to send him running, but Ollie had a job to do. Hollis sat on his bed with his back turned to Ollie, watching Big Chew's match against Gorgeous Gordon Gussett.

He rewound the ending over and over, watching as Big Chew finished his pin and their mom held his hand high in the air. On Hollis's desk, Ollie saw the elbow pad he had given him.

Well, the elbow pad Hollis had taken from him.

Hollis hadn't planned on washing Big Chew's signature from his forehead, but when he remembered he had to go to school on Monday and face his eighth-grade friends, he'd spent all Sunday night trying to wash it off. He was mildly successful, but instead of getting everything off, he just looked like he had black splotches all over his forehead.

So that day, he'd gone to school wearing a hat. Ollie had overheard Hollis telling his friends that he was cold (even though it was, like, superhot outside), but Ollie knew the real reason. He didn't want them to know that he actually liked wrestling.

The video of the match ended. Hollis stretched his arms. He pounded down the rest of his soda and tossed the can in the direction of his overflowing trash can.

It almost hit Ollie in the head on its way there, but he ducked just in time.

The room was somehow even messier than when Ollie had

snuck in to grab the laptop the other day. Hollis seemed content to navigate around the piles of smelly, soiled clothes. He'd made a temporary path from his bed to his desk chair through the discarded remains of snack wrappers and empty discount sports-drink bottles. One thing was for sure: Hollis had never been this messy when he shared a room with Ollie.

Hollis turned his attention back to the cracked screen. He clicked into another tab that he already had open. On the tab was a search for "how to talk to girls."

Ollie snorted. He couldn't help himself. Hollis whipped around.

"Hey!" screamed Hollis. Ollie was pretty sure that he had scared him. "No trespassers. Don't you know how to read?" And then he noticed the sign.

"What?! Come on! It took me like a whole hour to make that sign, Ollie! You really need to learn to respect other people's stuff. First my laptop . . ."

"*Our* laptop."

". . . and now my sign!"

Then Hollis noticed that the search window was still open. And that Ollie had seen it. Ollie could practically see the steam coming out of his brother's ears.

"That's it! You asked for it!" shouted Hollis.

Hollis charged toward Ollie, tackled him to the ground, and put him in a headlock. Ollie had lost all wrestling matches to his brother since the "great growth spurt."

But this was before Ollie had a growth spurt of his own.

He knew he couldn't use the gum to beat his brother. But he had just wrestled in his first real wrestling match and, in doing so, had learned the importance of a proper costume.

As he was forced to look down at his brother's shoes—his headlock didn't give him much range of motion—he saw they were untied. Ollie had learned the hard way just the other day what untied shoes could do to someone.

Which meant that maybe he could use that to his advantage.

He kicked free of the headlock, wheeled around, and forced Hollis to charge again. When he did, Hollis stepped on his own shoelace. His brother lost his balance and tumbled forward. Plastic bottles and wrappers went flying all across the room.

Ollie took his chance and pounced on top of him.

"One! Two! Thr—"

Hollis shoved Ollie off him, grabbed him by the shirt, and pinned him.

"My turn," said Hollis. "One! Two! Thr—"

He and Hollis were ripped apart by their mom.

"Hey! No beating up on your brother. Both of you," she said as she looked from one brother to the other.

"But he started it," said Hollis.

"I don't care who started it. There will be no unsupervised wrestling in my house. I don't want it to happen again."

Ollie and Hollis both stood there silently.

Their mom sighed. She hadn't even had time to shower after rushing home to make dinner for him and Hollis. The sweat stains on her shirt—not to mention the stench—clued him in that she had just recently finished an epic workout with a client.

Her hard gaze softened as she took a knee between them.

"Listen, you two. You each only have one brother. Be nice to each other. Understood?"

They both nodded.

Their mom sniffed the air. Her face turned a bit pale. "And I think we could *all* use a shower. And then you're gonna clean this room, mister. Who knows what's crawling around in here."

"I'll tell ya what's crawling around in here. Little bug-eyed brothers," said Hollis.

Ollie ran back to his room and closed the door. He couldn't believe he had been only one second away from beating his brother in a wrestling match. He hadn't gotten that close in *years*. And even though it was technically a loss, it wasn't a *total* loss.

Ollie felt energized by his almost-win. He felt a wave of confidence shoot through him that he hadn't felt since beating Gorgeous Gordon Gussett.

He picked up his smack-talk note cards and stared into the mirror.

"Your tongue may be silver, but silence is golden . . . ," he read.

He was going to practice and practice, even if it took him all night long, in order to get it right. He *had* to beat Silvertongue.

CHAPTER 24

THE following morning, Ollie slept through his alarm. He had stayed up most of the night practicing smack talk and remembered that he had to finish answering his questions for "The Deadliest Pigeon" presentation just as he was getting into bed.

"School waits for no one!" his mom shouted when she found him still fast asleep. He had just enough time to throw on clothes, grab the note cards that he had prepared for his presentation, and sprint to the bus.

At school, he told Tamiko that he had practiced his smack talk all last night. He cleared his throat and, in his deepest voice, said, "You know why they call you Silvertongue? Because second place is all your lil' smack-talk game is good for."

She inhaled sharply. "That hurt my emotions and I'm not even Silvertongue."

"I know, right? It cuts deep. They cut *real* deep!"

"Hey," she said. "I'm proud of you! Great work!"

It felt good to impress Tamiko. She had really helped him come up with the best lines. After all, her voice, like Silvertongue's, was her strongest asset.

She would never turn down an opportunity to yell at the top of her lungs.

Ollie could barely stay awake as the day went on, and by the time he got to math class he was practically asleep at his desk. Being Big Chew *and* Ollie was hard.

"Just five more minutes," he muttered when Ms. Glenbottom tried to wake him up.

The only thing keeping him awake at all was the anxiety of having to get up in front of his English class and read his cards. He didn't like it when all eyes were on him.

And he *had* read the short story. Well, more like skimmed. But it was really boring and hard to follow. Besides, he was busy worrying about his upcoming match with Silvertongue and how to beat her.

"I'm so nervous I think I might pass out," he confessed to Tamiko as they walked into Mr. Fitzgerald's class.

Tamiko rolled her eyes. Whereas Ollie was a mess—Tamiko pointed out that he had put his shirt on inside out—she was beaming with confidence. She'd even tucked her shirt in for the occasion. But then again, talking in front of the class never fazed her at all.

"Dude! You got in the ring in front of an entire arena," she said.

"But that wasn't me. That was Big Chew," he argued. "And besides, that was like, what, five people including you and Hollis?"

"You *are* Big Chew!"

"It's not the same," said Ollie. "When I'm him, I'm huge and awesome and I have long, flowing hair that is always magically conditioned. Big Chew can do or act however I want. It's like I'm playing a character on television. But when I'm me, I'm, well, just me."

Tamiko shook her head. "First off, we're a tag team on this. I got your back up there. And second, Big Chew didn't collect all the items for his costume. You did. Big Chew didn't infiltrate Hollis's room and come up with some awesome smack talk. You did!"

Maybe she was right.

No, she *was* right. Ollie had done all of that stuff on his own. Tamiko was always good at making him feel better. If he could get in the ring and wrestle in only his underwear, surely he could read a silly presentation in front of his class.

He tried to keep his eyes open during the other presentations. But he felt himself drifting in and out of sleep. He dreamt that he was standing in the ring with Silvertongue.

Only, it wasn't Big Chew standing in the ring. It was Ollie.

In the dream, he tried to speak, but when he did, no words came out of his mouth.

"What's wrong?" asked Silvertongue. "Cat got your tongue?"

The arena, which was filled to capacity, exploded with laughter.

Ollie felt small. Smaller than usual. He turned to run away, but he ran directly into the ropes and was sent flying back toward his opponent. Silvertongue tackled Ollie to the mat, picked him up, and threw him over the ropes. He had the sensation of falling and suddenly woke up back in class. Tamiko was shaking him and telling him that it was their turn.

"We're up, Ollie!" said Tamiko.

He breathed heavily. It was just a dream.

No. A nightmare.

He reached into his backpack and pulled out the note cards for the presentation. It had taken him until the sun had almost come out to finish. But there was no way he was going to let Tamiko down. He shuffled himself to the front of the classroom.

He stared ahead while Tamiko described the main themes and motivations of "The Deadliest Pigeon." He tried not to make any eye contact with his classmates. Luckily, they seemed more interested in doodling on their desks, sneaking glances at their phones, or—in one case way in the back of the room—picking their noses rather than hearing whatever Tamiko had to say.

"And now my partner, Ollie, will walk us through what the pigeon was feeling when he finally confronted his brother," finished Tamiko. She turned to him. "Take it away, Ollie!"

Ollie looked down at his note cards.

He gasped. He shuffled through them and realized that he hadn't grabbed his presentation note cards at all. He'd grabbed his *smack-talk* note cards!

"Take it away, Ollie!" echoed Mr. Fitzgerald.

Ollie didn't know what to do. He could try to recite the report from memory. But his mind was going blank. His throat was getting dry. And the longer he was silent, the more his classmates raised their heads and stared at him, presumably wondering what was going on.

"Umm. Is there any way we could finish the presentation on Monday?" he asked.

Tamiko shot him a confused look.

"Not feeling prepared is not a good-enough excuse here," Mr. Fitzgerald responded. "Ms. Tanaka has done a great job so far. I believe in you, Ollie. You look prepared. You brought your note cards. Why not just start by reading what you wrote on them?"

"I really don't think I should," he insisted.

"Ollie. I can't give some students second chances and not others. It wouldn't be fair." Mr. Fitzgerald smiled. "Now, just read the note cards. Otherwise I will be forced to give you and Ms. Tanaka a failing grade. Do you think that would be fair to your partner?"

Of course he didn't think it would be fair. But he didn't know what was worse: getting a failing grade, or reading the smack talk he had written for Big Chew.

He could feel Tamiko's eyes on him, but he didn't dare look at her.

He knew that he didn't have any choice. So he cleared his throat and shuffled the note cards, hoping to find one that wasn't particularly offensive. It was one thing to say smack talk in the ring, but in front of your class? He knew it wouldn't end well.

He strained his mind and attempted to pull something—anything—from memory.

Think, Ollie! You read the whole story. Mostly. Just move your mouth.

"Umm. So there's this pigeon and he's deadly. And then . . . he confronts his brother and says, 'Coo! Coo!'"

"Go on . . . ," said Mr. Fitzgerald. "Just read from your note cards."

But nothing else came. He looked down at his note cards.

"Okay. Here it goes." He cleared his throat. "What's on the tip of your tongue?" He paused for dramatic effect and looked up at the classroom. "Oh. yeah. My fist."

Tamiko's face turned green. Some of his classmates laughed. Others seemed confused. It looked like Mr. Fitzgerald didn't really know what to say.

Ollie wanted to crawl into a hole somewhere.

"Ollie," said Mr. Fitzgerald. "Just stick to what you have written on your note cards."

"I swear I am!"

"You're telling me that Virginia Borjenowitz wrote, 'What's on the tip of your tongue? Oh, yeah. My fist'?" asked Mr. Fitzgerald. "Not likely. Unless you've found some lost chapter that I've never read?"

"No, I don't think she did." Ollie gulped. "Sorry, I don't know how that got in there."

"Proceed, Mr. Evander."

Ollie sighed. He brought up the next card.

"You look hungry. Well, here's my elbow on a silver platter ..." Then he instinctively mimicked elbowing the air in front of him like he had practiced all last night.

"I don't know what's gotten into you," said Mr. Fitzgerald, his tone rising. "Nor do I know what's up with the silver- and tongue-themed insults. This is your final warning, Ollie. Just read your note cards."

"Seriously, Ollie. Quit it," said Tamiko through clenched teeth.

Ollie was racked with nerves. Surely someone had turned

up the heat? He was all sweaty and had to keep wiping his hands on the back of his pants. But Mr. Fitzgerald was waiting for him to continue. He had no other option.

He felt like everything was moving in slow motion. He raised the note card up to read, his lips started to move, and the words spilled out of his mouth.

"Your tongue may be silver, but silence is golden . . . ," he read.

Then everything sped up very quickly.

"Give me those cards right now."

Ollie handed Mr. Fitzgerald the cards. He shuffled through them and gasped.

"I don't know what this is, but it certainly isn't for your presentation. I have no other option than to give you and Ms. Tanaka a failing grade. Now take your seats. I don't want to hear another word about tongues or silver or whatever."

Ollie took his seat while the next group went up to the front of the classroom. Tamiko slumped down next to him.

"Dude, what just happened?" she whispered.

"We just failed the presentation," he whispered back.

"I counted on you to do your part. I did mine."

"I did, Tamiko. I swear. I stayed up all night and everything. But I could have sworn that I grabbed my presentation note cards this morning on the way out. I know I messed up. I'm really sorry."

Tamiko sighed. "That's really going to hurt my grade, Ollie. I know you don't really care about school and your grades, but I do."

"I know. I know. I said I was sorry. It won't happen ever again," he promised.

She buried her face in her hands and then started quietly giggling to herself.

"I mean . . . That line about your elbow on a silver platter *was* pretty funny."

CHAPTER 25

SATURDAY arrived and with it Ollie's match versus Silver-tongue. He got to Slamdown Town earlier than usual. After the debacle with the note cards in class yesterday, he didn't want to leave anything to chance.

"Just wanted to make sure I got a good seat for the show," he told his mom as he was leaving.

"But, Ollie, your seat has your name on it." Her eyes narrowed. "Illegally, I might add."

"Can't be too careful!"

This was a joke, of course. There were always hundreds of empty seats, and Ollie always sat in the same one. But, fortunately, his mom didn't question it further.

"All right, then. I'll see you afterward," she said as she gave him a kiss on the forehead. "And remember, no wrestling. You're there to watch, not to tangle with your brother."

"I promise to not wrestle Hollis," he assured her. Which was true, because he needed to wrestle Silvertongue instead.

He stuffed his costume into his bag, triple-checked that he had the correct note cards on hand, and retrieved the gum from its super-secret hiding spot under his desk.

When he entered the locker room, he did what had now become routine: popped the gum into his mouth, chomped down on it, and transformed into Big Chew.

He stared into the small, round mirror in his locker and practiced his smack talk.

"What's on the tip of your tongue?" he snarled. "Oh. yeah. My fist!"

Then he pretended to punch the mirror. He tried another.

"You look hungry. Well, here's my elbow on a silver platter!"

Then he elbowed the mirror.

It *was* intimidating, but he felt like he was missing something. With only a few minutes left to prepare before the big match, he hopped up and down, trying to ramp up his energy, and ran the lines again.

"What's on the tip of your tongue?" he snarled. "Oh, yeah. My fist!"

This time, he wound up, closed his eyes, and swung as hard as he could.

But instead of hitting the mirror, he hit something much meatier. He opened his eyes to see that he'd accidentally punched Big Tuna, his locker mate, who at that exact moment had bent down to pick up a lip balm he had dropped.

"Hey! That really hurt!" said Big Tuna.

"Oh! I'm sorry, Tuna. I didn't mean to punch you—"

"Not the punch. What you said! Nobody mocks the Tuna! Nobody!"

Tuna grabbed Ollie by the torso and tackled him into the lockers. The two titans rolled onto the ground. Ollie tried to grapple Tuna, but he was too quick. Tuna flung Ollie into a trash can. He bounced off and landed with a crash on the floor.

"Prepare yourself for the Tidal Wave!" screamed Big Tuna.

Ollie knew that the Tidal Wave was one of Big Tuna's signature moves. He stumbled to his feet in the hopes of reaching higher ground, but he wasn't quick enough. In seconds, Tuna grabbed Ollie by the back of his shirt, bent him over his knee, and raised his arms as high as they could go. Ollie knew that he had no other choice but to ride the wave.

Big Tuna lowered his arms and *slammed* them onto Ollie's back.

The impact knocked the wind out of his lungs. Not just the wind. He watched in horror as the gum shot right out of his mouth. In an instant, he felt himself losing all height, muscle, and attitude.

But the Tidal Wave sent him, and his smack-talk cards, straight over the lockers. Ollie landed with a thud on the other side, hopeful that Big Tuna was too angry to notice. Where the cards had fluttered away to, Ollie had no idea.

"Ready for round two?" bellowed Big Tuna from behind the other side of the lockers.

Ollie, small again, did the thing that he did best in a fight. He hid.

Ollie crawled into the nearest locker and shut the door behind him. Through the grate, he could see Big Tuna lumbering around and searching for him.

"Come out and face me, Big Chew! You can't hide from Big Tuna!"

Tuna stalked out of the locker-room doorway.

Phew, thought Ollie. *That was a close one.*

Suddenly, Screech Holler's voice drifted into the locker room from the stadium. "Our next matchup is gonna be a smack-talk smackdown of epic proportions. How is new guy Big Chew supposed to hold his own against the viper herself, Silvertongue?! Well, you won't have to wait long to find out. Put your hands together for *Silvertongue!*"

Oh, no.

His match was starting without him. He needed to find his bubble gum now. He knew he had only a minute, maybe two. Silvertongue would waste no time walking down the ramp, entering the ring, and taking hold of a microphone.

Ollie slipped out of the locker and crawled around on the sticky floor looking for the gum. It had to be around here somewhere, and he had to find it. *Fast.* What if his mom saw him back here? She'd escort him out and then he wouldn't be able to wrestle today. Or ever again if he didn't find the gum.

"And now, Slamdown Town," said Screech over the loudspeaker. "It's my pleasure to introduce our second contestant. Put your hands together for Big Chew."

Hurry, hurry, hurry.

He crawled around, past The Bolt, who was taping her gauntlets—

"Hey, kid, did you short-circuit or something? You're not supposed to be back here!"

—past Mack Truck, who was greasing his wheeled shoes—

"Seems like you got off at the wrong exit. Beat it!"

—and past Granny, who was sending her granddaughter a birthday card filled with the earnings she'd won betting on Big Chew's last match.

"Back in my day, kids weren't allowed backstage. My how times have changed."

He managed to locate his smack-talk cards, which had scattered all over the four corners of the locker room. But his gum was nowhere to be seen.

"I *shouted* louder so that people who are supposed to be wrestling in the ring by now could hear me. Give it up for Big Chew!" bellowed Screech over the loudspeaker. There was an awkward pause. "Where has that guy gone to? Has he gotten cold feet?"

At last, Ollie spotted his gum. And while he didn't have cold feet, his bubble gum sure did. He found his bubble gum stuck to the foot of the coolest wrestler in Slamdown Town: Snowman Steve.

Snowman Steve, or The Snowman, was bundling up for his forthcoming match. He had on his hat, his scarf, his parka, and his gloves, and he was lacing up his famed snow boots. And when Ollie's gum went flying, it had come to a stop right on the heel of The Snowman's icy snow boot.

Fortunately, The Snowman was too caught up in his pre-match ritual to notice. Ollie snuck over and went to pry the gum right off. At that exact moment, The Snowman took a step backward. Had Ollie's hand been a few inches forward, Snowman Steve would have crushed his fingers. Fortunately,

The Snowman brought his boot, and the gum, close enough for Ollie to pull the gum off instead.

Ugh, gross, thought Ollie.

"Well, if Big Chew doesn't get here soon, he'll forfeit the match," announced Screech.

Ollie looked up and saw The Snowman staring at him with an icy look.

"Hey there, Snowman." Ollie waved the gum around. "First off, you're totally awesome and there's no way that Sunstar should have beaten you. But yeah. I noticed you had some gum stuck to your boot there. No need to thank me. Unless you want to give me your autograph or something."

"What are you doing back here, kid?" asked The Snowman in a chilly voice. "Now get outta here, or there'll be trouble in your forecast."

He didn't need to tell Ollie twice. Ollie scrambled away into a nearby deserted hallway. Alone now, he stuck the gum into his mouth. And chomped.

Big Chew was back. And not a second too soon.

He ran as quickly as he could toward the entrance ramp.

CHAPTER 26

OLLIE sprinted down the ramp and dove into the ring.

"Sorry! I'm here! I'm here!"

Silvertongue stood there and licked her lips. She was hungry for wrestling.

With a double portion of smack talk.

"So, you were dumb enough to show up," yelled Silvertongue.

Silvertongue's outfit was as colorful as her commentary. She wore a leather jacket with a bright pink shirt underneath. She sported cyber-yellow nail paint and electric-blue pants, and her hair had recently been dyed rainbow. Everything about Silvertongue was designed to be loud. Just like her.

Ollie looked down at the first card in the stack and read his carefully chosen first line aloud. "If you want the win so bad, Silvertongue, then why don't you take it from me?" he asked as he pointed to the bold white letters emblazoned on his chest.

"Or are you too scared?" he added with a sneer.

Ollie saw Silvertongue's concentration waver for a moment before she returned back to normal. But for that brief moment, her nostrils flared, her eyes bulged, and her normally cool attitude flashed red hot. Silvertongue really *did* hate being smack-talked to. Well, Ollie knew she had only taken the first bite of a full five-course smack-talk meal. He knew that with his cards he'd be able to beat her at her own game.

"Well, better late than never, folks," announced Screech.

Ollie's mom, on the other hand, didn't share Screech's non-chalant assessment of the situation. She marched right up to him and checked him into the match.

"You are way outside the entry-time regulations," she said as she pointed an accusing finger at him. "Trying to keep all your new fans in suspense?"

All my new fans?

Ollie looked around and couldn't believe his eyes. There were more people in the stands than he had seen in years. Granted, it was only, like, ten more people, but hey. It was something. But they couldn't all be here *just* to see him. Could they?

"Hey! Pay attention!" said his mom, snapping Ollie's focus back to the present.

"Oh, yeah. Sorry about that. I'm here now, though."

"You're just like my son! Running late every morning before school."

He gulped. The veins on her arms threatened to pop as her black-and-white-striped shirt struggled to contain all her muscles. But it wasn't her muscles, or her size, that made him, and other wrestlers, melt with fear. It was how quickly she could verbally slap you with a rule, or a penalty, or in Ollie's case, a time-out in his room.

"No respect for the law," muttered his mom. "I'll be watching you."

With that, she stomped off.

"And I'll be the one beating you," warned Silvertongue. "Normally I'd insist that a lady be allowed to go first. That'd be me. But it'd be rude not to offer the first move to a baby. I wouldn't want you to start crying, after all."

Then she proceeded to mime a baby crying.

"Gadzooks. That one has gotta sting." Screech sucked in his lips. "Even I felt that one from over at the announcer's table. Someone find me a bandage."

"My turn, Silvertongue."

Ollie whipped out his note cards. Tamiko had urged him to memorize them, but he had insisted on having the cards with him. He didn't want to miss a single word. It was time to show off what he had worked so hard on. He felt more than a little confident.

"What are those?" demanded Silvertongue.

"Your doom!"

Ollie pulled up the first card. He pushed a strand of his long blond hair out of his face and cleared his throat.

"You know why they call you Silvertongue?" he read.

He savored the setup. The cards had been arranged to offer a setup and then a payoff. For now, he needed her to ask why. And he got his wish.

"Why?" she asked.

The next card had the payoff. He licked his lips, relishing the impending verbal takedown. "Ah, no can do, Silver! I have you scheduled for a beatdown right now. Saved the date and everything. See?"

Wait, he thought. *That doesn't make any sense.*

"Now, folks, that don't make no sense," said Screech.

Ollie panicked. His cards were out of order! He was pretty sure his question was supposed to be followed up by something about a tongue, but he couldn't keep it all straight. Was this going to play out just like his disastrous presentation? He recalled Mr. Fitzgerald and the entire class staring at him, and then became very aware that he was in the middle of the arena with all eyes on him. Ollie felt a bead of sweat trickle down his neck.

The cards were in the wrong order. He'd arranged them to start with setup and end with payoff. But they must have gotten mixed up after he got hit with the Tidal Wave.

Silvertongue could win the crowd and defeat her opponent with words alone. In fact, the crowd had come to expect it. He *had* to give them *something*. Or else.

Ding, ding, ding!

"I'm in trouble," Ollie said aloud to himself.

His fingers fluttered over the cards as if he were preparing a game of solitaire. They needed to be shuffled into order. And fast.

"You want trouble? Well, come get some!" shouted Silvertongue. She wasted no time as she grabbed on to Ollie and launched him into a power slam.

He shook off the hit and scrambled back to his feet. A quick rearrangement of the cards and Ollie was sure he'd gotten some semblance of order back. Then he read from the next card as he bounced off the ropes and ran at her at full speed.

"Oh, you wanna do this another time?"

So far, so good.

He pulled out the next card as he raised his arm to clothesline her.

"Because second place is all your lil' smack-talk game is good for."

"What in the world are you even trying to say?" asked Silvertongue.

Ollie wasn't sure, to be honest.

Meanwhile, Silvertongue ducked his clothesline, spun behind him, and grabbed Ollie by the back. Then she squeezed, like a cobra trapping its prey.

"They don't call me the viper for nothing!"

Ollie felt the air rush out of his lungs. He couldn't talk if he couldn't breathe.

He had been trying to say the payoff about schedules and calendars from earlier. If this continued, he'd be done for. He'd have to rearrange them on the fly. He began to shuffle the cards with increasingly twitchy fingers.

"I don't know about you folks," said Screech, "but does it seem like Big Chew just can't deliver the smack-talk goods?"

This sent a wave of laughter around the arena.

But Screech was right. Looking around, Ollie noticed that the Slamdown Town crowd—minus Tamiko and Hollis—was chanting and cheering for Silvertongue. The wrestler who dished the best smack tended to win over the crowd. And the wrestler who had the crowd behind them was able to use that advantage to emerge victorious. Silvertongue used the crowd as her armor. Ollie needed to get his smack talk in order as soon as possible, or Silvertongue would be able to use that armor to take any punishment he dished out.

Cards flitted between and around each other in a blur. He'd have these cards organized in a few short seconds.

But he also needed to pay more attention to the match. Silvertongue scooped him up and pulled off a brain buster, a throw noted for its ability to bust one's brain and leave the recipient dazed and confused, which made Screech Holler yelp.

"Less reorganizing, more wrestling, Big Chew!" he heard Tamiko yell from the stands.

Stumbling to his feet, Ollie wobbled. He shuffled back. And forth. And back one more time for good measure. He had eaten an intense brain buster. But it had all been worth it, because he had finally gotten his cards in order. Pulling off his cape, which had become wrapped around his head in the throw, Ollie returned his attention to the cards clutched firmly in his right hand. He made sure to read the next insult from start to finish before opening his mouth. Then he knew he'd deliver his first stunner of the match.

"Prepare to be amazed," he said. He climbed to the top rope and pointed at her. "What's on the tip of your tongue? Oh, yeah. My fist!" He dove off the ropes and onto Silvertongue. But instead of crushing her, Ollie was caught by his opponent in midair.

Oh, no!

Even with his best line, Silvertongue remained unaffected. She held him aloft as the crowd roared.

"You've got the words but not the venom," she hissed. "You're way out of your league. Maybe Slamdown Town Tiny Tykes is more your size."

Then she dropped him to the mat and body-slammed him. The move sent not only him flying, but his note cards, as well.

"Not again!" he shouted as he found himself hurtling toward the corner of the ring.

She grinned. "Seems like the forecast calls for a large chance of pathetic insults!"

He watched, helpless after still being dazed from his turn-buckle collision, as Silvertongue gathered up the cards from the mat.

"Let's do something about that."

She jumped out of the ring and grabbed a trash can from the first row of spectators. Ollie, clambering to his feet, watched as she climbed back into the ring while holding it. His mom immediately charged over.

"Hey! No waste bins in the ring." She motioned to the trash can. "Get that outta here!"

"If you say so! But first . . ." She held the cards above the trash can. Ollie's only hope of matching her smack talk was about to be thrown away.

"You wouldn't," he pleaded. She bared her teeth.

Silvertongue dumped his cards inside the bin. Then she raised the trash can overhead and readied herself to throw it at Ollie. She leaned forward and . . . only pretended to.

But Ollie still flinched.

"Got you," said Silvertongue with a laugh.

The crowd roared with amusement. Ollie felt like he was

back in the lunchroom on the day Hollis had gifted him the gum. He *knew* he was big, but he didn't *feel* big.

And *feeling* big was the key to smack talk. The very same downfall had happened to Ollie when Hollis made him feel like he could never be as big as his older brother. Right now, Ollie felt that same feeling of being smaller than small.

With the trash can still held high over her head, Silvertongue turned and chucked it over the ropes and clear out of the ring. And with it, any chance of Ollie's going toe-to-toe—or rather, smack talk–to–smack talk—with the viper.

"No more cheat sheets," hissed Silvertongue with a devious smirk.

CHAPTER 27

SILVERTONGUE had Ollie pinned in the corner. His mom circled as Silvertongue landed (legal) kick after (legal) kick. He would not be able to withstand her attacks for much longer. And yet, he could not break himself free.

"Come on, Big Chew!" Hollis's drawling voice drifted down from the crowd. "Silvertongue's a pushover. You got this! You can stop pretending to be terrible now."

Ollie groaned. Hollis had a voice that reminded him of the feeling he got each time his alarm clock woke him up to go to school. But even more annoying. He could just imagine how Hollis would be up in the stands right now: wearing his band shirt with the rip on the front and breathing his infamous room-clearing breath and exhibiting his know-it-all attitude, gorging himself on snacks that would only make his stubborn acne worse.

And that's when it clicked.

Ollie adored Silvertongue. Insulting her was difficult. But he had been wrestling with Hollis his whole life. And during their matches, they insulted each other all the time. With his brother, it was all fun and games. Well, at least it used to be. Now Ollie was pretty sure that Hollis meant all the nasty things he said. But before, they'd try to one-up the other with the most insulting, gross, and mean things imaginable. Just like their favorite smack-talking wrestler, Silvertongue. Usually, it would end with both of them on the floor, laughing until their stomachs hurt. And when Hollis's stomach hurt he would burp, or fart, or do both at the same time, and then they'd start laughing even harder.

Ollie shut his eyes and pictured himself a few years younger, back in his own room, caught in another wrestling contest with his brother.

And just like that, loads of insults popped into his head.

"You smell like a pair of unwashed gym shorts dipped in old cheese," he said, recalling the time Hollis had worn their mom's unwashed gym shorts on his head and shoved his mouth full of cottage cheese. Hollis stood proudly on the bed and declared himself the Cheese Monster. He dove off the bed, landed on Ollie, and blew cheese in his face. It was hysterical, until their mom made them clean it all up.

Ollie opened his eyes. The flurry of blows had stopped.

"What did you just say to me?" she asked.

"That you smell like a pair of unwashed gym shorts dipped in old cheese."

Her jaw hung open in shock. The fury in her eyes was replaced with embarrassment. The once-proud wrestler now appeared to be a bundle of nerves.

He had *finally* poked a hole in her armor.

"Hey, I have a condition, and three times a day I have to—" she started.

But before she could detail her daily hygiene routine, he took advantage of the break. He stepped forward, placed his golden gloves on both sides of Silvertongue's face, whipped his head backward and forward, and delivered a headbutt.

She reeled backward into the center of the ring, which allowed Ollie to, at last, escape the corner. He closed his eyes.

There was imaginary Hollis, in front of him again. They were wrestling and, in between headlocks, Hollis was telling him he knew the best way to talk to girls and get them to think you're cool. But Ollie knew Hollis had never talked to a girl in his life.

So he said, "You can't even talk to girls. And you think you're cool?"

Now when Ollie opened his eyes, Silvertongue's face was white with anger.

"Um, I mean, I probably should speak to my sisters more. But then, I needed my own personal space and—" explained Silvertongue.

This time he was ready and landed a superkick as Silvertongue allowed herself to get distracted again. The slightly scuffed sole of a golden boot planted itself firmly into her side. She bounced, hard, into the ropes.

He closed his eyes again and remembered the time when Hollis had used his electric guitar to play his own wrestling entrance music. Hollis thought he was some kind of musical genius, but since he never actually practiced his lessons, he didn't know how to play. Hollis just said that he was "misunderstood," dropped the guitar, and charged him.

Ollie opened his eyes and addressed Silvertongue. "Your guitar-playing sounds like two clogged toilets flushing! Actually, two clogged toilets flushing sounds worse."

Silvertongue gasped, her eyes wide with shock. "Who told you about my guitar lessons? I shared that in confidence!"

Admittedly, Ollie was surprised that that one stuck as well. But a well-aimed leg drop, a bear hug, and a flip back onto the mat was the only answer he gave. She squirmed as she made her way toward the ropes. The tables had started to turn in his favor. And everyone knew it.

"I don't know whether to laugh or cry, but tears are coming out anyway, folks!" shouted Screech. "Looks like Big Chew has finally found his voice. And a steady stream of attacks to go with it!"

He had struck a nerve. The attacks took their toll on Silvertongue. She stumbled, unable to focus, because his verbal attacks opened up opportunities for him to land hit after hit. He savored the salty taste of impending victory.

Or maybe that was just sweat that kept rolling into his mouth. Either way, it tasted great.

"And another thing." He tossed Silvertongue into the corner. He was eager to return the corner beatdown he had received earlier. "You spend *way* too much time in the bathroom." He was thinking about the times when he and Hollis had wrestled after lunch. Hollis's stomach would always get upset, and then he'd run from the room and dive into the bathroom. You couldn't spend more than ten seconds outside the ring before you were disqualified, so wrestling after lunch was always an easy win for Ollie.

"Enough!" screamed Silvertongue. "My time in the bathroom is nobody else's business. Plus, I'm on a new diet that, while healthy, does not agree with my stomach."

He had celebrated too soon. The match wasn't over *yet*.

She blocked his incoming strike, placed both of her hands around his face, and delivered a headbutt of her own. Seeing stars and noting the fact that Silvertongue had a slight dandruff problem, Ollie tumbled backward.

But she didn't follow up the attack.

"Big Chew! Big Chew! Big Chew!" roared the tiny crowd in response.

"Hey! Knock it off," hissed Silvertongue. Not to him. She had grabbed a microphone and was now speaking to the crowd. "You losers need to focus on the real trash talker. Me."

Silvertongue was fuming. The crowd had turned against her. And she was not having it. She ignored Ollie's mom's efforts to pry the microphone away.

"Rules clearly state that verbal assaults directed to the crowd are not allowed," his mom said, fumbling for the mic. "You're toeing the line, Silvertongue."

"Why won't any of you listen to me?" asked Silvertongue as she swatted his mom's hand away. "*I'm* the master of smack. The viper with the poison tongue. Pay attention!"

"Silvertongue better pay more attention to the match and less to the crowd," observed Screech Holler.

He had a point. Silvertongue was completely focused on the

crowd. Ollie doubted she even remembered he was still standing there. With her full attention fixed on the two dozen fans in attendance outside the ring, she had left herself vulnerable inside it.

Ollie took advantage of the opportunity. He ran and bounced off the ropes. One, two, three times. Each time gaining more and more momentum.

He turned toward Silvertongue and ran at full speed. He extended his arm . . .

"Oh, no! Silvertongue. Look out!" yelled Screech.

Ollie gathered up a startling amount of speed after bouncing off the ropes. The red cape fluttered behind his massive body as the wind whipped past him. His outstretched arm was aimed straight at Silvertongue's back. And she had no clue!

But then he remembered that his planned attack would be illegal. Blows from behind were dirty. And his mom's career had ended on a dirty move. There was no way Ollie was going to stoop to that level. So, before he slammed into her, he opened his mouth.

"Hey, Silvertongue!" he shouted.

"Huh?" She turned just in time to see him charging at her like a runaway train.

"Catch!"

With a *thud*, his arm slammed into her chest. She flopped backward onto the mat. So Ollie threw himself over her.

Right on cue, his mom appeared next to the pair. She fell down on the mat and went through the count.

"Eight! Nine!! Ten!!! She's out," declared his mom.

"He's done it again, folks!" Screech let out a whoop. "Big Chew has laid the smackdown on Silvertongue and emerged victorious. Give a big Slamdown Town cheer for your winner. And possible new fan favorite?"

He had won yet another match. He soaked in the cheers and applause. With this win, Big Chew was one step closer to facing Werewrestler. The championship belt felt practically within reach. He let the dream of winning back the belt wash over him.

That is, until he noticed his mom had a rather stern look on her face.

"You were dangerously close to violating—" she began.

"—rule twenty, about illegal blows to defenseless opponents," he finished. "I know, Mom—*er*, ma'am. That's why I yelled at her. So she'd turn around. Totally legal move then!"

His mom looked impressed. Or at least, slightly less annoyed. She tilted her head to Silvertongue, who was still passed out on the mat. "I swear, you insulted her like my kids do. I can see why my oldest son likes you so much."

She gave him a close look, squinting as if to better assess him.

He laughed. Not an amused laugh, but a nervous one. Had his mom paid Big Chew an actual compliment, or had she finally seen through his act?

"Well, I better get going. Other matches and all that. Gotta clear the ring."

Under his mom's watchful eye, he swung himself over the ropes.

On his way out of the ring, Ollie looked up and found Tamiko in her usual seat. Only, unlike his match with Gorgeous Gordon Gussett, she wasn't hopping up and down or cheering. She wasn't looking at Ollie at all.

Instead, she was staring at the empty seat next to her.

Ollie's seat.

He wondered what was wrong. But he didn't have long to wonder, because his mom started yelling at him from the ring to clear the entryway for the next match.

He sprinted up the ramp, exited through the wrestlers' entryway, turned the corner, and saw Hollis. Like before, he was hanging over the barricade trying to get his attention.

"Hey, Big Chew! It's me! Remember? Boy, you sure showed Silvertongue," blabbered Hollis. "That was intense. I felt, like, personally attacked. Now *that's* the mark of good smack talk!"

So he *had* noticed. Even on some subconscious level, his brother picked up on what Ollie had said in the ring. After all, he and Hollis had said that stuff to each other for years.

Ugh. Why did Hollis have to ruin his victory high?

But then Ollie had a brilliant idea. No insult that he said to his brother as his eleven-year-old self seemed to work. Ollie was too small, his voice too high, to do any damage. But as Big Chew? Big Chew was someone Hollis admired—maybe even feared.

If Big Chew delivered a can of smack talk to Hollis, it might have an impact.

A big impact.

Ollie opened his mouth, practically salivating at the idea of *finally* getting to his brother. The words flowed out beautifully.

"You know why you were named Hollis? Because Smelly Nincompoop wouldn't fit on the birth certificate."

Hollis stood there, dumbfounded. Then he said, "Pinch me. I must be dreaming."

What? He isn't mad?

"You remembered my name? And wrote me a personalized smack-talk line?" Hollis let out a cheer. "I don't even remember telling you my name. Now that's what I call treating your fans right. You can do no wrong, Big Chew! Oh, and check it out!"

Hollis held up his elbow. He was wearing the elbow pad.

Ollie's heart sank. He had failed to get to his brother.

Again.

"What do you think?" asked Hollis.

But Ollie was too confused to think. As Ollie, he was too hated. As Big Chew, he was too loved. Ollie turned and stormed off toward the locker room, leaving Hollis behind.

"You must be tired! Rest up, champ! You're gonna go all the way!"

Despite winning in the ring, Ollie couldn't win against his brother.

CHAPTER 28

OLLIE checked to make sure the locker room was clear. It was a high-traffic area, and he needed to ensure it was empty before he turned back to his normal self.

He wanted to change back into regular-size Ollie as quickly as possible. Something about the way Tamiko had looked—or rather, *not* looked—out in the stands had stayed with him. He didn't know why, but he felt bad. He couldn't shake it.

The room seemed empty. Or as empty as it would get. He turned around, poised to pop the gum out of his mouth.

And found himself face-to-face with Big Tuna.

Oh, no, thought Ollie. *Is he back for round two?*

He assumed one round of revenge had been enough. But perhaps Big Tuna was hungry for more. He *did* have a reputation for both large appetites and revenge.

"What's up, Big Tuna?" Ollie asked with a hint of caution.

He made sure to chew the gum with extra oomph. He was not about to lose the gum. Not this time, anyway.

"Um, hey there. Big Chew. I, uh . . . ," stuttered Big Tuna.

Big Tuna was nervous. That was not the reaction Ollie had been expecting.

"Look. I'm . . . ," started Big Tuna for the second time.

But Big Tuna chose to look away instead of finishing his thought. Ollie, unsure of what was happening, kept his mouth shut.

"That was some killer smack talk out there," said Big Tuna finally.

"Oh. You thought so?" he asked.

Big Tuna nodded. "Silvertongue is as snarky as they come. And you made her look like a kid on the playground who just had her lunch money stolen."

"That's a good one! I'll remember that for next time."

Then, more awkward silence.

"Listen, about before. My bad about the whole shoving-you-into-and-through-a-bunch-of-lockers thing," said Big Tuna.

"Are you kidding? I got a front-row seat to the Tidal Wave. It was so awesome."

Big Tuna slapped his belly and laughed. The tension in the room evaporated.

Ollie's eyes went wide. "You just did the Fin Slap!"

"Wait . . ." Big Tuna eyed him up. "Tidal Wave. Fin Slap. Do I detect a fan?"

"Is something fishy? 'Cause it's about to be!" said Ollie, parroting Big Tuna's famous catchphrase.

"Yep, that's the one." Big Tuna laughed. And slapped his belly again. "I never would have pegged you for a fan of mine."

"Are you kidding me? I wrote a whole essay about you back in fourth grade. We were learning about sea life in Mrs. Boredesky's science class, and I told her my favorite fish was tuna, because you know, you're Big Tuna, and then she was like—"

Ollie stopped the compliments. He had to remind himself that here he wasn't Ollie.

Here, he was Big Chew.

"But anyway," he continued, "it was a *long* time ago."

Big Tuna smiled. "Well," he said, walking toward the exit, "consider me a fan of yours, as well. If you ever think about going toe-to-toe in the ring, not just in the locker room, maybe give me a holler." And with that he walked away.

Ollie's mouth opened and closed. He must have looked like a fish gasping for water.

He double-checked that the coast was clear. Then he popped the gum out of his mouth, placed it in the wrapper, and stuffed it in his back pocket. And not a moment too soon.

Because another wrestler had walked into the locker room.

"Hey, sorry, I was just—" started Ollie. But he stopped right there. Because the wrestler who had just entered the room sent a chill up his spine.

Werewrestler. With his smug frown permanently plastered on him. Ollie wanted to wipe that frown right off his face. He wished he was still Big Chew. He knew his eleven-year-old self couldn't do anything to hurt a wrestler that size.

"What are you doing back here, pip-squeak?" growled Werewrestler.

"Um, I got lost looking for the bathroom," he lied.

"This area isn't for puny little punks. Get lost."

Ollie wasn't sure if another opportunity for a one-on-one outside the ring with Werewrestler would come up. He needed to find a way to get Werewrestler interested in facing Big Chew for the belt. Then Big Chew would teach Werewrestler all of Professor Pain's thirty-two moves to make your enemies feel soul-crushing pain.

"Did you hear me, shrimp? You aren't allowed back here," repeated Werewrestler.

"You think you're so tough. But you're not. Big Chew is going to stop you!" he said.

"Big who? The newbie? He wouldn't last five seconds in the ring with me."

"He beat Gorgeous Gordon Gussett *and* Silvertongue," Ollie spat back. "And he'll beat whomever he has to in order to get at you."

"What are ya? His manager or something? Why do you care so much?"

He fought the temptation to chew the gum and face Werewrestler right there in the locker room.

"I care because it's time for a new champion. And that champion is Big Chew."

"You think I'm scared?" scoffed Werewrestler.

Werewrestler pointed to the gold championship belt around his waist. "Listen, kid. I've defended this belt so many times I've lost count. Even if I bother to challenge this Big Chew fool, he'll fail just like everybody else. Then again, I do love making examples of people. Maybe I'll do it just to break the newbie's spirit."

"Oh, yeah? We'll see about that!" shouted Ollie.

"Ollie!"

His mom stood in the doorway. She must have been walking past and noticed him and Werewrestler inside the locker room. He did not need a second look to know she was furious. He wondered if she was angrier at him or at Werewrestler.

"Ollie, this is a wrestlers-only area. What is going on here?" she demanded.

"Oh, I see." For the first time in the conversation, Werewrestler smiled. He looked from Ollie to Ollie's mom. "He's your son. Is that it, Banshee?"

Red splotches flashed across her face. "It's Referee now. And it's no concern of yours."

"But it's like you said, *ref*. This is a wrestlers-only area. And considering I'm the only wrestler here, it is very much my concern."

Ollie hardly dared to breathe.

"I didn't realize you cared so much about the rules. I seem to recall that they don't apply to you very much," said his mom.

"Rules are for chumps. Which is why you and your son should hit the road, ref."

The two stared each other down. He hoped his mom would slam Werewrestler straight through the wall.

But instead his mom pulled away. She handed the stare-down victory over to Werewrestler without any fight at all.

"Come on, Ollie. We're going home."

Werewrestler is the worst, he thought as he followed his mom out of the room.

Ollie expected his mom to punish him for being where he shouldn't have been. But she seemed lost in her own thoughts. He had somehow avoided getting into trouble.

Best not to push his luck.

His mom steered him back to the lobby in silence, where Hollis waited in line for more nachos.

"Hey, dweeb-face! Did Big Chew write *you* a personalized smack-talk line?" asked Hollis as they passed by. "Because he wrote me a personalized smack-talk line. I'd tell it to you, but you wouldn't understand it. We're close like that."

Or maybe Hollis *is the worst.*

Ollie decided to call it a draw in the championship title of the worst person ever.

"Where have you been, dude?" asked a concerned Tamiko when he finally made it to his seat. "You missed a good one with Big Tuna and Mack Truck."

"Well, buckle up again," said Ollie. "Because I have a lot to tell you."

CHAPTER 29

"WAIT a second," said Ollie to Tamiko as he searched his book bag. "I know for a fact I put my drawing in here earlier."

The school day had, mercifully, just ended. So he'd been watching Professor Pain's next video in the *Anyone Can Be a Wrestler* series by his locker while Tamiko collected her things to bring home.

"So you think you can 'rassle?" asked Professor Pain.

The Professor was seated in an empty classroom. How he had managed to fit into one of the kid-size desks, Ollie had no clue. But there sat Professor Pain, with his pen and paper at the ready.

"Well, let's see. You know how to work a stylin' costume."

He wrote *costumes* on the paper.

"And you've mastered your own unique brand of smack talk, too."

The words *smack talk* were added underneath.

"But what's next? Well, that's easy. It's a signature move. Now that everyone can see and hear ya, it's time to make your opponents feel the utter defeat of being beaten by a move that's all your own."

Ollie, who had been wrestling his brother his whole life, was more than familiar with the basics when it came to wrestling moves. Throws and grapples, strikes and suplexes, pile drivers and chops were all standard fare for any match. But what he did not have, at least not yet, was a move specific to Big Chew.

"Just like your costume and your smack talk, you need to tailor your signature move to what sort of wrestler you are. Some wrestlers prefer high-flying kicks. Others like using parts of the ring. Still others like to build up their finishers with a bit of theatrics. I'm sure you're all familiar with my own ridiculously awesome stunner: Surprise Quiz to the Face."

Ollie had watched countless footage of the Professor executing his signature Surprise Quiz to the Face move on his hapless foes. The finisher involved a big meaty fist to the face instead of complicated long-division problems, followed immediately by a soaring corkscrew takedown. His students never passed the quiz, and he did not grade on a curve.

"With your signature move, you show the crowd exactly how you like to tango. Or in this case, wrestle. Think of your move as a powerful exclamation mark, a way to demonstrate what sets you apart from the run-of-the-mill jabbers and body slammers."

Ollie hoped for inspiration and, soon, for a signature move of his own to use against Big Chew's next opponent: Barbell Bill.

Barbell Bill had two traits: strong and stronger. And an

insane list of special moves to back it up. The Pain and Gain. The Morning Jog Kick. But none more deadly than his patented finisher, the Kettlebell Kick.

Slamdown Town attempted to outlaw the move after Four-Leaf Clover caught the full impact and became the less popular Three-Leaf Clover. Fans had demanded the return of one the league's most-feared moves. So the league caved, much to Ollie's mom's dismay.

Ollie now regretted signing that petition.

"I mean, maybe you just forget it, Ollie?" said Tamiko, referring to the drawing. "You've been forgetting a lot of things lately," she added, probably recalling his broken promise to protect her father's pants and their failing presentation grade.

Ollie had spent the previous evening drawing an awesome picture of Big Chew wrestling Gorgeous Gordon Gussett, Silvertongue, and Barbell Bill all at once. He had already defeated the first two, and if things went his way, he would soon defeat Barbell Bill, too. But as he searched through his bag, he could not find it. The drawing wasn't there.

"I don't get it. I put it in here this morning and . . ."

Now he remembered.

"And what?" asked Tamiko, her eyebrows raised. All around them kids rushed past. The school hallways were abuzz with students desperate to get home.

"Hollis!"

Hollis had snooped around his book bag that morning. He kept asking to see the drawing and saying that Big Chew was his favorite wrestler. He had begged, pleaded even, for Ollie to give him the drawing. Of course, Ollie refused. So

Hollis must have grabbed it out of his bag when he wasn't looking.

Tamiko furrowed her brow. "Well, can't you just draw another one? We've got to walk Mrs. Ramirez's dogs. You know how she gets if we're late."

Ollie noticed that Tamiko hadn't been as excited to talk about Big Chew stuff lately, which was annoying because that's all Ollie wanted to talk about. He'd asked her what was up at the arena on Saturday after filling her in on everything that had happened with Werewrestler.

But she had just brushed it off.

"You're here now, so let's just enjoy the matches. Okay?" she had said with a huff.

As they headed toward the school exit, Ollie spotted Hollis chatting with his eighth-grade friends. He leaned against his locker while they (probably) discussed boring, eighth-grade things like acne, or graduation, or being the worst.

Ollie marched directly up to his brother.

"What did you do with my drawing, Hollis?" he demanded.

Hollis felt the eyes of his friends draw toward him. Being confronted by his little brother put him directly in the spotlight. "What are you talking about?"

"My drawing of Big Chew. I know you stole it from me," insisted Ollie.

Hollis looked uneasily at his friends, who had begun to laugh and hiss like a bunch of hyenas, then back to Ollie.

"I didn't take your stupid drawing. Now buzz off before I get really annoyed."

Ollie knew that staying in such close proximity to a bunch

of eighth graders could prove disastrous. But he refused to leave without his drawing, which he *knew* Hollis had.

"Don't lie, Hollis. You took it from me. I bet it's in your locker right now."

A vein throbbed in Hollis's neck. But then it settled.

"Why don't you go ahead and take a look?" asked Hollis as he spun the combination on his locker.

"All right. I will," Ollie replied.

Ollie outstretched his hand and opened the locker. But all that was inside was a pair of dirty socks, never-opened text-books, and a crushed soda can.

Huh. Maybe Hollis didn't steal the drawing? But then where did it—

He suddenly felt himself being shoved from behind and pushed inside the locker. With a laugh, Hollis slammed the door in Ollie's face. He could hear Hollis and his friends laughing from the other side. Inside, it was pitch-black and super tight.

"Hey! Let him out!" shouted Tamiko.

"Fat chance!" said Hollis. "That's what he gets for accusing me of stealing his stuff."

Ollie pushed with his arms and legs, but the door wouldn't budge. For one, it was locked. And two, Hollis was leaning against it.

"What's the matter wittle baby? Can't open a siwwy wittle door?" mocked Hollis in a high-pitched baby voice from the other side.

Ollie was too weak. But Big Chew wasn't.

Ollie reached into his back pocket, found the gum, and

placed it in his mouth. In an instant, he transformed into Big Chew's hulking mass, filling up the entirety of the locker.

With no trouble at all, he head-butted the door open and, in the same movement, spat the gum out into his hand and transformed back to Ollie, all while the door still concealed him.

The door went flying off the hinge, sending Hollis and the eighth graders tumbling backward onto the floor. Ollie stepped out of the locker with fists clenched.

"What the . . . ?!" said Hollis.

The eighth graders scrambled away, confused and maybe even a little scared of Ollie. Ollie walked up to Hollis and stood over him, huffing and puffing. He took a deep breath.

"Okay, you were right. I didn't see my drawing."

"How did you do that?" demanded Hollis from the floor.

Ollie shrugged. "Maybe I've been working out."

Tamiko dragged him away before anything nasty could happen.

"Come on, Ollie. We have to walk Mrs. Ramirez's dogs anyway."

She was right. They had a job to do. Tamiko and Ollie ran off down the hallway, and as they did, they could hear Hollis and his friends talking about how they had watched a video about freak kids with super strength online, and that maybe Ollie should join the carnival.

Now safely outside, Tamiko and Ollie walked down the sidewalk toward Mrs. Ramirez's.

"So, Professor Pain had a lot of good tips for solving Big Chew's signature finishing move," said Ollie after he'd calmed down. "I was hoping we could talk it over. Come up with some cool options."

"Oh, good, more Big Chew talk." From Tamiko's tone, Ollie noted that she was not excited at all.

"Come on. You always think of the best stuff. You totally saved my butt with the smack talk."

"Yeah, I did. So what did he say?"

"Something about being true to yourself," he said. "Making sure you put your mark on your opponent."

"So, start there. What makes Big Chew, Big Chew?" asked Tamiko.

He chewed on that question. Which is why he didn't notice the huge wad of gum in front of him until it was too late. *Spletch!*

Ollie pulled up his shoe to find a string of gum, which now tethered him to the sidewalk.

"Hey, Ollie. Are you a detective?" asked Tamiko.

"You know I'm not."

"Well, you are now, gumshoe!" Tamiko giggled at her own joke.

Ollie tried to pry and pull his shoe free of the sidewalk, but it wouldn't work. With a huff, he untied his shoe, firmly grabbed hold of it, and pulled with all his might.

This was one stubborn piece of bubble gum. Finally, the shoe sprang free from the sidewalk and sent Ollie flying backward onto the pavement.

"Ouch!" said Tamiko, running to his side. "Are you okay?"

Ollie lifted his elbow to reveal a pretty nasty scrape.

"That looks pretty bad. You should get that cleaned up."

"Yeah," said Ollie. "Lemme run right home and grab a bandage."

"That sounds good. I'll head over to Mrs. Ramirez's."

Before he stood up, Ollie inspected the shoe that he still clutched in his hand. He had freed the shoe from the sidewalk, but he hadn't freed the gum from his shoe. The gum stuck to the bottom of his shoe like . . . gum stuck on the bottom of someone's shoe.

He struggled to yank the gum off, but it just snapped back every time.

"Ollie?" asked Tamiko.

"Sorry," he said as he stood up and looked at his elbow. "I'll be right back!"

He sprinted toward home, one shoe on, one off.

"But hurry!" cried Tamiko after him. "This is a two-kid gig."

He was glad he did not live too far away. Otherwise, run-hobbling home on one shoe would have been much weirder than it already was. He thankfully made it home without stepping in any other offenders—the sidewalk was a minefield of chewed gum.

He heard the loud, moody music that blasted out of Hollis's room from all the way downstairs. A wave of fresh annoyance from earlier washed over him while he washed his cut and applied a bandage. He knew he should just run up to his bedroom, grab his other shoes, and leave. But he hated that Hollis kept winning.

He had the power to stand up to his brother in Big Chew, but he couldn't do it as himself. And to make matters worse, Hollis loved Big Chew. Would he still love him if he knew that Big Chew was his "annoying little brother"? So, instead of walking away, Ollie approached his brother's closed bedroom door.

"Hey, Mom told you to stop playing that horrible music so loud!" he shouted. Ollie had added the word *horrible*. But the volume of the music was too high for Hollis to hear. Either that, or he was ignoring him.

He banged on the door and noticed the sign had been changed.

~~NO BABIES~~ NO OLLIES ALLOWED!!! EVER

"Hollis. Seriously. This isn't even real music!"

Stupid lyrics about being misunderstood were Hollis's only response. Now Ollie was losing his patience. This time he banged on the door using the shoe in his hand.

"Hey, bro. Come on. Turn that down!"

The shoe collided with a *splat* on the door and hung there. In his anger, Ollie had forgotten the gum was even stuck to the shoe. He was surprised how sticky the gum was. Probably from years of baking in the sun on the sidewalk. His shoe hung there, suspended on the door. Then Ollie got a good idea. A *very* good idea.

He *yanked* the shoe off the door and headed into his room. He placed his trash can in front of his bed, slipped his shoe back on his foot, and tied his laces tight.

He *wound up* and kicked the can as hard as he could with his gum-covered shoe. Just as he'd hoped, the trash can stuck to his shoe. And if cans could stick to gum-shoes, maybe faces could, too. Specifically, Barbell Bill's face.

His plan was simple. Take an extra-sticky piece of bubble

gum, tuck the chewy wad safely behind his ear, slap it on his shoe in the ring before the big finish, and introduce his opponent to a new kind of sticky situation.

He had found Big Chew's signature finishing move.

And that's when he heard it. Outside, several dogs barked while a high-pitched, panicked voice cried for help. When Ollie poked his head out the window, he saw that the high-pitched, panicked voice didn't belong to just anyone.

It belonged to Tamiko.

He had completely forgotten about walking the dogs. He had told Tamiko he'd be right back, but had gotten distracted by Hollis and then by his finishing move. And of course, she had been left alone to deal with Mrs. Ramirez's dogs. All ten of them.

He threw on a new pair of shoes—sans gum—and bolted down the stairs.

He needed to help Tamiko before it was too late.

CHAPTER 30

THE situation turned out to be even worse than he feared.

He found Tamiko being pulled on her butt by a pack of poodles. She was being dragged through the dirt and struggling to hold on to the leashes.

"What happened here?" he asked.

"What happened here?" repeated Tamiko, incredulous, as she attempted to rein in the dogs. "What happened with *you*? You were supposed to come back right away."

"Sorry. I got held up a bit."

"Well, start holding these a bit." She tossed a few of the leashes she was holding into his hands, then dusted herself off and climbed to her feet. Immediately, the dogs began to drag Ollie down the street.

"Whoa, hey now. Slow down. Come on, guys," he said as the dogs yanked him across the lawn so that they could follow a bushy squirrel. He immediately felt guilty. He had only half the dogs, and they were unusually energetic today—no wonder Tamiko hadn't been able to wrangle them all!

"I didn't hear back from you!" she shouted as she stumbled up next to him. "So I thought I'd take all ten poodles myself and meet you at your house."

Ollie struggled to keep his hold on the leashes. "But you know we've never been able to manage more than five at time!"

"Yeah, well, you weren't there. And these poodles were getting antsy. So I didn't have much of a choice."

Ollie counted the dogs again as he was pulled through a prickly hedge. "Unless I'm wrong, I'm being dragged by four dogs right now. And you only have five," he said.

"Yeah, genius. Congrats, you can count to nine," mocked Tamiko.

He looked over the dogs. "So where's number ten?!" he asked.

"She slipped free a few minutes ago. I've been looking for her."

It took them nearly an hour to locate poodle number ten. She'd discovered a nearby neighbor having a cookout and had been enjoying the best feast of her life when Tamiko and Ollie finally found her. They promised to pay back the man for the cost of all the food she had eaten.

All the money they had earned walking dogs, wasted because of one poodle's appetite for grilled meats.

But at least they had every poodle accounted for. With all the dogs rescued, Ollie and Tamiko began walking them home. Tamiko refused to say anything to him during the entire walk back to Mrs. Ramirez's house.

"My poor poodles!" shrieked Mrs. Ramirez when Ollie and Tamiko, covered in dirt and dripping with sweat, told her what had happened.

She scooped up poodle number ten and held her close as she planted kisses all over her face. The poodle let out a gassy meat burp, which made Mrs. Ramirez even angrier, as she fed her dogs a strictly vegetarian diet. Then she turned her gaze on Tamiko and Ollie.

He realized in that moment how much Mrs. Ramirez looked like his mom when she caught him breaking a rule.

He gulped.

"Irresponsible, outlandish, and downright unforgivable," scolded Mrs. Ramirez.

He and Tamiko stood there silently. He was afraid that anything he said or did would be wrong. Mrs. Ramirez was *really* angry.

But since they said nothing, she grew even angrier.

"Well," she snapped. "How do you explain all of this?"

"I'm so, so sorry, Mrs. Ramirez," said Tamiko.

"Yeah, it's all my fault—" Ollie started. But Mrs. Ramirez cut him off.

"Your fault?"

He shrank back under her unwavering glare.

"Yeah. You see, I stepped in some gum. Which was kinda funny actually."

He knew as soon as he'd said it that he had made a huge mistake. Mrs. Ramirez seemed to expand with rage. Her eyes bulged. Her nose flared.

"Funny?!" she shrieked. "You think my poor little pooch running free and eating hamburger and hot dogs and who knows what else is *funny?*"

"N-no," he stammered. "That's n-not what I meant to say."

Tamiko tried to calm her down. "See, what happened was, Ollie was *supposed* to go home and get new shoes. But he never came back. So I decided to—"

"—to put my darlings in mortal danger?"

Ollie thought Mrs. Ramirez was overreacting. She made it seem like they had walked the dogs past lava or strapped jet-packs to their backs to see which dog flew best.

"But no one got hurt," he insisted.

Mrs. Ramirez shook her head.

"Maybe not this time. But the next?" She held the poodle caught in her grasp even closer. She squeezed so tightly, the poodle's tongue popped out of her mouth.

"Well, I won't make the same mistake twice. You're both fired," she declared flatly.

"Fired?" moaned Tamiko.

"But, Mrs. Ramirez, can't we make it up to you?" he asked.

Without any reply, Mrs. Ramirez walked inside her home and slammed the door shut. He could hear her comforting the dogs through the door.

"Don't worry, sweetums," came her muffled voice from the other side. "Mommy won't let those reckless children come near you anymore. Now you all need nice long baths. Come to Mommy."

The scratching on the door proved that the dogs thoroughly rejected the idea of bath time. Ollie turned to make a joke to

Tamiko. But her scowl made him decide that now was not the best time.

"Where were you?" asked Tamiko with anger.

"I was at home," he repeated.

He tried to avoid her glaring eyes. But she wouldn't let him off the hook.

"What were you doing?" she demanded.

"I was coming up with Big Chew's finishing move," he admitted.

Her mouth fell open. "What?"

"Yeah, I came up with this awesome new idea," he said. "I actually am gonna chew the gum. Well, another piece of gum, and then use it with this big epic kick, and—"

"You can't keep doing this." Her voice was thick with disappointment. "It's not fair."

"I said I was sorry. I can fix this," he insisted.

"No, Ollie, you *ruined* this. And not just this. You did it to my dad's outfit. You did it again with the presentation. And now all of my wrestling money is gone with no way to even get it back."

He *had* done all of that. There was no denying it. But each time something went wrong, Big Chew had won as a result. He figured that whatever mistakes he made were worth it. At least for him anyway . . .

If she had an issue, why hadn't Tamiko brought this up before? He tried to reason with her. "It's not like I'm trying to mess stuff up. I'm doing this all for a reason. You know that. And I'm so close to Werewrestler that I can practically taste his wet dog stench."

She sighed. "All you care about is Big Chew and wrestling and revenge."

"I thought you *liked* wrestling," he countered.

"I don't like wrestling, Ollie. I love it," answered Tamiko.

"Then what gives?"

"Ever since you became Big Chew, the *only* thing you care about is wrestling," she said as she crossed her arms.

"Hey, that's not true."

At least, he didn't think it was.

Besides, winning as Big Chew was important. Super important. He'd defeat Werewrestler. He'd become champion. He'd avenge his mom's loss from all those years ago.

And he'd bring the fans back to Slamdown Town.

And since Tamiko was his manager, that meant she'd probably get cool stuff, too. He wasn't sure exactly what a manager got for a championship, but he figured at least a Slamdown Town stapler or a stress ball. What was so wrong with that?

"I promise it'll be worth it."

But Tamiko just shook her head.

"For Big Chew maybe. But not for me," said Tamiko. "And I've had enough."

"What are you saying?"

"I'm saying that you need to find yourself another manager." She gave him an icy look. "But since that's a Big Chew thing, I'm guessing you won't forget *that*."

She left him in front of Mrs. Ramirez's house.

Later that night, Ollie tried to reach out to say he was sorry. To help her understand why he needed to focus on Big Chew. But she ignored all his messages.

He figured this was an argument she would need more time to get over. So he turned his attention back to Big Chew.

His match was still happening, whether Tamiko wanted to help or not. He needed to keep working on perfecting his signature finishing move.

Barbell Bill was the very last opponent standing in his way. Ollie knew that once he beat him and won his chance to wrestle Werewrestler for the belt, Tamiko would see why Big Chew was so important.

She was his best friend, after all.

He knew she'd come around.

CHAPTER 31

THE day of Big Chew's match against Barbell Bill arrived.

The car ride over was way less fun than usual. Hollis, clutching a paper bag too close to his chest, kept giving Ollie suspicious looks. The strange locker feat of strength from the other day still appeared to be rattling around his teenage brain. Ollie had never heard back from Tamiko. And she'd refused to talk to him at school. Which only convinced the eighth graders even more that he was a weird loner with freakish strength.

He figured she wanted to get her own ride to the arena. He'd join up with her after he had won the match, and he would make things right.

Ollie arrived backstage and took out a regular, nonmagic (yet delightfully fruity) piece of bubble gum. After a few minutes of dedicated chewing, Ollie plucked the now-sticky chewed-up gum and tucked it behind his left ear.

Now that his gum for the finishing move (he still hadn't thought of a clever name) was taken care of, Ollie popped Professor Pain's gum into his mouth and chewed. He transformed without any trouble: a first for Big Chew. He took that to be a good sign.

Ollie waited just out of sight on the entrance ramp. The arena buzzed as the fans inside took their seats, snacked on their snacks, and waited for the match to start.

He chomped on his gum. Today was going to be the day he'd punch his ticket to a match with Werewrestler. Then Tamiko would *have* to forgive him.

Once she saw his epic finishing move, things would go back to normal.

"Slamdown Town! It's wrestling time," declared Screech Holler's electrifying voice from inside the arena.

That was Ollie's cue. He walked down the ramp to gnarly rock music and flashing lights.

His cape billowed behind him, his conditioned hair shimmered and sparkled, and his boots squeaked on the sticky ramp as he made his way down to the ring.

With a quick motion, Ollie vaulted between the ropes. He waved to the crowd while pacing the ring. Soaking in their cheers never got old.

"And his opponent, the mustached muscle monster himself. The titan of fitness. Barbell Bill," announced Screech.

Barbell Bill appeared. His outfit had no style. And he didn't care. His entrance also had no flair. And he still didn't care. The only defining feature Barbell Bill possessed, outside of his extremely ripped physique, was a well-oiled, bushy handlebar mustache. Legend had it that Barbell Bill was born with the impressive 'stache, shocking the hospital staff so much that the doctor fainted.

Other than the mustache, Barbell Bill had no spark or pizzazz. His simple wrestler singlet was draped over only one shoulder, cinched at the waist by a large belt. His long, flowing locks draped down past his meaty shoulders.

Ollie knew that Barbell Bill's personal philosophy was "hit hard." It was simple (just hit hard) and effective. No bells. No whistles. Only barbell strength.

Barbell Bill ignored fans leaning over the railing for a high five. He had one focus. And it was directly in front of him.

He hoisted himself over the ropes and into the ring. The two wrestlers stared each other down. Ollie spotted a nearby microphone and, with a flourish of his red cape, leaned over to scoop it up.

"Hey, Barbell Barf," he said. "I know you were probably busy pretending that listening to moody music makes you cool. But I'm happy you showed up so I can totally kick your butt."

Barbell Bill flexed his biceps. "Foolish man of bubble gum. How can weak, puny wrestler like you hope to defeat strong, great wrestler like me? I laugh at you now."

Then Barbell Bill threw his head back and laughed only once.

"That's rich, coming from a guy who probably hasn't bothered to wash his socks for six months, because you claim to like the smell."

"Is boring," declared Barbell Bill. "Me hit now."

"Bring it on, peach fuzz," Ollie said as he tossed the mic out of the ring. His golden gloves practically squeaked with anticipation as he opened and closed them in preparation for the match to come.

Ding, ding, ding!

Both wrestlers wasted no time.

Ollie threw a huge spinning backfist, which Barbell Bill immediately blocked. He countered with a Pain and Gain blow to his hip. The hit sent Ollie to his knees.

Barbell Bill followed up with a series of strikes.

But Ollie broke free of the barrage with a sweeping leg kick. Barbell Bill collided with the mat. Ollie dove after him and tried to pull off a leg hold.

Barbell Bill saw it coming. He threw a knee that caught Ollie right between the words *big* and *chew* on his chest. The move sent him tumbling backward. Wasting no time, Barbell Bill shot forward with a Morning Jog Kick. Then another. And, of course, a Dumbbell Slam into the corner of the ring.

Ollie came roaring back. A diving stomp created some distance. A suplex sparked an early opportunity to pin Barbell Bill.

"One! Two!" tallied his mom as she pounded out the count.

But Barbell Bill kicked out before she got to three. That allowed him to stand back up.

And immediately dish out a blistering Exercise Bicycle Kick.

"My goodness, Slamdown Town!" bellowed Screech Holler. "Looks like we are in for a moves showcase the likes of which I have never witnessed."

There was no question that Barbell Bill's endurance was legendary. He had recorded some of the longest fights in Slamdown Town history, including an epic all-night match. Ollie's best chance of winning was to end the match fast.

"It's been fun, Barbell." And he meant it. "But it's time for my ultimate finishing move. Hmm, I should probably give it a name to sound cooler. How about—"

He was abruptly cut off as Barbell Bill made a move to grapple with him. But Ollie spun out of the way. He used the surprise dodge to send Barbell Bill toppling forward into the ropes. Ollie used that opportunity to run into the corner of the ring and firmly set his footing.

The one directly across from where Barbell Bill had just bounced into the ropes.

"Oh, I know! Prepare for the Bubble Buster!" he shouted.

Ollie pulled the second piece of bubble gum, the nonmagic fruity one, from behind his ear, and slapped it on the bottom of his golden boot. Then he raised his foot and aimed it straight at Barbell Bill, who was running at him full speed.

He pulled his attention away from Barbell Bill for just one moment. With victory in his grasp, he wanted to see the look on Tamiko's face for himself. Only, he discovered a problem.

Tamiko wasn't there.

CHAPTER 32

IT seemed impossible. But when Ollie did a quick skim of the stands, Tamiko was nowhere to be found. He wondered if perhaps she had drunk way too much soda and had to run to the bathroom. (It had happened before.) But then he realized Tamiko would *never* leave a match the moment before someone was about to lay the pain on their opponent.

So where was she?

"Knock, knock."

Ollie snapped his attention back to the match. But he realized too late that his leg was no longer in position for the Bubble Buster finishing move.

Instead, Barbell Bill pounced on Ollie with a clothesline, extending his arm as he slammed into him. The blow sent Ollie hurtling backward, up and over the rope. The world spun, then flipped, and then he crashed on the floor outside the ring.

"You take seat," said Barbell Bill. He pointed to the outside of the ring.

"Big Chew certainly left himself out to dry on that one, and all Barbell Bill did was supply the clothesline," said Screech.

Ollie groaned. There went his chance to finish early. He pulled himself off the grimy floor and made a mental note to wash his hands after the match. Ollie went to reenter the ring before stumbling on an unfortunate discovery.

Owing to the gum that was stuck on the bottom of Big Chew's golden boot, he found himself securely fastened to the Slamdown Town floor. The gum belonged on his opponent, not on his shoe. As he attempted to free his boot, he scanned again for Tamiko.

He found his mom, not Tamiko, as she waved her muscular arms in his face.

"Wrestlers need to be in the ring at all times!" she shouted. "If you're outta the ring for ten seconds you're disqualified. The clock starts now. One . . ."

"Yeah, I know," he grunted. "I'm just looking . . . for someone." The second it came out he knew it sounded ridiculous. He needed to get his head back in the match.

"Four . . ."

He wanted Tamiko to share in Big Chew's awesome victory. Just like they always had. But since she was apparently busy somewhere else, he'd just have to finish this match on his own. He hoped she hadn't accepted the all-you-can-eat nacho cheese challenge again. That had taken weeks to recover from last time.

Ollie felt his boot begin to rise, little by little, off the grimy floor.

"Eight . . . nine . . ."

He realized he would not be able to free his shoe before the count ended. In a last-second decision, Ollie yanked his foot out of his boot. Leaving the boot outside the ring, he pulled himself back through the ropes just in the nick of time.

His mom glared at him. "Hey," he said with a shrug, "you said wrestlers need to be in the ring. Not their boots."

But Barbell Bill had been watching.

And he was prepared.

"Enough. I finish now," said Barbell Bill.

Ollie's adversary wasted no time. He began to do cartwheels around the ring. Faster and faster he wheeled. The time had come for *his* killer finishing move.

"Take cover!" screamed Screech. "Barbell Bill is prepping the Kettlebell Kick."

But Ollie had planned for this.

Ollie had watched the Kettlebell Kick countless times. Over and over, Barbell Bill's opponents made the same mistake. Everyone tried to run away from it. And anyone who tried to run only found themselves kettlebell-kicked in the chest.

If running away didn't work, maybe *not* running away would.

However, none of that planning would matter if Ollie didn't have his boot—the one currently being held by the gum outside the ring.

Ollie didn't want to risk an earful from his mom again by vaulting outside the ropes on his own. So instead, he collided straight into Barbell Bill, who was distracted by his pre–Kettlebell Kick hamstring stretches.

The pair toppled over the ropes together.

"Looks like this fight is going outside the ropes!" Screech could barely contain his excitement. "New and uncharted territory, folks."

Ollie had hoped to scramble over to his lone boot, but Barbell Bill was the first to act. He clasped his huge, muscled hands on either end of Ollie.

With barely a grunt, Barbell Bill lifted Ollie straight into the air with a gorilla press, as if he were simply a free weight. From where they were located, Barbell Bill threatened to send Ollie straight into the stands.

In an instant, sensing the rule violations at hand, Ollie's mom stomped over.

"Now this is really getting out of hand," she said in a huff. "Wrestling is to be done inside the ring only. Put him down."

"Is not my fault," argued Barbell Bill as he held Ollie aloft.

"I said. Put. Him. Down. *Now*," ordered his mom.

With a grumble, Barbell Bill let Ollie slip out of his grasp.

Ollie sprang forward. He had one objective. Quick as he could, he ran to his stuck boot. He placed both of his gloved hands on the shoe and pulled as hard as he could.

"Listen up, you two." His mom pointed inside the ring. "Get back inside, or I will disqualify you."

"Come on," grunted Ollie. "Give . . . it . . . back . . . please . . ."

Maybe Slamdown Town was listening. Maybe the gum had been loosened just enough. Either way, the arena floor relinquished its claim on Ollie's boot. With a pop, it shot right up.

Ollie gave a cheer. Then, under an intense glare from his mom, Ollie launched himself back into the ring for what he hoped would be the final time today.

Barbell Bill had almost finished his stretches. Ollie didn't have much time. Without further delay, he shoved his foot into his boot. Big Chew's costume was back in working order, with both boots accounted for.

With everything where it belonged, Ollie placed himself back into the center of the ring. He knew just what he wanted to do as Barbell Bill, who had completed his buildup for the Kettlebell Kick, leapt out of his last cartwheel and soared through the air, foot leveled straight at Ollie's chest.

He did the last move Barbell Bill expected: nothing at all. He stood absolutely still. And waited.

The second before the kick hit him, Ollie caught the attack out of midair.

"By gum, that took some guts. I've never seen anything like that!" shrieked Screech.

Neither had Barbell Bill, whose mustache twitched in shock. Ollie swung the captive leg with all his might. Barbell Bill shot backward, straight into the ropes. As he sprang forward off the ropes, Ollie carefully tiptoed across the ring. He needed to be mindful to not get himself stuck again as he wedged himself into the corner.

Ollie raised his leg up and aimed a bubble gum–filled sole straight at his opponent. Barbell Bill's momentum off the ropes meant he was headed straight for him.

This time, Ollie kept his focus squarely on Barbell Bill.

And this time, Barbell Bill collided straight into his gum-covered boot.

"Is pain," muttered Barbell Bill.

He tottered. He teetered. Then Barbell Bill took a monstrous fall to the mat floor. Ollie immediately launched himself forward. He covered Barbell Bill to start the count.

His mom stepped toward them. But instead of counting, she crossed her arms.

"Now listen here, Big Chew," said his mom. "Chewing bubble gum is one thing. But slapping it on your shoe and using it as a weapon is another."

"Seriously?!" yelled Ollie. He swung himself around on top of Barbell Bill to look up at his mom. "Can't we talk about this later? Like, after you've counted?"

"Rules clearly state that no outside weapons are allowed," insisted his mom.

"Sure, but I am allowed to have accessories," he said. "Rule sixty-two, subsection B. And since it's on my boot, this gum counts as a fashion accessory. Not a weapon."

Ollie liked to be prepared. *Especially* when his mom was the rules enforcer.

"That seems like quite a stretch." She considered for a moment. "But bubble gum is also stretchy, and since you didn't *outright* violate any rules . . ."

His mom dropped to the mat and banged out the count.

"Eight. Nine. Ten. He's out!"

Ding, ding, ding!

The match was *finally* over.

Screech Holler screamed and fell out of his chair. "He's done it again! Big Chew is the comeback king, the piece of gum that will never lose its flavor!"

Ollie scanned the crowd again. He hadn't noticed them before, but there were *definitely* more people in the stands. Maybe Big Chew was becoming a bit of a draw.

But still no Tamiko.

"Big Chew! Big Chew!" chanted the audience.

Over the roar of the crowd, Screech Holler proclaimed that Big Chew was the most exciting new wrestler in years, and Ollie's mom droned on about food-safety regulations and how they impacted fashion statements. But Ollie wasn't paying attention.

He was still busy scanning the crowd, wondering where his best friend was.

"Is there anyone that can beat Big Chew?" asked Screech Holler.

"Arooooo!"

Goose bumps broke out on Ollie's arms and the back of his neck. He knew that howl. The arena crowd howled in response and broke out into raucous applause. That howl indicated the impending entrance of Slamdown Town's most notorious bully.

Werewrestler.

CHAPTER 33

WEREWRESTLER'S sudden introduction sent shivers down the spines of everyone gathered in Slamdown Town. Ollie remained where he was in the ring. Barbell Bill still lay facedown on the mat, passed out.

The world seemed to hold its collective breath.

Then smoke filled the entrance ramp. It billowed forward and blocked out everything. And then *he* emerged from the smoke.

Werewrestler.

He looked down on the ring and raised a microphone to his mouth.

"What do we have here?" snarled Werewrestler. "A chump who thinks he's a champ?"

Werewrestler made no move to head toward the ring. This wasn't an impromptu match (Ollie's mom made all efforts possible to ensure that no unauthorized wrestling would occur on her watch); this was a challenge. Ollie had witnessed these encounters countless times before. Werewrestler was sizing up his opponent like a hungry wolf. Ollie's heart beat against his chest at the thought that Big Chew's chance to face Werewrestler for the championship belt might finally have arrived.

Ollie couldn't find a microphone of his own in the ring, so he climbed through the ropes and headed to the ringside announcer's table to seize one.

"I'm being overrun. Send backup!" yelled Screech, who retreated into his cheaply made bright orange suit like a turtle into its shell.

Ollie took the mic straight out of Screech's shaking hands. "I'll give this back once I'm done teaching this no-good, cheating jerkface a lesson."

From the stands, Hollis let out a cheer. "Yeah, you give it to him, Big Chew!"

Ollie knew that Hollis wanted to see Werewrestler toppled from his throne as much as he did. Pretty much every fan in Slamdown Town wanted to see Werewrestler defeated. But now wasn't the time for his brother's commentary.

"Zip it, Hollis," Ollie said into the mic.

Hollis squealed. "Big Chew just said my name during an actual match!"

"What part of 'zip it' do you not understand?"

"He said it again!"

"I said, what part of—"

Werewrestler growled and cut him off. "Quiet. You're just a big dumb kid, Big Chew."

"Big dumb kid says what?" Ollie said.

"What?" asked Werewrestler, genuinely confused.

"Gotcha," said Ollie.

The entire arena broke out in laughter.

"Oh, boy, I *do* love classic humor," cried Screech. "You got him good with that one."

"If you're done being an idiot," interrupted Werewrestler, "I'm here to tell you that your wish is about to come true."

Ollie froze. He had waited for this moment ever since he became Big Chew.

"That's right, Big Chew. No more stalling. I've been watching you. You think because you got a fancy outfit, a big mouth, and some pathetic moves, you can beat me?"

"Of course I can beat you," Ollie replied.

"Well, then, consider yourself challenged. And trust me, once I'm done with you, the only thing that's gonna be chewed up is your face," said Werewrestler.

He pointed at the ring and licked his lips with his huge tongue. Then he walked back up the ramp and vanished into the smoke.

Ollie tossed the microphone back to Screech as he headed toward the ramp.

"My goodness, folks." Screech fumbled with the mic. "We have ourselves a challenge! Why, this will be a championship match for the ages. The new kid on the block, Big Chew, versus the undefeated, reigning champ, Werewrestler. Next Saturday. Winner takes the belt."

He'd finally scored his chance to take on Werewrestler.

He was certain Linton Krackle was busy calling Tamiko

right now to arrange the particulars. Ms. Manager would be demanding floor-to-ceiling banners of Big Chew, calling it the match of the century. No, the best match of *all time.*

Not to mention local TV commercials, exclusive Slamdown Town Big Chew championship shirts, and of course the revival of one of their favorite video game series ever: *Slamdown Town Brawlmania Supreme*, this time with Big Chew on the cover.

Ollie giggled to himself at the thought. Tamiko'd be so relieved that the plan had finally worked that, whatever was going on, they'd be right back to normal.

This was all going to turn out all right. He knew it.

He walked away from the ring and through the entrance ramp.

"Big Chew!" shouted Hollis as he jumped up and down behind the fan barricade, which was barely holding him back. "It's me. Lil' Chew."

Lil' Chew? What's a Lil' Chew?

Ollie turned to see his brother wearing an outfit that looked like a cheap knockoff of Big Chew's costume. He wore heavy winter gloves to sub for the leather ones. Instead of combat boots, Hollis wore rain galoshes that were several sizes too small. He'd wrapped a bedsheet around him to pass for the wrestler singlet. He even had gold underwear, which looked like it was colored with gold crayon and, unfortunately for Hollis, looked *extra* brown on the backside.

His brother beamed with pride.

"I spent so much time making this. Like, I didn't study for two tests or do my biology homework or do my chores or anything," admitted Hollis.

Ollie had ended up having to do those chores because Hollis was slacking off when he claimed to be studying. Like always, Hollis's love for Big Chew harmed Ollie.

"And check out this drawing," said Hollis, pulling a piece of paper from his pocket. It was the drawing that Ollie had done of Big Chew wrestling Gorgeous Gordon Gussett, Silver tongue, and Barbell Bill. The drawing that Hollis *had* stolen from him.

Only, Hollis must've made some edits. Alongside the other wrestlers, Hollis had drawn a stick figure of himself, dressed as Lil' Chew, holding hands with Big Chew.

"See?! It's me and you! What do you think?"

"I think . . . ," started Ollie. Ollie wanted to hang his brother up by the underwear. He wanted to sit on top of him like Hollis had sat on top of him so many times before.

"You're gonna be the next Slamdown Town champion!" continued Hollis. "I just know it! With your outfit, and smack talk, and moves, you can't lose!" Hollis mimed doing Big Chew's finishing move.

"Give me that!" said Ollie. He reached forward with his giant hand and snatched the drawing away from Hollis. He dangled it in front of his brother's face, like Hollis had done with the flyer.

Hollis stood there, wide-eyed and mouth hanging open. Ollie wanted his brother to jump up and down for it, like Ollie had jumped up and down for the flyer.

But that didn't happen.

"Yeah! I was going to give it to you anyway! I bet you

get a lot of fan art. Maybe you can hang it on your fridge, and every time you open it, you'll see it and think of me, Lil' Chew!"

Ollie buried his head in his hands. Of course, it seemed that nothing Ollie did as Big Chew would ever break his brother. Big Chew was Hollis's idol, after all. He might as well give up, because all his efforts only ever amounted to Hollis having that stupid grin on his face.

And that was worse than doing nothing at all.

Hollis fumbled for his camera. "Hold on. I need a picture of us. Lil' Chew and Big Chew, together at last. The number one wrestler with his number one fan!"

Hollis snapped a photo of them before Ollie could react.

"Wait till my little brother sees this! He's never gotten a selfie with a wrestler. I can't wait to post this on my Officially Unofficial Slamdown Town Fan Club. I'm a web developer, in case you didn't already hear."

But Ollie had heard all that he could handle. He pocketed the picture and marched down the hallway toward the locker room. There were more important things to tackle than dealing with Hollis.

He needed to find Tamiko.

As quickly as he could, he walked back into the locker room. Wrestlers came forward to congratulate him or offer him phone numbers for reliable medical care to call after his match with Werewrestler. But he waved them all away.

He found a quiet corner and spat out the gum. Then he ran all around the arena.

He checked the stands. He searched the lobby. He asked the concession-stand workers.

Nothing.

He tried to reach out to Tamiko multiple times. His messages remained unread, his calls unanswered. After nearly a half hour of searching, he couldn't escape the truth.

His best friend—the one who had helped him become a better wrestler, the girl who somehow knew as much about wrestling as he did when he figured that was impossible, the one who stood up for him after his brother turned on him—was *not* here.

Instead of coming to watch him wrestle, she had stayed home.

He had won the fight against Barbell Bill. And secured his title match against Werewrestler.

But without Tamiko there to celebrate, he found he wasn't as excited as he should have been about the win. Without his best friend, he wasn't very excited at all.

CHAPTER 34

OLLIE slumped back in his seat in the stands, dragging a soggy nacho through some congealed neon cheese. His match with Barbell Bill had been scheduled early, so there was an entire evening of wrestling to enjoy.

Only, he couldn't really enjoy himself, knowing that Tamiko was mad at him.

He looked over at the empty chair next to him. Since they'd become friends, he had never sat here before and watched wrestling without Tamiko. Now that he was, it didn't feel right.

He observed as Gorgeous Gordon Gussett revealed his new spring lineup of outfits in his bounce-back match against Petey Paradise. Apparently glitter was in style. The cleaning crew took some time to scrub the ring down. But Ollie was certain that, hundreds of years from now, people would still be finding flecks of glitter in the ring.

That match was followed by a spat among the Sánchez Sisters. When Ana revealed that she was leaving the ring to go to college, her sister Mariana became enraged. But when Ana clarified she planned on majoring in headbutts with a minor in civil engineering, the two sisters reconciled. With the controversy behind them, they delivered a resounding defeat to the Infinity Squad who, ironically, lasted only three minutes in the ring.

Then Big Tuna managed some long-overdue revenge when he interrupted a match between Jesse Five-Fingers James and Doctor Destruction. Big Tuna swam into the ring and dramatically Fin-Slapped Jesse, who never saw it coming. He was knocked out cold.

Ollie's mom got so angry that her head threatened to pop off.

"The rules are very clear that any wrestler who intends to invade another match must submit the request to me at least twenty-four hours before those intentions are carried out!" she shouted as she barred Big Tuna from the ring.

The knockout allowed Doctor Destruction to secure a victory.

The matches were great. Some of the best he'd seen in months, actually.

But without his best friend there, Ollie found himself having far less fun than normal. Or rather, no fun at all.

But he couldn't leave. After all, his mom was his ride home, and there was still a whole evening of matches ahead. So, for the first time in his life, he walked out in the middle of a match, hoping to find something—anything—to take his mind off Tamiko.

First, he made a pit stop at the pinball machine. The left flipper didn't work properly, and Hollis had tilted and rocked the machine so often that half the lights refused to blink. But the game spat out tickets that could be redeemed for prizes at the counter.

Ollie scored a decent amount. Not nearly as much as Tamiko ever did. She was the video game extraordinaire, and it was she who, naturally, held the top score. Normally, he and Tamiko would pool their tickets together to get one of the top-tier prizes.

But now he had only enough for the bottom row.

"Here's your cheap garbage—*er*, I mean, cherished prize," said the ticket taker as he handed Ollie a plastic replica of what he could only assume was The Bolt, but looked more like a blob with mismatched, googly eyes that fell off after two minutes of play.

Then he ordered a supersize slushie from the concession stand. It was not advisable to go in on a supersize slushie alone. The drink contained the largest legal sugar content allowed in the tristate area. Which is why he and Tamiko usually split it.

The icy slush turned his teeth and gums and tongue blue. He bounced up and down in his seat as the sugar overload made its way through his body.

But it didn't help him feel better, either. He still felt blue— and now he literally was.

No amount of sugar or cheaply made toys or awesome matches made the sinking feeling that he had *really* messed up go away.

Tamiko wasn't here.

And since she wasn't here, he started to realize that he hadn't really been there for her a lot lately. This was the first time since becoming Big Chew, after all, that he had not stayed backstage with the other wrestlers post-match. He wondered if Tamiko felt the same loneliness he was feeling right now each time he had gone away to wrestle.

He felt bad. Then he remembered all the other stuff he had ruined. Her dad's costume. The presentation. Mrs. Ramirez's dogs. He hadn't been a good friend the past few weeks.

The admission made him feel *even worse*.

For the first time in his entire life, Ollie was relieved when the final wrestling match ended. The ring emptied and the wrestlers cleared out. Screech Holler entered the ring, prepared to make the final announcement for everyone to go home.

But the show wasn't quite over. Ollie watched as none other than Linton Krackle, the Slamdown Town CEO, walked down the entrance ramp.

"As I live and breathe, folks, it's the man who makes it all happen. Give it up for . . ." Screech paused, pulled out a piece of paper, and read the following from it, ". . . the most successful business tycoon in the history of forever: Linton Krackle!"

The usual showering of boos and hisses rained down as he descended the ramp toward the ring. He waved off the crowd, struggled getting over the ropes, fumbled his way into the center of the ring, and held a microphone to his lips.

"Is this thing on?"

"Boo!" yelled Ollie. "Linton socks!"

"I'll take that as a yes. I have an announcement to make. So shut it."

More boos and hisses rained down.

"Yeah, yeah. Get your fill of that. Because you won't be able to do that for much longer. As of next week, Slamdown Town is closing. Permanently."

The arena suddenly went silent. Even Screech had no words. He just stood there next to Linton, head down, speechless.

Ollie wondered if he had heard wrong. Clearly, Linton had made some sort of mistake. Or Ollie had entered into a nightmare.

"Next Saturday's championship match between Big Chew and Werewrestler will be the final match here at Slamdown Town," confirmed Linton.

As quickly as they had gone silent, the people in the arena erupted with shouting. Ollie saw the devoted stragglers turn from silent shock to outraged yelling. They were the fans who had come to the arena through thick and thin, rain and snow.

Through years of boring, nasty Werewrestler being champion.

Several rows down, Hollis looked just as shocked as he was.

"But wrestling is life!" cried Hollis. He rolled up the sleeve of his Lil' Chew costume and pointed to a peeling splotch on his arm. "My temporary tattoo says so."

The crowd roared their disapproval. Linton motioned for them to be quiet.

"Listen!" shouted Linton over the yelling. "I appreciate that you fools—*er*—fans show up every week and pay full-price admission. But the point is, there ain't enough of ya. Which means

there ain't enough to keep this place open. Plain and simple. So I'm shutting Slamdown Town down. For good."

Sure, Slamdown Town was a little rough around the edges. It hadn't had a makeover in years, and most of the talent was, well, lacking talent.

But the arena was home. The fans were family. The thought of it closing . . .

Ollie wasn't the only one in shock. His mom stood there, mouth hanging open. She held on to the rope for support. Ollie hadn't ever really seen his mom look so uncertain.

"This can't be," moaned Screech. "Slamdown Town, closed?! Without even a fight?"

"What exactly does everyone expect me to do here?" demanded an annoyed Linton. "I tried bringing in new talent, but still, no one showed up!"

"What do we expect?" responded Screech. "Folks. Seems like our previously esteemed owner wants to know what we expect."

Screech Holler walked to the edge of the ropes. His voice shook with a fiery passion as he began to lead the crowd in a chant.

"Keep it open! Keep it open! Keep it open!"

Ollie shouted as loud as he could. Everyone in the arena joined in. They may not have been a large crowd, but those gathered gave it their all. Linton Krackle surveyed the scene. His eyes narrowed and his fingers instinctively flexed toward the wallet in his pocket.

"You all love this place so much?" asked Linton.

The crowd roared their approval.

"Then put your money where your mouth is!" The corners of Linton's mouth curled into a dollar-sign-esque sneer. He looked like he was ready to make an arrangement.

One that definitely would be skewed in his favor.

"Here's the deal, Slamdown Town. I got one week to keep the arena operating before the investors walk. If it were just on me, I'd keep scamming you suckers—*er*—fans for the rest of my esteemed life."

Linton looked around, his demeanor serious. "In order to keep Slamdown Town open, we need butts in every seat. And I mean *every seat*. Those are the very clear and highly unreasonable, if you ask me, terms I've been given. If every seat in this arena is filled by the end of next week's championship match, then you win. And also, I win, because more butts equals more money. So . . . everybody wins! But we all know that ain't happening. This arena hasn't been filled to capacity in years. Why would it happen now?"

No one, not even Screech, had a response for that. Ollie knew Linton had set the bar high. Too high. And yet, Slamdown Town's very survival depended on meeting that bar.

"Well? What do you all say? You want to fight my battles for me? I mean, are we in this together as a team and symbolic—emphasis on 'symbolic'—family?"

The people in the arena roared louder than they ever had, as if their life depended on it.

Linton grinned. "Well, that's settled. Now if you'll excuse me, I have *perfectly legitimate* offshore bank accounts to look over in my office."

Linton waved off the crowd and walked away. Ollie couldn't believe that Linton would so easily dangle the future of Slamdown Town like that. If the arena were in his hands, he would *never* let it close.

He sat there, alone.

In one afternoon, he had earned his shot against Werewrestler. He had also let his best friend down. His older brother still seemingly hated his guts no matter what he did. He'd discovered that his favorite place in the entire world was going to close.

And apart from the impossible task of somehow filling every seat in the arena, there was nothing he could do to stop it.

CHAPTER 35

OLLIE figured that the fact Slamdown Town was going to close next Saturday would have been enough to make Tamiko speak with him again.

But he quickly discovered he was wrong.

He had reached out to Tamiko multiple times since the announcement. She never responded. So that Monday, he resolved to talk to her directly. She couldn't ignore him if he was standing right in front of her. Sure, she might be mad at him. But the arena was *closing*.

She had to realize that nothing was bigger than that.

He looked for her on the morning bus ride to school. She sat all the way in the back. Her face was fixed firmly on her phone.

She didn't even look at him when he approached.

"Can I sit here?" he asked.

She shrugged. Ollie took that for a yes. He sat down next to her.

Her tapping seemed to have more force behind it than usual.

"So, I guess you were busy this weekend?"

The faint sound of in-game battle music was the only answer he got.

"Yeah, that's okay. I figured you were. Since you didn't respond to me and stuff."

"Do you want something, Ollie?" she asked in an annoyed tone. She continued to stare at her phone rather than face him. "I'm a little busy digging for treasure."

"Yes, I want something. Slamdown Town is going to close. We've gotta do something about it," he answered. A bit sharper than he'd intended.

But that finally got her attention. Tamiko smashed the Pause button on her game and turned to face him. He had seen her look like this in the past, but she had never looked at *him* this way before. It was the way she looked at Hollis when he walked into a room.

Annoyed.

"What can *we* do about it?" snapped Tamiko.

"Well, I was thinking that maybe Big Chew could—"

She cut him off.

"See? Right there. You're back to Big Chew again."

The other students turned around to stare at the two friends as they argued. He could feel their eyes on them. He hated the feeling of being the center of attention.

But he hated the way Tamiko was acting even more.

He lowered his voice. "Seriously. Unless you have a better idea that you haven't told me about, you have to know that Big Chew is our best shot at saving the arena, right?"

"What good is saving the arena if I won't have a friend to watch wrestling with?" said Tamiko.

His cheeks burned with a mix of guilt and anger. "Look, I said sorry. Like, a thousand times. What more do you want?"

"I want my friend back."

"I haven't gone anywhere!"

"Oh, yeah? Show me what's in your pocket."

Ollie paused. He reached into his back pocket and pulled out the bubble gum.

"As long as you still have that, you'll never really be back."

She returned her attention to her phone. Ollie couldn't believe she would just sit there and do *nothing* while the fate of wrestling hung in the balance.

"Fine," he retorted. "I'll do it *myself*."

He stormed off to find another seat.

He and Tamiko didn't say another word to each other that whole day. He was furious. And disappointed. And a mishmash of uncomfortable feelings that made him feel slightly sick to his stomach. She was supposed to be his manager. She was supposed to be his *friend*.

If she won't save wrestling, then I will, thought Ollie.

After all, *he* had beaten Gorgeous Gordon Gussett. And Silvertongue. And Barbell Bill. Compared to all that, saving Slamdown Town would be a piece of cake.

Only, it wasn't. Ollie could not think of a single plan or idea or crazy scheme that might prevent the arena from shutting down. The day dragged on with no solutions.

How was he supposed to single-handedly fill every seat in the arena?

Later that evening at the dinner table, Ollie pushed his food around his plate. Even Hollis, who usually had two helpings (he was a growing boy, after all), didn't eat much.

"Ollie, why aren't you eating?" asked his mom. "Beets are good for digestion. And you know the rules. You gotta finish all your vegetables."

"I'm just tired," he lied.

Instead of focusing on the nutritional value of beets, Ollie's attention focused solely on a drawing he was making. The words *Save Slamdown Town* were written on top of the page. Underneath, the beginnings of a sketch took shape. A half-finished Big Chew stood in front of the Slamdown Town Arena entrance. But Ollie felt that Big Chew was out of place. Something wasn't right.

He started to erase Big Chew. Before he could finish, an overwhelming feeling of helplessness washed over him. The drawing wasn't good enough to save Slamdown Town. And in that moment, he felt like the drawing would never be good enough. Why would *any* drawing ever be? Plus, he'd never be able to put up enough posters completely on his own anyway. So instead of adding anything, Ollie tossed the pencil down.

He went back to pushing beets around his plate.

His mom looked at her two moping boys with a raised brow. "Such serious faces. You know we're all going to be okay, right? No matter what happens with the arena."

"Yeah, right," muttered Hollis. Ollie knew Hollis had taken the news hard when his brother hadn't even bothered to catch him in a headlock since the announcement. In fact, Hollis had barely said two words to Ollie since Saturday. Ollie was grateful;

he was in no mood to deal with his brother's bullying on top of everything else going on.

"Now, come on, none of that," started his mom.

"But what are we gonna do without Slamdown Town? Wrestling is my whole reason for existence," moaned Hollis.

If only his eighth-grade friends could hear him now, thought Ollie.

"You both are far more than just wrestling," said their mom as she shook her head. "I know how many good memories we all have there. But when it closes—"

"*If* it closes," interjected Ollie.

A weak smile spread over his mom's face. "Right. *If* it closes, we'll still have each other. Wrestling's been a big part of this family, but if it goes away, we'll still have our family."

Will we? thought Ollie as he glanced over at Hollis. Without wrestling, he and Hollis would have nothing in common anymore.

"But what about your job?" asked Ollie.

He thought he saw a shimmer of doubt spread over his mom's face, if only for a second. But if so, she was quick to hide it.

"I'll just take on more clients," she said without any doubt. "I've been meaning to save this town from the evils of nonregulation daily exercise. Everything will work out." She paused. "Get it? 'Work out.' That's a little personal-trainer humor to lighten the mood."

Ollie laughed a little, mostly to make his mom feel better, and pushed his plate away. Beet juice splashed all over his drawing. But he didn't even bother cleaning it up.

"Can I be excused, please?" asked Ollie.

He didn't want to listen to how life would be *after* Slamdown Town closed. Not when he was too busy trying to brainstorm ways to save it—and failing, it seemed.

His mom's face scrunched up with concern, but she nodded. Ollie scooped up his plate and the beet-stained drawing. He placed the plate in the sink. Then, without a second thought, he crumpled up the drawing and tossed it right into the trash.

He trudged upstairs, closed the door, and flopped down onto his bed.

Taking the championship belt back from Werewrestler was supposed to be the goal. And he'd just scored the match.

But now he needed to somehow stop an unbeaten champion *and* fill every seat in the arena. Problem was, he was just a kid. A kid with magic gum in his back pocket.

He heard a knock. The door swung open, and his mom poked her head in.

"Requesting permission to enter the ring—*er*—room?" she asked.

He shrugged and she stepped inside. She closed the door and took a seat next to him. Normally, she would have commented about how his bed was unmade, or how he'd left his dirty clothes strewn about the room, or the hundred other household rules he'd broken.

But instead, she overlooked the infractions and sat in silence.

"So I know that when I'm overwhelmed, I like to talk it out to make sure I have everything in order," said his mom after a moment. "That and a vigorous cardio session work wonders for the stress and the glutes."

"Why won't Tamiko help me? I already apologized. What

more does she want from me?" he blurted out. He hadn't meant to ask, but the question had been boiling inside him since their fight.

"Oh, you're fighting with Tamiko?" his mom asked in surprise. "I thought you two were the unbreakable tag team. You both have practically been inseparable since the day you met."

They had been. But then again, so had Ollie and Hollis. And that hadn't turned out well. Were he and Tamiko doomed to the same fate?

"I don't know what else to do," admitted Ollie.

"Well, what is Tamiko saying about everything?"

"She keeps saying I'm not there for her or something."

"Time out," interrupted his mom as she reflexively made a time-out symbol with her hands. "*Have* you been there for her, Ollie?"

He sat up. "Of course. I've always been there for her."

His mom arched her brow. The way she was looking at him made Ollie feel like she could see right through him. And even as he had said it, Ollie knew that ever since he'd become Big Chew, he'd been there less and less for Tamiko.

Ollie sighed. "But, okay . . . Let's say there was this other me. Not me, of course. But, like, an older, bigger me with crazy long hair."

His mom laughed. "All right. Let's say there is this other you. Who definitely is not you," she clarified with a smile. "What has this other, long-haired you got going on?"

"Let's say that this other me also has an awesome best friend. But this me, the tall, big one, he's got this really cool shot at making his dream come true. Because he's so big and strong, he can make it happen. And his awesome best friend is totally helping, too. But then everything gets really complicated and being that guy, that cool, awesome, strong guy who could win it all, seems to be the problem. What should he do?"

Ollie bit his lip. He knew his mom could help steer him in the right direction.

"Seems to me like this other you is missing the point," said his mom after a moment.

"He is?"

His mom nodded. "This other you, the one you keep saying is the big, strong one. You really like that other you, don't you?"

"I really do! Or would, I mean," he added hurriedly.

"I bet you look at that other you and you think that having all those imaginary muscles makes him strong."

"Super strong. Like you," shouted Ollie.

His mom flexed her arms. "I'll admit, that's pretty strong. This other you doesn't skip leg day. Or arm day. Or any other day, if he's the same as me. But this other you isn't the strong one, Ollie." She pointed at his chest. "*You* are."

Ollie rolled his eyes. "Come on, Mom. You know I can't even beat Hollis anymore."

"Who said strength is all about muscles? Did muscles help save Barbell Bill on Saturday?" asked his mom.

Ollie hadn't considered that. "No, I guess not."

"Silvertongue is able to go toe-to-toe in the ring with wrestlers twice her size. Do you think she's weak?"

"Not one bit." Ollie knew firsthand that Silvertongue was anything but weak.

"And it only took one dirty hit to stop me, the Brash Banshee,

from holding on to the belt. My muscles didn't save me then, did they?"

Ollie chewed on that. Maybe he was putting too much faith in Big Chew's colossal body to win out.

"This other you may appear to be stronger, but that's only on the outside. The Ollie I know is strong in lots of ways. You're passionate and dedicated and admittedly not great at cleaning your room or doing your homework," she observed. But her eyes held no hard edge when he looked up at her. "But most of all, you, Ollie Evander, are loyal. You've always been part of a tag team. Sure, you've changed up who with—"

"That was Hollis's decision, not mine," insisted Ollie.

"Trust me, I know," said his mom. "And that's what I'm saying. You always stick to one rule: Be a good friend. So why would you start breaking that rule now? I don't think any dream is worth that."

When she put it like that, Ollie found it hard to disagree.

His mom scooted up closer to Ollie on the bed. "You know, when I stopped being the Brash Banshee for good, all everybody kept telling me was how I had been robbed from winning the belt."

"But you were," pointed out Ollie.

She nodded. "I sure was. An illegal targeting of the funny bone with a portable seating device is well outside the guidelines. But turns out, it may have been the best thing that ever happened to me."

"But why?" Ollie asked, shocked. He shook his head. The thought that Werewrestler cheating to steal the championship belt was the best thing that ever happened to his mom threatened to make his mind into mush.

"Losing that match meant I could be true to who I was. Who I *really* was," she answered. "Beneath the Brash Banshee, I was me. Not the other way around."

He considered that. And realized he had broken that rule with Tamiko. A lot.

"And you know what? I found I kinda liked being a ref. In fact, I loved it! The Brash Banshee wasn't really me." She nudged Ollie playfully. "I'm more of a rule-keeper than a rule-breaker. If you hadn't noticed."

He giggled. They sat for a moment in silence.

"I just want to save the arena. But I don't know how," he admitted.

His mom pulled him into a big hug.

"I know, Ollie. I know," she said. "But don't think you have to somehow do that alone. Because, honestly, you never have done it alone, and that's where your strength comes from."

For one moment, Ollie allowed himself to be just an eleven-year-old kid getting a hug from his mom—a kid who didn't have to worry about wrestling for a title belt or getting butts in seats in order to save an arena. Or repairing his friendship with his best friend.

He hugged his mom back. Then he felt much better.

"Thanks, Mom," he said. He gave her a kiss on the cheek. "I don't know how I'm going fix all this. But I'm going to."

"Good," she answered with a smile. "And I know you're going to work just as hard at saving the arena as cleaning your room back to acceptable health-code standards."

CHAPTER 36

LATER that night, Ollie paced his room. His confidence had returned after talking with his mom, but even with that renewed passion, he was no closer to figuring out how to save Slamdown Town.

A knock at the door drew his attention. The voice that shouted from the other side of the door stopped him in his tracks.

"Yo, Ollie. Open up," demanded Hollis.

Ollie considered leaving the door closed. Didn't Hollis know that this was no time for messing around? Slamdown Town hung in the balance!

But Ollie knew that Hollis could overpower him if he were left out there. So Ollie dragged himself over to the door.

As slowly as possible, he opened the door. His brother slouched on the other side. Hollis looked like he would rather be anywhere else. His arms were folded tightly across his chest as he refused to even look at Ollie. So why in the world was he here then?

"What do you want, Hollis?" Whatever his brother had in store, Ollie figured it was best to get it over with quickly so he could go back to saving the arena.

Hollis shoved a slightly damp, crumpled piece of paper into Ollie's hand. To Ollie's great surprise, he found himself holding the drawing he had thrown out after dinner.

"You know I threw this out for a reason, right?"

"I want in," said Hollis. His tone suggested he wasn't asking at all.

"Listen, Hollis. I can't let you in to wrestle now. I've got a lot to—"

But Hollis cut him off. "No, ya dingus. Not into your room." Hollis pointed to the drawing. "I want in on your master plan to save Slamdown Town. So let me have it."

Ollie's brain threatened to burst. He could barely comprehend what was happening.

"Master plan? Hollis, I got nothing. Okay? Besides this"— Ollie waved at the drawing—"which isn't even good."

"Um, yeah it is," countered Hollis. "'Save Slamdown Town.' That's what it says. I noticed it in the trash wedged in between some meat loaf."

"I was wondering what that was," said Ollie as he sniffed the drawing.

"You think I just pick random pieces of paper out of the trash for fun?" Hollis shook his head. "And if I can notice a slightly crumpled piece of paper in a trash can, then other people would definitely notice it hanging up somewhere. So what else besides the poster do you have going on?"

"Like I told you before, nothing," admitted Ollie.

Confusion and disbelief spread over Hollis's face. Without asking for permission, he pushed forward into Ollie's room.

"Hey, I didn't say you could come in here," whined Ollie.

But Hollis rounded on him. "Do you think I want to be in here? Because trust me, the answer is no. If anyone found out, I'd be done for. But Slamdown Town is at risk. So I don't care about all that, and I don't care if you don't want to work with me. Get used to it, because this is happening."

The fact that Hollis was in his room insisting—no, *requiring*—that Ollie work with him after spending the last few years doing everything in his power to keep Ollie away was so outrageous that he began to laugh.

"What's so funny?" demanded Hollis as Ollie bent over laughing.

Ollie, confident his laughing fit had passed, looked up at his older brother.

"How many times do I have to tell you that I don't actually have a plan before you're gonna believe me?" asked Ollie.

"But you always have a plan. That's your thing," Hollis pointed out. "You may only be a sixth grader, but you know . . ." Hollis rubbed his arm with nervous energy, his eyes fixed on the ceiling. "I remember you coming up with some cool ideas. With our tag team and all that. Back then, of course. You're totally not cool now."

Ollie opened his mouth. But no words came out. Hollis had, completely unprompted, paid him a compliment. Sort of.

"I mean, now I always come up with plans with Tamiko," admitted Ollie. "But she won't even talk to me at the moment. And I've been trying, but I can't come up with a way to save Slamdown Town on my own. Outside of making some sort of poster, I'm kind of lost on what to do."

"The loudmouth won't talk? That's a first," muttered Hollis. "Well, you better get her talking again. There is way too much at stake to have some sort of toddler tantrum between you two mess everything up." Hollis took a menacing step closer. "Because if you don't, I will give you a noogie every hour of every day until you do. We are saving Slamdown Town. All of us."

"Why?" Ollie found the question spilling out of his mouth before he could stop it. "Why all of us? This is because you like Big Chew, right?"

Hollis rolled his eyes. "You really can be a sad sack sometimes. My seat is right next to yours, remember? The original one, not some sixth-grader knockoff. I watched all those matches, too, same as you. And did you forget that I'm the web developer and moderator of the Officially Unofficial Slamdown Town Fan Club? Face it. Slamdown Town doesn't just belong to you. It belongs to all of us."

Hearing his brother's reminiscence about the arena reminded Ollie of when hanging out with Hollis had been the only thing he ever wanted to do. And there was no place they'd rather have hung out than Slamdown Town.

His brother may have morphed into an eighth-grade jerkface, but Hollis really seemed to care about the arena and all the memories contained there.

"And don't get any ideas. Once we save the arena, everything goes right back to normal," clarified Hollis. "Now, say you're gonna help me or I'll sit on you until you do."

That was not a threat that Ollie could take lightly. He reviewed his options.

Hollis had the raw strength that he didn't. Strength he used to get results, one way or another. His strength made people listen to him. And when Hollis put his fists to something, people generally gave him what he wanted.

Tamiko was the loudest best friend ever. At least, he hoped she still was. She'd never willingly work with Hollis. Hopefully, if he hadn't totally messed up, she'd still be willing to work with Ollie. With her help—and her loud mouth—getting the word out would be easy peasy.

And Ollie was pretty good at doodling drawings of wrestlers. Pretty much everyone told him so. With a few sketches posted to the right places, enough people might realize what was at stake. Maybe, just maybe, a drawing or two could help save Slamdown Town.

This plan, however crazy, was the only plan he had, and also the one option that did not immediately include his brother sitting on top of him. After all, he was a sixth grader. There was only so much he could do. But he resolved to try.

"I'm in," answered Ollie.

"Good. Stay there," ordered Hollis.

Ollie stood rooted to the spot, fearful that Hollis might sit on him anyway if he didn't obey. "Where are you going?"

"To get your homework," said Hollis as he marched out of the room in a hurry.

Ollie waited and marveled at what had just occurred. A day

ago, he and Hollis had been enemies. Now, as Hollis barged back into the room clutching supplies for a new poster, Ollie realized that, somehow, Slamdown Town had brought him and his brother back together.

At least for a temporary alliance.

This was what the pigeon felt like after his brother said, "Coo! Coo!" thought Ollie.

CHAPTER 37

THE next day after school, Ollie found himself standing in front of Tamiko's house. There was tons of work left to do considering his match with Werewrestler was only four days away. But he had, finally, worked up the courage to talk to his best friend.

That and the looming threat of a lifetime supply of Hollis noogies had spurred him into action.

He had given Tamiko her *space*, something that his mom and several online articles had told him was necessary sometimes after a fight. So he waited. Besides, he needed to take care of a few tasks before being able to offer a proper apology.

But the entire school day had gone by without her saying a word to him, and he felt completely alone without his best friend.

While having Tamiko around would certainly help the efforts to save Slamdown Town, Ollie found he didn't care so much about that. He didn't even care so much that Tamiko's advice always helped him calm down leading up to his matches as Big Chew. With all the work to be done in order to keep the arena from closing, it seemed almost mind-boggling that Big Chew still had to face Werewrestler for the belt.

Despite all that, Ollie found that he really just missed joking with Tamiko on the bus ride to school each morning. Or stuffing their faces with too many snacks during lunch. Or complaining about homework while walking the poodles.

Or watching wrestling matches together.

He wanted his friend—no, his best friend—back. He needed her friendship in his life, because he knew that it would outlast Slamdown Town, whether it closed in a few days or several years down the line. Now all he needed to do was say that to her, and hope that she would listen.

He took a deep breath. Then another. And then he rang the doorbell.

Tamiko opened the door.

"Hey," he said.

"What's up?" she asked.

He just stood there. And so did she. He'd stand there as long as it took.

But that didn't mean it wasn't awkward.

"Do you want, like, a soda or something?" she asked.

"Yeah," he answered. He guessed the Tanakas were off their health kick.

He followed her to the kitchen. She opened the fridge and pulled out the last orange soda. She gave it to him. Orange soda was his favorite. So he felt that was a good sign. Then she grabbed a grape one for herself and moved to the table.

They sat and drank their sodas in silence.

A quiet Tamiko was a rare thing. A quiet Tamiko who also wasn't playing a game on her phone was a sight he had never witnessed before. He wondered what she could be thinking about. But sitting here drinking sodas wouldn't answer that question.

So Ollie cleared his throat. "I'm really sorry," he began.

She said nothing.

"I get if you're still angry with me and stuff. But I wanted to let you know that I've felt like a total butthead because of what I did," he admitted.

He had. So he decided to go about fixing everything he had messed up.

"My dad told me you talked to him," she said finally.

"Yeah," he said, relieved she was talking now. "I told him that you had covered for me and that I would work to give him the money for a new pair. Then he started getting really excited about the new pants having even more glitter than the last pair."

"But how?" she asked. "We got fired. Remember? Plus, you wrestle for free."

"Actually, I spoke to Mrs. Ramirez, too. It took a lot of begging. And a *lot* of poodle bath time," revealed Ollie, holding up his still-pruney hands.

"I was wondering why you smelled like wet dog," she acknowledged.

"But she agreed to let us both come back," he said. "So I can pay your dad back once I earn enough. And I'm gonna use all my money. You don't have to use any of yours. Plus, I spoke to Mr. Fitzgerald, and he is letting us do extra credit. So that way, we can make up the failing grade. But I'll do the bulk of the work."

The words spilled out of his mouth. Tamiko blinked rapidly as she absorbed it all.

"You did all that? For me?" she asked.

"Yeah. When I said sorry this time, I wanted you to know I meant it," he said.

He had taken his mom's advice to heart. This time, he *was* sorry.

She took a few moments to think about that. Ollie thought, hoped, she looked a lot happier than when he first came in.

"Good. Glad to hear you stopped being a massive jerkface," she teased Ollie.

"Me, too," admitted Ollie with a big smile.

He liked that they were back to having a normal conversation again.

"So yeah, listen. I really am sorry," he repeated.

She nodded. "I know. Me, too."

"You? What for? I was the jerk," he said.

"Nah. I mean, yeah, you kinda were, but I know how important all this is to you. And I was sort of jealous I guess."

"Jealous?" That surprised him.

"No, not of the gum. Of Big Chew," said Tamiko. "You got to spend all this time with the wrestlers. And that meant you couldn't spend time with me. So, I don't know . . ."

She looked down at the table.

"I guess I wished I was as awesome as Big Chew was, and then you'd want to hang out with me again."

He shook his head. "What are you talking about? There's no one as awesome as you."

"Really?" she asked.

"Of course." He was surprised she didn't know. "You're the coolest, most awesomest friend ever."

She laughed. "Yeah. I guess I am."

"We good?" he asked.

"We're good," she answered.

"So," he began in a nervous tone. "I find myself without a manager. Know anyone who might be interested in working with a wannabe champion who promises to not be a jerk anymore?"

"I can make a few calls," joked Tamiko. "Speaking of which, I'll have to reach out to Linton. You would not *believe* how many voicemails he's left."

They spent the next few hours hanging out like they always did. Tamiko kicked his butt in video games. Then she and Ollie enjoyed triple-mega-chunk peanut-butter-and-chocolate ice cream. With extra sprinkles, of course.

This was how things were supposed to be. He and Tamiko, hanging out and having a great time. Ollie couldn't stop smiling.

For one afternoon, they could just be kids, and friends, before saving the arena.

Ding, dong!

The doorbell echoed down the hallway. Ollie, caught up in having fun with his best friend, had forgotten to tell Tamiko about the arrival of what would surely be a very unwelcome guest.

"Oh, maybe that's a package for me," said Tamiko with excitement. She ran off down the hall toward the front door. She apparently had ordered a new gaming headset and was eagerly awaiting its arrival. Ollie knew she would be disappointed.

Ollie sprinted after her. "No, wait. Tamiko."

By the time Ollie rounded the corner, Tamiko already had her hand on the doorknob.

"That's not a package," said Ollie. "It's—"

Tamiko yanked the door open and found herself staring face-to-face with—

"Hollis?!" shrieked Tamiko at the top of her lungs.

"What did I say about yelling?" said Mrs. Tanaka from upstairs. "Inside voices, please."

The look on Tamiko's face was one of sheer horror at finding her least favorite person outside her very own house. For his part, Hollis looked like he was trying to hide under his sports jacket.

Hollis opened his mouth to speak, but before he could, Tamiko shut the door right in his face. She spun on her heel to face Ollie.

"Explain why the sweaty menace is currently standing on my front porch."

"Hollis and I are working together to save Slamdown Town," answered Ollie.

It took the better part of a minute for Tamiko to stop rolling on the floor with laughter. When she realized that Ollie wasn't joking at all, her mouth hung open in shock.

"You. And Hollis. Working together?" She shook her head. "I don't buy it."

"And I don't blame you. But it's real," he confirmed. "Trust me. I'm as confused by it as you are. But he really, really loves Slamdown Town. So much so that he's willing to work with us to save it."

"Us?" hissed Tamiko. "I'm not working with him."

"Hey!" shouted Hollis from the other side of the door. "Are you two done with your little reunion? Kiss and make up yet?"

Tamiko opened the door. "When I want your opinion, I'll ask for it. Which will be in . . ." Tamiko looked at the clock on her phone. "Never minutes." And she shut the door in Hollis's face again.

"Look, I know this is crazy," started Ollie.

"It is. It really is crazy," confirmed Tamiko.

"But the fact that Hollis wants to actually help for once instead of dishing out wet willies shows that he's committed, at least for as long as the arena is under threat of closing."

Tamiko still look unconvinced. But after a moment's consideration, she opened the door again.

She pointed a finger straight at Hollis's face. "State your business here, eighth grader."

"Really?" He sighed and looked over at Ollie.

Ollie shrugged. "It's her house. Her rules."

"I'm here for Slamdown Town. After me, you two are easily some of the biggest wrestling fans I know. What else do I have to say?"

Tamiko scoffed at that. "As if. We totally blow you out of the water."

Hollis's nose flared, but he held his retort in check.

"If you want to save the arena as much as I do," he said through clenched teeth, "then we need to work together. Just until Saturday, and then you can go back to . . ." Again, Hollis swallowed the insult on the tip of his tongue. ". . . whatever you want after that."

"Wow. That looked painful," chided Tamiko. She sighed a

long sigh. "But not as painful as me agreeing to work with you only until Saturday."

Ollie, who had been on pins and needles the whole time, let out a cheer. "Awesome. With the three of us working together, there's no way Slamdown Town will close."

They made their way into the living room. Ollie sat down on the couch, keeping the peace between Tamiko, who was seated to his right, and Hollis, who standing to his left.

"Don't touch or breathe on anything," warned Tamiko, staring daggers at Hollis.

In an effort to turn the conversation toward the real objective of saving Slamdown Town, Ollie pulled out the stained drawing he'd been working on and showed it to Tamiko. "It's not finished yet. I could really use your help with how to improve it."

"It's pretty good, though," approved Tamiko. "Me likey where this is heading."

Hollis nudged Ollie in the shoulder. "See? I told you."

"So I figured we could all discuss how to get started," proposed Ollie, rubbing his shoulder. "Linton was very clear. A butt in every seat or the arena will close."

Tamiko's face split into a proud smile. "Actually, I've already been mentioning it to my fans on my *Griddle Royale* streams." *Griddle Royale* was the newest gaming obsession of Tamiko's, and of the world for that matter. It was a free-for-all game in which one hundred players fought to the death on a giant griddle filled with oversize pancake, bacon, egg, and sausage environments. Since she first learned how to play, Tamiko had placed first in almost every game. And since the game was so popular, her dozen subscribers had turned into two hundred.

Hollis snorted. "Can't believe people actually voluntarily choose to have their earbuds exploded by you."

"I know, right? It's awesome," said Tamiko.

"On my end, I've already started talking to my friends—" started Hollis before Tamiko interrupted him.

"Eww, eighth graders!" she shrieked.

"Tamiko," said Mrs. Tanaka in a tired voice from the other room. "Please keep the volume to an acceptable level."

Hollis scowled at Tamiko. "Yes, eighth graders. You know, the kids who you'd never be able to convince to come. But I totally can. Once I, you know, tell them that I actually like wrestling and try to find a way to convince them that it's cool. I'm thinking my extremely awesome Officially Unofficial Slamdown Town Fan Club can help with that. One look, and they'll see how amazing wrestling really is."

"Eighth graders and a site with zero traffic. Well, that doesn't inspire confidence," declared an unimpressed Tamiko.

Hollis turned red in the face. "I'm working on it, okay?"

"Seems to me like we all have a good start," said Ollie. "If we all work together, maybe we can pull this off."

As it turned out, despite the constant flow of smack talk and minor bickering, the trio was able to cover more ground than Ollie could have ever hoped for.

After sharing ideas with Hollis and Tamiko, Ollie used his drawing skills to design a poster of a larger-than-life Big Chew wrestling a colossal Werewrestler on the roof of Slamdown Town. ONLY YOU CAN SAVE SLAMDOWN TOWN was written across the top, with the match info on the bottom of the page.

Over the next few days, he, Hollis, and Tamiko made sure to stick the poster all over school: in all the hallways, the class-rooms, the lunchroom, and the gym, and even on the school mascot's back during the big coed kickball game.

The word got out and, after the trio endured a brief trip to the principal's office for hanging up unsanctioned posters and a clever framing of the endeavor as a "confidence-building exercise" by Tamiko, the posters were able to remain. The principal even let Tamiko guest-host the morning announcements, where she told the entire school to come and that there would be free pop-corn, and ice cream, and carnival rides—none of which was true.

Meanwhile, Hollis tended to bring his bullying out when attempting to convince people to attend Saturday's match. Ollie and Tamiko had agreed that, for once, Hollis was allowed to use bullying and intimidation in order to convince people to go.

It was for a good cause.

"But please keep the wedgies to a minimum," said Ollie.

"I don't tell you how to draw the posters," said Hollis. "You don't tell me how to bully."

Hollis immediately plucked out the first seventh grader he could find.

"What are you doing Saturday?" demanded Hollis.

"Going to my sister's graduation ceremony."

"Cancel it. You're going to Slamdown Town and watching wrestling. Got it?"

The terrified student nodded.

"Good. And bring your whole family. Immediate. And extended. Or else."

Hollis bullied and muscled his way through the hallways with ease, easily convincing measly sixth and seventh graders to attend the match that weekend. With each gulp and nervous sweat, Hollis became more and more emboldened, as if he derived more and more energy from bullying. Ollie was just happy that he was picking on someone else.

But Ollie had never seen Hollis more nervous than when he stood in front of his eighth-grade friends and prepared to confess his long-held secret.

"Everyone, I have a confession to make." Hollis took a deep breath. "I love wrestling."

A sharp intake of breath from the group met Hollis's confession. Ollie waited, tapping his foot with impatient energy.

A large eighth-grade boy with a splotchy peach-fuzz mustache came forward. "Hey, dude, that must have been hard to share," said the boy as his voice cracked.

"We, like, so appreciate you putting that trust in us," said a squat girl with braces. "Trust is, like, so key to healthy friendships and stuff."

"It's really adult of you to share your truth," said another girl in an oversize sweater.

Ollie buried his face in his hands. The eighth graders thought they were so mature, and it annoyed him to no end. But he knew that beggars couldn't be choosers. The group went on about stuff like this being a safe space and supporting one another and how proud they were of Hollis for opening up to them.

"Does that mean you'll all come to Slamdown Town on Saturday?" Hollis asked. "I need your help."

To Ollie's great surprise, a good portion of Hollis's friends agreed to come. Those that didn't commit had their online friend statuses reduced from "Friends" to "Acquaintances."

"It was brutal but necessary," assured Hollis.

As the week went on, Hollis continued to work his magic.

But Ollie was afraid it wouldn't be enough.

"I got the eighth graders, didn't I?" said Hollis. "Don't worry. Once they start talking about it, all the seventh and sixth graders will get on board, too. That's how it always works."

"Great. But there are more seats in the arena than there are kids in school," said Ollie.

"Exactly. Which means we need to think bigger."

"Bigger?" asked Tamiko. "I didn't know your tiny brain could form big thoughts."

"Who said that?" demanded Hollis as he looked around, pretending not to see Tamiko. "Must have been some itty-bitty sixth-grade baby in need of her nappy time."

Ollie stepped between them.

"What do you mean by 'bigger,' Hollis?" asked Ollie.

✾✾✾

That night after school, Ollie and Tamiko sat on the living room couch and watched as Hollis bent over his cracked laptop screen. He would type a few words, delete them, type them again, and delete them again. Tamiko tapped her foot impatiently.

By "bigger," Hollis had been referring to the Officially Unofficial Slamdown Town Fan Club. He said that if people had a place like the fan club to gather and discuss the upcoming match, then they could pledge their support and drum up additional interest and spread the word.

Hollis insisted on writing a blog post to greet newcomers. But he was taking hours to actually finish it, and time was not on their side.

"Think you can hurry up?" asked Tamiko.

Hollis rolled his eyes. "You can't rush greatness, Tamiko."

"I'm not. Hollis, you're the one who forgets to finish your own articles. The one leading up to Barbell Bill's match literally ended with 'I'll finish this later' in parentheses."

"I think that's dramatic and engaging material," declared Hollis. "And speaking of dramatic and engaging material . . ." He held up his laptop for them to read the blog post.

Greetings fellow Slamdown Town fans, and welcome newbies. We're here for one reason and one reason only. Because we all LOVE wrestling. (That, or I said I'd give you a super wedgie if you didn't sign up for my website and show up this weekend. I stand by that statement.) As you know, Linton Krackle (booooooooooooo) is threatening to shut down the arena because it's not making any $$$$$$$ or something. Well, I'm here to tell ya that THAT ain't happening. Slamdown Town isn't just an arena. To me, Slamdown Town is a second home. I've been going there every weekend with my mom since I was a baby. It's where I took my first steps, and where I learned how to do my first head lock on my little bro. I've had some of my best memories there, like the time I ate so much cotton candy that I burped cotton and then threw up blue for two days straight. Besides, where else is it perfectly acceptable to walk around in your underwear AND have terrible body odor? (I'm not talking about ME, I'm talking about the wrestlers!) This weekend is the big championship match between BIG CHEW (yayayayayaya) and the reigning champ, WEREWRESTLER, who is a total loser who is gonna totally lose this weekend. BIG CHEW needs all our support. So make sure to come out this Saturday, buy a ticket, and put your butt in a seat. If not, I'll personally kick yours!

"Well, what do you think?" asked Hollis.

"Honestly," said Ollie, "I think it's the best post you've ever written."

"I thought so myself," said Hollis, pleased.

Tamiko clutched her stomach. "All this brotherly bonding is gonna make me hurl like that cotton candy story. I wonder what color it'll be."

Hollis, who had no interest in finding out the answer, stepped away from Tamiko. "Now all it needs is your artwork, bro."

One by one, they scanned in all of Ollie's drawings and placed them on the website.

On the front page was the final drawing of Werewrestler versus Big Chew on top of the arena. Other drawings of Silver-tongue, Barbell Bill, Gorgeous Gordon Gussett, and Lil' Old

Granny appeared on the various pages. And across the top banner, in big bold letters, was the rallying call:

ONLY YOU CAN SAVE SLAMDOWN TOWN

The site had finally become the awesome fan page Hollis had always envisioned.

"Now we just have to get people to click on it," said Ollie.

✳✳✳

Hollis was, remarkably, right about the eighth graders. Once they started posting about the Officially Unofficial Slamdown Town Fan Club, every other middle schooler took notice. In the span of a single lunch period, there were more than a hundred users liking, commenting, and blogging away on the website.

"I knew I was destined to be a web developer," said Hollis with tears in his eyes.

Ollie and Tamiko shook their heads but kept quiet.

Tamiko continued to mention the event on *Griddle Royale*. She spent every evening unlocking each piece of apparel and, after she had unlocked the highest-level gear, outfitted her game avatar in a vaguely Big Chew–inspired purple, gold, and red outfit. With her popularity soaring due to her skill, other players started to emulate her outfit, and support for Big Chew—and the arena—was high.

"Hey, everyone," shouted Tamiko into her mic as she fought for breakfast glory. She'd kept the stream up constantly, giving her viewers a barrage of thrilling victories. "Looks like we have yet another pledge to attend Slamdown Town this Saturday. You will *not* be disappointed. And be sure to check out the Officially

Unofficial Slamdown Town Fan Club for all the info. Remember, only *you* can save Slamdown Town. Now let's see if we can score another five backers while I win again!"

Alone, they would not have been able to accomplish nearly as much as they did together. As the week drew to a close, the trio walked home from school that Friday buzzing with excitement. The past few days were a blur of getting anyone and everyone they could to agree to join them on Saturday.

"I'm pulling a massive five-hour stream tonight." Tamiko's eyes shimmered with pride. "Longest ever for my channel. That's sure to bring in the viewers."

Hollis and Ollie parted ways with Tamiko and headed toward home.

"Do you think we got enough?" asked Hollis as they turned onto their street.

Ollie felt confident that, after all their hard work, they would succeed.

"Let's hope so!"

They had done all that they could think of to try and save the arena. More important, they had done it together.

CHAPTER 38

THE day of the match had finally arrived. That Saturday, Ollie piled into the car along with his mom and brother.

"Don't worry. We got this," assured Hollis, who was already wearing his Lil' Chew outfit.

"Fingers crossed," said Ollie. The knot in his stomach tightened.

They picked up Tamiko and headed straight for Slamdown Town.

Tamiko eyed up Hollis.

"I like your costume," she said without sarcasm.

Hollis had been prepared to verbally retaliate but was caught off guard by the compliment. "Thanks," he mumbled.

Ollie caught his mom smiling at them all through the rear-view mirror. The look on her face when glancing between Ollie and Hollis was one of relief. As if she had been waiting for this moment for a long time.

To be honest, so had Ollie.

"Outside of getting everyone to come, here's to hoping Big Chew kicks Werewrestler's butt!" shouted Hollis.

Ollie gulped. He certainly hoped that would happen. But with all his focus on saving the arena, Ollie'd had little time to think about the match itself.

"What do you think, Mom? Can Big Chew defeat Werewrestler?" asked Ollie.

"With his hands tied behind his back!" shouted Hollis.

Tamiko nodded. "Werewrestler isn't gonna know what hit him!"

Ollie beamed at Tamiko, who winked at him.

"I don't know, kids. I wouldn't get my hopes up," cautioned his mom.

"You don't think Big Chew can win?" Ollie's heart sank.

"No, I didn't say that. But Werewrestler is . . ." She left the thought hanging.

But Hollis was more than willing to finish the thought for her.

"Werewrestler is the worst wrestler ever and a lousy cheating bum and I hope Big Chew kicks his hairy butt into next week!" said Hollis.

They made it to the arena. And they could hardly believe their eyes. There were more cars in the parking lot than there had been in years. The ticket takers, busy for once, ushered Ollie through the turnstile after he handed over his stub. Once inside, they found tons of fresh new faces. Kids and eighth graders (*ugh*) and adults and everyone in between.

The word had gotten out, thanks to all their efforts. Ollie stood, wide-eyed, observing the actual throng of people jostling into the arena. He didn't know if it would be enough to fill every seat. But the possibility no longer seemed outlandish.

"We did it! Wrestling is saved!" shouted Hollis. He pumped his fist in the air.

"Not yet, it isn't," said Tamiko.

"Yeah, we need to make sure that *every* seat has someone in it. Or we're doomed," Ollie pointed out.

"Arena-saving work really makes you hungry," said Hollis. "I'm gonna run to the snack line to grab some hot dogs. Who knows. Maybe this time there will be an actual line!"

Hollis sped off, leaving Ollie and Tamiko alone.

"You got this," said Tamiko.

"Thanks."

"Join me right after you win, okay?"

He smiled. "Deal."

With that, he made his way backstage and into the locker room. The roar coming down from the arena was louder than he'd ever heard it. Soon, he'd be out there in front of all those people. But first things first.

The coast was clear. After sticking a fresh wad of gum behind his ear for his finishing move, Ollie chomped on Professor Pain's gum and transformed into Big Chew.

Time to kick some Werewrestler butt, he thought as he checked himself out in the mirror. There was no way Slamdown Town was going to close on Big Chew's watch. He took a long look around the locker room for what he hoped was not the last time. Then he headed out into the hallway that led toward the wrestlers' entrance.

To his surprise, he found a crowd of wrestlers had lined up on either side of the hallway leading to the ring. As he walked past, they shouted out words of encouragement.

"Great job getting the crowd to show up. Haven't seen this many people in a long time. Go end that wolf cub's streak!" cheered Big Tuna.

"Watch his left hook. And his right one. And his legs, too," advised Devastator.

"Zap that good-for-nothing cheat into next weekend," said The Bolt. "And whatever you do, don't turn your back on him."

Lil' Old Granny offered Ollie a cracked breath mint that, for all he knew, had decades on him. "Last thing you want is to fall victim to the perils of stinky breath," she exclaimed, waving the mint in his face.

He pocketed the mint and soaked everything in. The other wrestlers seemed to be as eager as he was to see Werewrestler lose his belt. He was more than happy to make that happen.

By the time he stood just outside the entrance ramp, Ollie was pumped.

"Ladies and gentlemen, boys and girls. Have we reached the final match of Slamdown Town?!" screamed Screech. "I certainly see a lot of folks pouring in. But will it be enough? And who will be the champion? Well, I know a certain newcomer looking to claim the belt. Give it up for the challenger: Big Chew!"

Ollie made his way down the entrance ramp.

The arena had filled up quite nicely. Fans loaded in from all sides.

Ollie's heart soared. There were so many fresh faces.

He saw Hollis, who had already scarfed down all the food he'd bought only moments ago, flanked by his eighth-grade friends, plus a bunch of sixth and seventh graders he'd promised to pile-drive if they didn't show up. They looked nervous, but hey, it had worked.

He spotted Tamiko, as well. Just above in their usual spot. She was surrounded by a large group of people wearing *Griddle Royale* apparel. So her streaming had paid off, too. There were still a few empty seats around her as fans piled in. But it looked like they had a real shot at pulling this all off.

Ollie felt his spirits lift. No matter what happened in the ring, having Tamiko back in Slamdown Town made him feel like everything was going to be all right.

She waved at him. He waved back. Then he turned his attention completely on the not-so-easy task of beating Werewrestler and claiming the championship belt.

Besides the fact that Werewrestler weighed nearly half a ton, Ollie knew that this would be the most difficult opponent he had faced yet. Werewrestler didn't only excel at one element of wrestling like the others. He was a true master of the ring.

But that didn't matter. Ollie would come out on top. He had practiced. He had trained. All the pieces had come together for this exact moment.

His mom checked him and cleared him for the match.

He was ready.

Now all he had to do was wait for Werewrestler's entrance.

Screech Holler's voice rang out. "Oh, no. Big Chew. Look out!"

Too late. Something massive collided into Ollie from

behind. He lurched forward and was thrown outside the ring. It took all of Ollie's focus to keep chewing. The force of the impact had nearly knocked the gum right out of his mouth. After all, Big Chew transforming into a tiny eleven-year-old kid would have been quite an awkward start to the championship match.

"Knock, knock," came Werewrestler's voice in his ear.

He turned. Werewrestler stood there. With his piercing blood-red eyes. He heaved from the force of the blow. That somehow made him look even more like a savage wolf.

"What are you . . . ?" Ollie started.

But Werewrestler was on him in the time it took Ollie to blink. Werewrestler tackled him straight through the ropes and into the ring.

He was pinned. And the match hadn't even started yet!

CHAPTER 39

OLLIE struggled under the massive weight of Werewrestler, who had him pinned in the center of the ring.

"I'm here now," declared Werewrestler. "And the belt stays with me."

"What in tarnation, folks?!" yelled Screech. "Werewrestler's skipped his entrance and decided to get things started early."

"Knock it off, Werewrestler. The match hasn't even started," Ollie's mom said as she moved in to separate them.

Ding, ding, ding!

"It has now," snarled Werewrestler.

Before he could be pulled off of him, Werewrestler began to unload strikes on Ollie.

"Get off me, you cheater!" he yelled. Ollie dug out the mint Lil' Old Granny had given him and shoved it in Werewrestler's face. "I think you need this more than me."

"It's a dirty and apparently smelly start, but it's gonna stand now!" shrieked Screech.

Werewrestler batted the breath mint away and left Ollie on the mat. He climbed the ropes and launched himself off them, intent on hurtling himself at his opponent. He fell straight down on Ollie.

But Ollie was back on his feet. And he dished out an upper-cut that rocked Werewrestler, who countered with a back elbow. So he ducked and landed a hard leg kick to Werewrestler's shin. He took Werewrestler down.

"A ripped shirt and a wolf necklace?" asked Ollie as he kept Werewrestler in a tight grip. "You seriously thought that could compete with my awesome cape and Big Chew underoos?"

"I didn't know they sold diapers for babies your size," said Werewrestler.

Then Werewrestler escaped and took *him* down. They traded blow for blow, grapple for grapple. But Werewrestler absorbed any hit Ollie gave and dished out more. Ollie wondered how long he could keep this up.

He clasped his hands together and swung them straight into Werewrestler's gut. The hit managed to drop Werewrestler to a knee.

"Don't you know gum belongs in the trash," sneered Werewrestler.

And with that, Werewrestler delivered an eye poke. An *illegal* eye poke.

Ollie shook his head. He couldn't recover in time to see Werewrestler charging toward him. But he sure felt the collision.

"Get back!" he heard his mom yell.

When his vision cleared, Ollie saw her speaking to Werewrestler.

"That was dirty, and you know it," she was saying.

"A little biased, aren't we, Margaret?" asked Werewrestler.

"You know what you did. Don't do it again," she warned.

Werewrestler rolled his eyes. His mom cleared them both to fight again. So Ollie answered the cheap shot with a clean spin kick. The blow made Werewrestler double over. That one had stung, in a very legal and acceptable manner.

"That's gonna leave a mark, folks," observed Screech.

"How does that phrase go again? All bark and no bite?" asked Ollie.

Werewrestler bared his teeth. "Let's see how you handle the Jaws of the Wolf."

"The Jaws of the Wolf!" shrieked Screech. "Sweet sarsaparilla, anything but that!"

Werewrestler launched himself forward in a rage. He locked his titanic arms around Ollie. Werewrestler squeezed and squeezed and squeezed until Ollie felt like he might be snapped in two like a candy bar.

"You know what my favorite thing about bubble gum is?" asked Werewrestler with a snicker. "Popping it."

"You should . . . really try . . . breath mints," grunted Ollie.

He brought a few headbutts down on Werewrestler. The first one dazed his opponent. The second one managed to free Ollie from his grasp.

"Big Chew's broken free. I thought his bubble was burst for sure!" yelled Screech.

Werewrestler was back at it again. A rib-breaker. Then a

superkick. And then a striking spear. Then he spun around and used his wolf pendant to strike Ollie in the face.

The more they wrestled, the more obvious it became that Werewrestler was no joke. The brute force, the biting tongue, the costume; each element of Werewrestler's game was worthy of a champion. The blows started to pile up.

Ollie needed to slow down the fight. He thought back to the wisdom of Professor Pain, words that had lulled him to sleep the previous night.

"The mark of a true 'rassler," said the Professor from Ollie's phone as he lay under the covers, "is knowing yourself. Only once you know yourself can you know your opponent. Stop fighting the fights in here"—he said, pointing to his head—"and start fighting the fights out there," he said, pointing away from him. "Time to get out of your own head and into theirs. And then put that head in a headlock."

So he tried to get into his opponent's head.

"You're like that swamp monster from those movies, but hairier," he said. "Enjoy hanging around swamps? Is that where you feel at home? You certainly smell like a swamp monster. I can practically taste your body odor!"

"You want a taste? Here!" shouted Werewrestler. He launched a cannonball somersault that sent Ollie backward. It took everything he had to even remain on his feet.

"I don't think they make deodorant strong enough to cover that up!" he shouted.

Werewrestler snarled.

"And trust me, I've walked enough dogs in my life to know that what you need right now is a muzzle!" yelled Ollie.

There! Werewrestler opened himself up for just a moment. So Ollie wasted no time. He spun out of the way. He avoided Werewrestler's attempted takedown to land a forehand chop, which caused Werewrestler to stumble.

Ollie quickly followed up with a knee to the chest and then a swift elbow to the back.

"Watch those shots to the back," barked his mom.

She hated breaking rules even more than she hated Werewrestler.

"That's why I didn't aim for the head," he argued back.

"Right, but just make sure to—"

Wham!

Stars appeared in front of his eyes. Werewrestler had hit him while his back was turned. With a chair. He knew this because Werewrestler promptly hit him with it again.

"I just said watch the attacks from behind!" shouted Ollie's mom.

She placed herself between him and Werewrestler.

"And no chairs allowed in this match," she added.

"Guess I didn't hear you, ref," said Werewrestler. "Too busy defending my belt."

He tapped the shiny gold belt around his waist.

"But you wouldn't know what that feels like."

Ollie saw his mom's face turn red. She pointed a warning finger at Werewrestler. Ollie was grateful for the break. It allowed him to clear his head. And to set up a Big-Chew-flying-cape special attack aimed right at Werewrestler's rule-breaking face.

"Eat this, you dirty cheater!" he yelled.

But Werewrestler caught the cape before it wrapped around his face.

"Sticks and stones may break my bones," Werewrestler said with a scowl. "And I don't even need dirty tricks to beat ya."

"Sounds like someone's been to the local slam poetry contest!" shouted Screech.

"I'm gonna drop you straight into the floor," declared Werewrestler.

He was true to his word. Werewrestler plowed right through Ollie and landed a devastating—but definitely legal—gut-buster drop.

Ollie toppled to the ground. And this time, he stayed down.

He was exhausted. Nothing he threw at Werewrestler worked. He was running out of ideas. Maybe Werewrestler *couldn't* be beaten.

Ollie felt Werewrestler lift him up. He was powerless to stop him.

"It can't be. Is this the end of Big Chew?!" screamed Screech.

"Should have figured you wouldn't put up a fight," mocked Werewrestler. "There's only one champion in this league. And you're looking down at him. Enjoy your flight!"

And with that, Werewrestler tossed him out of the ring.

CHAPTER 40

OLLIE snapped out of his daze. He had just enough time to grab the top rope as he soared over it. The rope snapped and catapulted him back into the ring.

Directly at Werewrestler. His outstretched arm collided with Werewrestler's jaw. The added speed from the top rope gave Ollie the extra wallop he needed to finally astonish Werewrestler, who struggled to stay upright.

"What a tremendous display of acrobatics there by Big Chew," gushed Screech.

He was still in the match. And he intended to win it.

"You ain't getting that lucky," said Werewrestler. "In fact—"

Ollie grabbed the wad of gum from behind his ear while sending the shocked Werewrestler hurtling toward the ropes.

"I think it's time to burst your bubble!" Ollie shouted. He slapped the gum on his boot. Then he extended his right leg and aimed straight for Werewrestler's approaching face.

The finishing move did its job. Werewrestler swayed and fell like a ton of bricks onto the mat. Ollie ran over. Werewrestler was out cold.

"Werewrestler ate a faceful of gum!" yelled Screech.

This was his moment.

"It's been fun," said Ollie. He pulled Werewrestler up by his silver chain and lifted all four hundred and ninety pounds above his head. "But it's time for me to take that shiny gold belt for myself."

This was it. He was going to *win*.

All of his hard work. Everything Tamiko and he had worked toward was about to come true. All he had to do was toss Werewrestler onto the mat and pin him for ten seconds. He soaked in the roar of the crowd.

But then he saw it.

One. Empty. Seat.

The seat directly ncxt to Tamiko.

His seat.

Ollie let Werewrestler fall back to the mat as he walked to the ropes.

"What's he waiting for, folks?" demanded Screech.

The arena had been filled to capacity. Except for *his* seat. The one that had his name on it in permanent marker. The seat that he had sat in for years and years, but that had been empty ever since he became Big Chew. Tamiko had always made sure to keep his spot open for him. And it seemed there hadn't been enough fans for someone to take his spot.

They were one short.

At any other time, Ollie would have demanded his seat be

reserved just for him. It seemed almost a cruel twist of fate that his demand was fulfilled, today of all days.

Now, with victory only moments away . . .

One simple pin and Big Chew would be named the Slamdown Town champion. But then Slamdown Town would close forever. Linton had made the stakes clear. A butt in every seat by the time the new champion was declared.

Ollie knew he belonged in that seat more than he belonged in the ring. Unfortunately for Ollie, Werewrestler also felt that Big Chew did not belong in the ring. Which was how Ollie suddenly found himself careening up and over the ropes.

For the briefest of moments, Ollie had the sensation of flying. That sensation was immediately followed by Ollie crashing straight through a wrestling barricade and into a pile of ringside equipment boxes. He lay there, dazed, wondering what exactly had sent him shooting over the ropes with such force.

Moving aside the barricade to get a better look at the ring, Ollie saw Werewrestler standing on the mat with what appeared to be a pair of shiny silver brass knuckles on one of his fists. The Bolt had warned Ollie not to turn his back on Werewrestler. If only he had remembered.

"What in the worldwide sport of wrestling? Has Werewrestler lost his mind?!" yelled Screech. "That may be the dirtiest move I've ever witnessed in all my time here at Slamdown Town!"

Screech wasn't the only one who felt that way. Ollie doubted he had ever seen his mom angrier than she was at that moment. He could see the veins on her neck pulsing all the way from where he was now.

"Absolutely unacceptable!" she roared in Werewrestler's face. "The use of a class-five unsanctioned weapon combined with a blow from behind is not only illegal, but also indecent and immoral!"

"Ah, shut yer trap," snarled Werewrestler.

Werewrestler turned, grabbed Ollie's mom, and slammed her down onto the ground.

"Now he's attacking the ref!" shouted Screech.

He lifted her into the air and slammed her back down on top of his knee. Then he tossed her into the corner of the ring. She shook it off, wiped her brow, and stood.

"Werewrestler. You've crossed the line. The rules are very clear that—"

Werewrestler growled and pointed toward the direction of Big Chew. "You know the rules, don't ya? He's been out there for way more than ten seconds."

"Oh, I know the rules all right," assured Ollie's mom.

"Good," sneered Werewrestler. "Then name me the champion."

"And according to the rule book, attacking the referee is grounds for one of two punishments. One, the referee has the authority to disqualify the attacker. Or two, the referee could fight back. And the second option seems *way* more fun."

She charged forward and wrapped her arms around him and delivered an intense yet standard-abiding pile driver.

"What in blazes is happening?" demanded Screech. "Somebody get me a rule book! And did anybody see what became of Big Chew? Maybe we need to send out a search party."

Ollie had no clue what was running through his mom's head. But he knew that somehow, some way, what she was doing was staying true to who she was. Which meant that somehow, some way, what she was doing was all by the book.

A choice had presented itself to Ollie. He could either run into the ring as Big Chew to help his mom and claim the belt. Or . . .

It was just like their posters had said:

ONLY YOU CAN SAVE SLAMDOWN TOWN

After everything he had been through over the past few weeks, Ollie knew *exactly* what to do. But he needed to be fast, while the crowd was still distracted. So he spat the gum out of his mouth. Back to his normal self, Ollie had no issue tiptoeing out behind the equipment boxes unseen.

Everyone's attention was still firmly fixed on the chaos inside the ring.

He dashed up into the stands. Jogged up the stairs.

And he planted his butt firmly in the seat next to Tamiko. *His* seat.

"Ollie! What are you doing?!" yelled Tamiko.

"Saving the arena. We were still one short," he said as he pointed to the chair. "Slamdown Town needs me more than it needs Big Chew."

"But you've wanted that belt for, like, forever," said a stunned Tamiko.

"I know. And I still do." Ollie smiled. "But what would be the point if I couldn't come here every Saturday with my best friend in the whole wide world?"

"What about Werewrestler?"

They turned their attention back to ring, where his mom had Werewrestler in a very legal and very painful-looking chokehold.

"Seems that's already being taken care of," he answered.

"By gum, folks, today has a been a day of firsts!" shrieked Screech as he scooped up the mic from the wreckage. "I thought Werewrestler's blow was dirty. But a referee wrestling for the belt? Is this even legal?"

His mom, now holding Werewrestler in a firm-but-fair head-lock, found a nearby regulation microphone and switched it on.

"Actually, Screech, I'd advise you to turn to page four hundred and sixty-two of the official Slamdown Town rule book," she instructed.

An attendant brought the massive rule book over to Screech.

"If you look carefully at rule number seven hundred eighty-seven," she explained, "you will see that in the event of a catastrophic rule violation, such as attacking the referee, a referee may take it upon herself to enter the match."

"It looks like our esteemed referee is one hundred percent legitimate."

"And as such, I am, under those conditions, well within my right to stake my claim on the belt," concluded his mom.

Ollie couldn't believe what he was hearing.

She threw Werewrestler to the mat, leapt on top of him, and pinned him. The entire arena counted to ten in unison and, collectively, confirmed the victory.

Ding, ding, ding!

"Well, now, didn't y'all hear what she said?" demanded Screech. "The referee is your new, perfectly legal, by-the-book

Slamdown Town champion! And she's already got a kick-butt costume to boot. Give it up for the woman in the black-and-white stripes."

Ollie let out a cheer. He felt the rush of the entire arena as fans jumped to their feet. Finally, after all these years, Werewrestler had been defeated. His mom retrieved the belt from Werewrestler, who was too busy seeing stars to react, and held it high above her head. The audience roared their approval.

"Let's make sure that cheering remains at acceptable decibel levels," warned his mom. The arena quieted ever so slightly. "Much better. Also, will the owner of the white suburban with the license plate SCR33CH please make their way to the parking lot. It appears Lil' Old Granny got in your car by mistake and is currently heading toward the freeway."

"Goodness gracious, I gotta run!" shouted Screech as he grabbed his keys and jetted for the parking lot.

"Did *that* just happen?" asked Tamiko, turning to Ollie.

"Oh, it happened. My mom's a champion!" he shouted.

As if he sensed an opportunity to ruin a good mood, Linton Krackle appeared.

He casually walked down the entrance ramp. He soaked up all the boos and yelling without so much as a single flinch.

"Go back to the hole you crawled out from!" yelled Ollie.

"You're the worst person in the history of everything!" shouted Hollis.

"Your business skills are like your breath. They both stink!" screamed Tamiko.

Linton made his way into the ring. He held out his hand for Ollie's mom to shake.

She just stood there. That drew more cheers from the crowd, which she silenced with a warning finger. But Linton waved it off. He turned to speak to the audience.

"Not only do I have the unexpected privilege of witnessing history as our ref becomes the first ever Slamdown Town referee to ever be our champion—seriously, Cash Cow, I mean Big Chew, where'd ya go?—but I got other news for you," announced Linton.

The arena seemed to collectively hold its breath.

"Seems enough of you suckers—*er*, I mean patrons—showed up that my so-called 'smart investors,'" he said as he made exaggerated air quotes, "wised up. A butt in every seat by the end of the match. That was the deal. We sold every ticket today. Trust me, I saw the numbers. Those big, beautiful numbers. It was certainly a photo finish, though," he said, glancing in Ollie's direction. "So . . ."

Tamiko, wide-eyed, turned to Ollie. "Is he saying what I think he's saying?"

"In other words," continued Linton, "prepare to spend a lot of money here next weekend, because Slamdown Town will officially remain open for business. Seriously though, bring your money. Like, *all* of it. Because I'm raising prices."

Tamiko screamed so loudly that Ollie's ears rang. He didn't mind. He screamed right along with her. He screamed until his throat was sore. And then screamed some more.

Happy didn't seem like a happy-enough word to describe what he felt.

"We did it!" he screamed to Tamiko.

"We totally did!" shrieked Tamiko.

They both jumped around. He felt like he had the energy to run ten thousand miles.

Several rows down, he noticed Hollis clutching the person next to him, some eighth-grade girl Ollie recognized from school.

"We did it. We saved wrestling," sobbed Hollis loudly into the girl's shoulder. "And my mom won the belt! How cool is that?"

"Yeah, that's pretty cool," he heard the girl say as she gingerly patted an overwhelmed Hollis on the back. "And I'm not just saying that. It actually is cool!"

Hollis had successfully talked to a girl. His mom was champion. Slamdown Town had been saved. This was the best day of Ollie's entire life.

CHAPTER 41

THE following Saturday, Ollie got ready for wrestling just like he always did. He riffled through his closet for his coolest wrestling shirt. It wasn't a hard decision. He put on his ratty old Professor Pain T-shirt, which he wore only for extra-special occasions for fear it would fall apart. It was, after all, the first wrestling shirt he'd ever gotten, and it still fit him. He guessed that was one of the benefits of not having hit his growth spurt yet.

He then texted Tamiko to see if she was ready to take on Kragthar. They had just enough time before needing to leave for the match to face the menacing evil that had proved impossible to defeat.

I was born ready. Be on in five.

Then, as he waited for Tamiko to boot up *Revenge of Kragthar*, he rewatched Professor Pain's final video in his *Anyone Can Be a Wrestler* series.

"Listen, friends," said Professor Pain's voice through the lap-top speakers. "I've told ya about how costumes, smack talk, and moves are the key to making you a great wrestler. But I haven't told you the most important key of all to wrestling: *you!*"

Ollie smiled.

"Yes, you!" continued Professor Pain.

"Me?" said Ollie, playing along.

"The most important lesson is to be yourself. We can wish all we want, but until you believe you can be the best wrestler ever, well friends, you won't be. Remember, these videos here, they can teach ya *how* to be a 'rassler. But only *you* can make it happen."

Professor Pain waved to the camera, ending in a freeze-frame advertisement for the production company's various other *Anyone Can Be a . . .* series. Ollie wrapped up the Professor's magic bubble gum and shoved it into his back pocket.

His phone vibrated as he received Tamiko's message saying she was ready.

Ollie launched *Revenge of Kragthar.*

"Today is the day," declared Tamiko through the headset as her wizard and Ollie's knight made their way into the vast, creepy dungeon. "Kragthar is going down."

Ollie winced and lowered his headphone volume. "He won't know what hit him. But it's going to be a lot of fireballs and power attacks."

Ollie wasn't nervous, despite the fact that Tamiko was streaming and their game was being watched by hundreds of random internet strangers.

In the past few weeks, Ollie had beaten the best wrestlers Slamdown Town had to offer. What chance did a pixelated level ninety-nine boss have compared to all of them? Besides, he had the best tool available to take Kragthar down. And it wasn't the teleporting shoulder pads.

It was Tamiko.

"We can do this, Tamiko," said Ollie as they ran past the three-headed silver snake and headed into the final area. "As long as we stick together, we got—"

Just as Kragthar appeared on-screen, Hollis barged into the room.

"Hollis?"

"Oh, no, not again," moaned Tamiko through the speakers.

Hollis's eyes shot from Ollie, who remained frozen with uncertainty, to the cracked screen where Ollie's knight sat motionless. They had been so close . . .

"Well, are you just gonna sit there and let Kragthar beat you?" demanded Hollis. "Come on, I need to finish my blog post for the site. Chop-chop."

Ollie turned back to the task at hand. His fingers, slippery with sweat, banged on the keyboard. He licked his lips. Acid pits and icy blasts popped up everywhere. Kragthar spun around and absorbed blow after blow. With each hit, his health meter went down.

Finally it hit a critical level and Kragthar stood there, stunned.

There it was! The opening Ollie had been looking for.

"When I use my epic strike, go in for the finisher!" yelled Ollie.

"Set him up for me," said Tamiko, her voice tense with anticipation.

Ollie's knight charged forward and slammed into Kragthar. "Now, Tamiko!"

Tamiko gave a cry and used her highest-level spell, the Sunbeam Express. A wave of light washed over the entire screen. When it cleared, Kragthar was just a pile of ash.

"We did it!" shrieked Ollie.

"We are the best adventurers of all time!" shouted Tamiko. "Take that, Kragthar."

They received message after message of congratulations from T@M1k0's followers.

Ollie heard Tamiko's dad in the background. "Tamiko, we just got a call from the neighbors again. Please keep it down."

"But we beat Kragthar, Dad."

"Kragthar? Nice," said her dad. "Just celebrate a little quieter, okay?"

Hollis moved himself between Ollie and the laptop. "All right, my turn. Gimme."

"See you soon, Tamiko!" shouted Ollie into the headset.

Without wasting another moment, Hollis closed the game and scooped up the laptop. But considering his brother had waited until after Kragthar had been defeated, Ollie didn't resist.

"You aren't even going to say congrats?" asked Ollie.

Hollis rolled his eyes. "Please. Everyone knows Kragthar is way easier to beat in *Revenge of Kragthar*. Just wait until you play *Kragthar: Eye for an Eye*. You're gonna get stomped."

They made their way outside and piled into the back seat of the car. Hollis began typing away on the laptop.

"Gotta post my pre-match thoughts to all my adoring fans," he said.

His mom leapt into the front seat, started the car, and off they went.

True to his word, Hollis had officially ended their temporary alliance.

But life with his brother hadn't been all that bad. While the occasional sweaty headlock still caught him by surprise, and Hollis had continued to ban Ollie from talking to him at school in front of other eighth graders, he and Hollis were bonding over wrestling more now than they had in years.

"Who do you think is gonna take the matches?" asked Hollis as their mom drove them toward the arena.

"Pretty sure The Bolt will beat The Snowman," predicted Ollie.

"Nice. I can see that," agreed Hollis. "And pretty sure that Lil' Old Granny dominates Barbell Bill. Few minutes and he's done."

Ollie nodded. "Oh, he'll lose. She's stronger than she looks."

"How do you know that?" asked Hollis.

"Just a guess."

"Plus, Big Chew is *totally* going to make his return today," declared Hollis. He had a working theory that Linton Krackle had forced Big Chew into an early retirement in order to build up hype for his eventual return. "It's just a big money-making thing. But I don't care! Take my money, Linton!" Hollis held up his piggy bank and rattled it next to Ollie's ear.

Big Chew's disappearance had caused quite a stir. At first, amid the awesome chaos of Werewrestler finally ceding the belt to the referee and Slamdown Town being saved, no one had even noticed he was gone. But at the end of the day, Big Chew never reappeared from the pile of barricades he'd been tossed into. And that's when the conversations started.

Some thought that Big Chew and the referee had been working together as a tag team in order to defeat Werewrestler. Others believed Big Chew felt betrayed that the referee had stolen his moment of glory and had walked away from wrestling for good. One conspiracy theorist even posted on the Officially Unofficial Slamdown Town Fan Club, which still maintained a decent amount of visitors, that Big Chew had fallen through a crack in the arena floor and was biding his time before emerging from a subterranean lair. What was clear to everyone was that Big Chew, for whatever reason, was nowhere to be found. And nothing outside of Hollis's stubborn hopes seemed to indicate he'd be making a quick return.

"That one I wouldn't be so sure of," said Ollie. "But what I *am* sure of is that Mom is still going to be the champion after today. Right, Mom?"

Their mom laughed. "Trust me, I'll be keeping the belt nice and safe."

She had handled her newfound fame exactly as Ollie expected her to: by the book. The arena had hired a new referee since the old referee was now the Slamdown Town champion wrestler known as "The Referee."

Ollie thought her new wrestling persona was true to the mom he knew and loved.

"Most importantly, I'll be keeping the rules nice and safe," she clarified. "I may be the champion and a wrestler again, per the rules, but I'm a referee at heart. And the rule book clearly states that a referee's number one duty is to uphold the rules. Hopefully this newbie is up to par and has memorized all three thousand seven hundred wrestling bylaws. If so, that means there will technically be two referees when I'm in the ring. Double rules!"

Having the belt back where it belonged, draped over his mom's massive shoulder, brought a smile to Ollie's face. He wanted to be just like her when he grew up.

As they pulled into the parking lot, the familiar sight of Slamdown Town greeted Ollie. He knew Tamiko would be waiting for him inside, sitting at their usual seats, but he had one task to take care of before joining her.

Ollie strolled through the arena until he found himself in the trophy room. The shelves were lined with golden cups and silver medals, sparkling belts and colorful plaques. Various trinkets and props collected from Slamdown Town wrestlers over the years lay strewn all over the room. He knew each piece by heart, having spent many an hour poring over every nook and cranny.

Captain General's medal of ringside heroics for carrying his entire tag team to safety.

Lil' Old Granny's first walker, complete with tennis balls on the ends.

Tommy TV Remote's original factory-issue battery pack.

The piece he was looking for sat on a dusty wooden case under a flickering light in the back of the room: Professor Pain's original Slamdown Town championship belt.

The belt had been replaced after the Professor's retirement with an even flashier belt. An almost-forgotten corner of the trophy room was its final resting place.

Ollie had thought long and hard about what his next move would be. Contrary to Hollis's conspiracy theory, Linton had been calling Tamiko's phone nonstop to schedule Big Chew's next fight. But Ollie, like Professor Pain before him, had decided his time had come.

No, Ollie wasn't going to retire to spend more time sleeping on tropical beaches and being paid to make terrible local-business commercials. And he wasn't leaving because he didn't like wrestling anymore or something like that. In fact, being a wrestler was easily the coolest thing that had ever happened to him—and probably would ever happen to him.

But there was one part about wrestling that he loved more than being an actual wrestler, and that was watching matches with his best friend. Tamiko made wrestling a thousand times more epic and fun and cool. Being Big Chew had nearly taken all that away.

Besides, there would be plenty of time for Ollie to grow up and be an awesome wrestler himself. He knew he could do it all on his own, no magic gum required.

Ollie checked to make sure the coast was clear. Seeing that he was alone, he reached into his back pocket and removed the wrapped gum. He plucked it off the piece of the neon-blue flyer, the very same flyer from more than a month earlier. *That* he tucked back into his pocket. He'd planned on hanging it up in the first place, with all his other mementos. Crumpled and smudged and dirt-streaked as it was, the flyer had certainly earned its place on the wall.

Ollie took the gum in his hand and stuck it firmly behind Professor Pain's belt.

Maybe it would still be there for him if he needed it on a rainy day in the future. Maybe the gum would find its way into someone else's hands and, if they wished on it like he did, allow them to experience the thrill of transforming into a super-buff, powerful wrestler.

Either way, Ollie relinquished his claim on the gum. It had taught him a lot about wrestling, about family, and about friendship. He felt it would somehow be greedy of him to not share that with someone else.

The gum controlled its own destiny now.

He left the trophy room without looking back. He walked back into the arena, ran up the flight of uneven stairs, took a hard left at the first broken window, leapt over the old pothole that was created when Lil' Old Granny pile-drove Barbell Bill in an out-of-the-ring brawl, and—finally—arrived at the set of rickety seats that he and Tamiko claimed as their own.

"There you are!" said Tamiko, leaning back in her seat and glancing up from her phone. She had moved on from *Jewel Heist* after claiming all top-ten leaderboard spots and was now playing *Dance Party*, a music-rhythm game that forced her to use two fingers. Her new account, Salsa Boogiedown, was already climbing the ranks. She was wearing a lone lime-green sock today, paired with her favorite Silvertongue shirt. She already had her arms full of red licorice, extra-butter popcorn, and what looked like five gallons of soda.

"Did you do it?" she asked.

"Yup." Ollie had filled Tamiko in last night as to his intentions. As Big Chew's manager, she was devastated to lose her best and only client.

As Ollie's friend, she was happy to have him back.

"Ladies and gentlemen, boys and girls," crooned Screech over the speakers. "It's time to get to your seats, because the matches are about to begin."

"You ready for this?" asked Tamiko.

"You bet I am," answered Ollie.

Ollie and Tamiko smiled and readied themselves for another heart-pounding, blood-pumping afternoon of Slamdown Town wrestling.

ACKNOWLEDGMENTS

Maureen Smith, Gary Nicoll, Patty Nicoll, Lauren Palette, Olivia Smith, Lindsey Tews, Ryan Nicoll, Anne Heltzel, Jessica Gotz, Marie Oishi, Hana Anouk Nakamura, Michael Clark, Lena Buzzetta, Joseph Buzzetta, Jillian Vanek, Jess Landau, Steven Landau, Morgan Rubin, Michael Krouse, Joshua McHugh, Maya Carter-Ali, Amir Ali, Marielle Carter, Andrew Moriarty, Dwight Hahn, Maria Losada, Rachel Jackson, Rob Domingo, Patricia Melendez, Melinda Carr, Steve Palette-Nicoll, and Kitty Meow.